LOVE IN DISASTER

T0125637

By the Author

A Palette for Love

Love in Disaster

LOVE IN DISASTER

by

Charlotte Greene

2017

LOVE IN DISASTER

ISBN 13: 978-1-62639-885-6

This Trade Paperback Original Is Published By
Bold Strokes Books, Inc.
P.O. Box 249
Valley Falls, NY 12185

First Edition: March 2017

CREDITS
EDITOR: SHELLEY THRASHER
PRODUCTION DESIGN: SUSAN RAMUNDO
COVER DESIGN BY MELODY POND

Dedication

For my one, my only, my darling.
Love you forever.

Chapter One

K it stared out the window of the cab, her eyes shaded from the oppressive August sun. The airport in New Orleans was a good distance from downtown, where she was staying, and she was having a hard time keeping her eyes open. Flashes of brilliant green and long stretches of canals and bayous along the side of the road passed by her flickering lids before she finally gave in and closed them. She'd always struggled with jet lag and couldn't remember why she'd ever thought traveling from Europe to New Orleans without a break was a good idea. Ostensibly, it had meant more time at the archives she was visiting in the U.K. and Ireland, but in practice she was exhausted, and she knew she would remain so for most of her time at the conference.

Her department chair had asked her to attend the annual Irish Literature Association meeting last fall, long before she'd secured the funds for her archival visits. When she'd been awarded the money, it had meant some last-minute scrambling to cram everything into her summer. Well, here I am, she thought. Even if she walked and talked like a zombie through all her meetings the next few days, she would get her chair off her back for a while.

She must have actually dozed off, as the next thing she knew, the cab had stopped and the driver was shouting to wake her. She shook her head a few times to clear the cobwebs and apologized to him before climbing out. As she'd come directly from Dublin, she had far more luggage with her than her week-long stay in New

Orleans warranted, and she felt ridiculous as the driver pulled suitcase after suitcase from the trunk of the cab, lining them up neatly on the sidewalk next to her. Embarrassed by his efforts—he was a tiny man—she overtipped him, hoping her department would reimburse her later.

Not until he drove away did she realize he'd dropped her off in front of the wrong hotel. Sagging with exhaustion, she felt frustrated tears prickle the corners of her eyes. She stared down at the piles of suitcases next to her in blank dismay, unable to formulate a single idea about how to proceed. She glanced up and down the street, hoping another cab would appear, but she was almost completely alone out here. Only the hotel's doorman, who was greeting another guest, stood nearby. He finally spotted her and snapped to attention before bringing her a luggage cart.

"Let me help you with that, miss," he said, already slinging the first suitcase onto the cart.

"There was some kind of mix-up." Her voice was slightly slurred with sleep.

He must not have heard her, or chose to ignore her, as he continued to load her luggage onto the cart. Realizing that she had no better options at this point, she let him continue and decided to call her actual hotel from inside. Perhaps they could arrange a pickup. She followed him as he pushed the cart and her luggage into the large and impressive lobby of the wrong hotel. As no one was in line, she was led directly to the check-in desk and, after tipping the doorman, was left to explain her strange predicament to the clerk.

He stared at her, obviously confused. "So you don't have a reservation here at the Roosevelt?"

"No," she said, starting over. "You see, my cab dropped me off at the wrong hotel—"

"Unfortunately, miss, the hotel is completely booked," the clerk broke in. "There are several conferences in town right now."

"I understand that." She tried to keep the fury from her voice. Her frustration and exhaustion were making it harder for her to clarify her problem. "I just need to call my *actual* hotel to see if they can pick me up or arrange a taxi."

"I see," he said, clearly displeased. "Where are you staying?"

"The Ramada," she said.

"I see." His tone suggested exactly what he thought of the Ramada. "So how can I help you?"

"I just need a telephone."

He pointed at a bank of pay phones across the lobby, and disgusted by his rudeness, she grabbed her cart and pulled it over there. She spent several fruitless moments going through her things for change, finding only British pounds and euros. Getting out her credit card, she followed the convoluted instructions needed to make a call, finally getting through after twenty minutes of being continually disconnected.

She got her hotel's answering machine.

Too tired to do anything else, she pushed her luggage cart over to a sofa in the lobby and collapsed into it, covering her eyes with her hands. She leaned her head back on the sofa and sighed, trying to make a decision.

Once again, she must have dozed off, as the next thing she knew, she was being shaken awake, and not gently. "You can't sleep here, miss," a large man was telling her. He was dressed in a suit tight enough to show the outline of gun under the jacket. Hotel security.

"I'm sorry. I didn't mean to—"

"I don't care," the man said. "You can't sleep here. If you're not a guest, I'm going to have to ask you to leave."

Too tired to argue with him, she climbed slowly to her feet and pushed her cart back outside. As she passed the front desk, she saw the desk clerk's eyes following her and understood that he'd been the whistleblower.

Outside, she nodded at the doorman, who raised his eyebrows, seeming confused to see her and her luggage again. "Where is the Ramada from here?" she asked him.

"A couple of blocks that way." He pointed. "Down on Gravier to the right."

Without trying to explain herself, Kit began pushing the luggage cart in that direction. She heard the doorman call after her, but she kept pushing, knowing that he likely wouldn't chase her. She'd bring the cart back later. Maybe. That guy in there had been an awful prick. Also, she'd long ago realized that sometimes it was better just to do a thing than to ask permission.

She passed several people on the streets between the hotels, and they stared after her, apparently startled, but no one said anything. The heat was oppressive, and the sun, to her tired eyes, nearly blinding even with her sunglasses. The walk was also longer than a couple of blocks, and harder with the luggage cart, but she finally made it to her hotel. The doorman there was surprised to see her coming down the street with a cart, but he nicely held the door open for her.

"Welcome to the Ramada," the clerk said as she approached the front desk. The girl was very young, her face bright with helpful politeness.

Kit took off her sunglasses and sighed, trying to gather her strength for one last human encounter. "Hi. I have a reservation for Katriona—or maybe Kit—Kelly."

The clerk typed on her computer for a moment and then started frowning. "Can you spell your last name?" she asked.

"K-e-l-l-y," Kit said.

The clerk typed the name again but continued to frown. "When did you make this reservation?"

"Six months ago," Kit said, alarm pinching her voice higher.

"Do you have the reservation number by chance?"

Kit rooted around in her purse, finding nothing, and was forced to go slowly through each of her suitcases to find her hotel and conference reservations for New Orleans. As she looked, finding nothing but information regarding places in Europe, panic threatened to overwhelm her. She knew no one in town and wasn't sure if she knew anyone at the conference. Her friend Becky might be here, but she hadn't checked in with her in months. What on earth was she going to do? The information she was looking for, however, was, of course, in the last of the suitcases, crammed beneath most of her underwear. Too tired to be embarrassed by the explosion of her belongings all over the lobby, Kit pulled out the reservation sheet and handed it to the clerk before bending down in order to stuff things back in her bags.

When she looked back up, the clerk's face was red with embarrassment. "I'm sorry, miss, but this reservation is not for our hotel."

Kit's heart almost stopped beating. "What do you mean?"

The clerk handed back the reservation sheet, and Kit saw, clearly and without reading anything else, the words Holiday Inn at the top of the page.

Hearing laughter behind her, Kit turned, clutching the reservation page. Three people behind her in line she saw a woman about her own age. The woman had a hand over her mouth, trying to stifle her giggles.

"Is something funny to you?" Kit spat.

The woman was clearly amused. "I'm so sorry," she said between chuckles. Her voice was surprisingly low. "I don't mean to laugh. It's just so typical."

"Typical?" Kit almost shouted.

"Here you are, holding up the line, searching through everything you own, and you're not even staying here. It's just the kind of thing that would happen to me."

"I'm so happy for your amusement," Kit snapped. "Glad someone is getting some pleasure out of this."

The woman held up her hands. "Jeez! Don't bite my head off. I only meant to empathize. It's not the end of the world. You shouldn't get so worked up about something so trivial."

"You don't know the first thing about me, and you certainly can't tell me how to *feel* about something. Who the hell do you think you are?"

"Christ," the woman said, sounding disgusted. "Excuse me for living."

"Can I call you a cab?" the clerk interrupted, clearly trying to break up the argument. "We can have you at the Holiday Inn in minutes."

"Please do," Kit said, suppressing her anger one last time in order to be civil.

She spent the next few minutes repacking her bags as well as possible and then dragged the luggage cart back outside in order to wait for the cab. The heat hit her again, hard, but the clouds had rolled in, making the light easier on her eyes. Her sunglasses still firmly in place, she looked around, curious. This was a seedier part of town than she'd expected to see on her visit. Graffiti and trash were everywhere, and several homeless people had congregated near a bus stop about a block away. She had heard about a thousand warning stories from a colleague about wandering around New Orleans outside of the tourist areas, and she was starting to regret her skepticism. Living in San Francisco, she'd learned how to locate the safe blocks from the rougher ones, but it was clearly a little different here.

As she waited, she saw the woman she'd argued with inside appear in the doorway. The woman didn't see Kit, or pretended not to, and Kit watched her walk away and back toward the nicer part of downtown. The woman had the tight, firm body of an athlete and moved in her black jeans and T-shirt with a lithe grace. Her hair was dark and slicked back, but Kit could detect the hint of curls beneath the hair product that was holding it in place. Her forearms were roped with tattoos, and she was wearing heavy, motorcycle-type boots. Kit had immediately regretted making such an ass of herself inside and had almost apologized to her in there. Now, seeing that hot body walk away from her, she felt even worse.

The woman was just her type.

Kit sighed as the woman disappeared around a corner, and then she shook her head, amused with herself. There was no earthly reason why she'd ever see the woman again, so why be upset about how she'd acted? All those weeks working in Ireland and the U.K. had meant a long dry spell, but picking up strangers from the street was rarely her MO anymore. There were, after all, guaranteed to be plenty of lovely academic pickings at the conference this week.

The cab ride was a few short blocks, and relieved to finally be in the right place this time, she overtipped everyone who helped her get to her room. It was surprisingly large and airy, with high ceilings and a giant bed. She had a window that overlooked Dauphine, and, as she stood there in front of the air conditioner trying to cool down, she watched tourists scurry by on their way to fun and revelry in other parts of the French Quarter. While the last two hours had been one long headache, she was actually happy that her hotel was in the Quarter rather than downtown. It would be easier to see more of the city from here, and despite her fatigue, she was excited about her time in the Crescent City.

Chapter Two

K it must have fallen asleep immediately upon lying down, as the telephone startled her so badly that she yelped in surprise. The light outside had softened considerably, and she judged it to be early evening. Groping around on the bedside table, she finally found the phone and picked it up.

"Hello?" she croaked, then cleared her throat. "Hello?" she said louder.

"When are you ever going to get a damn cell phone? I've called every hotel in town."

"Hello? Who is this?" Kit asked, confused.

"It's Becky. You know, Rebecca Lee."

Kit sat up and moved her feet over the edge of the bed. Becky was a colleague. While they'd never attended the same schools or worked at the same university, they ran into each other at conferences fairly often, as they both specialized in Irish Literature. "Hey, Becky. Nice to hear from you. I take it you're here in New Orleans?"

"Yes, and I saw your name on the program. Since we're both presenting tomorrow, I assumed you'd be in town by now."

"I just got in a little while ago."

"Do you want to have dinner? I actually managed to get a reservation at this new place on Frenchmen. I think it must be because of a cancellation—the place is booked months ahead. It's supposed to be the new hot thing, and I'd hate to go alone. It has one of those celebrity chefs or whatever."

Kit yawned and looked around for a clock. "Sure. What time?"

"The reservation is for eight. We can either walk over there or take a cab."

Kit stood and stretched, still looking for a clock. "I'd love to walk, if we can. I was flying all night and day."

"Okay! I'll be over there in half an hour."

"How fancy should I dress?" Kit asked.

"No evening gowns, but nice. Probably nicer than you'd dress for work. I'll wait in the lobby."

Kit yawned again and then laughed. "Sorry to keep yawning in your ear. I'll be down in thirty minutes."

Months in the U.K. and Ireland had trained Kit to take quick, efficient showers, and she decided to wear a dark-blue silk blouse and a conservative gray skirt with flats, since they were walking. Her hair was still damp, but she pulled it up into a loose bun, hoping the heat would dry it before they reached the restaurant. She slid a couple of loose red curls out to soften the hairstyle and swiped a little mascara on her light eyelashes before grabbing her purse and heading downstairs.

Becky was already sitting in the lobby, staring into space. She was a large woman, and she was wearing a severe, men's-style suit and shoes. Her hair was short and poorly styled, but when she spotted Kit, her face broke into a beautiful smile. With a little grooming and styling, Becky could be incredibly attractive, but she apparently did okay just the way she was. She and Kit had actually slept together once in their early conference-going years, but neither of them had been interested in repeating the experience. Becky heaved herself up and walked over, wrapping Kit in a bone-crushing hug that smashed Kit's face into Becky's breasts.

"You did that on purpose," Kit said, blushing. She had the freckly pallor of her Irish and Nordic ancestors, and the slightest embarrassment was always obvious to everyone.

Becky hooted, loud enough that several people glanced over at them. "Of course I did. I'm a pervert." Becky looked her up and down, holding her shoulders. "You're looking great!"

"Thanks," Kit said. "I feel like tired dog crap right now."

"Well, you don't look it. You look as fresh as a daisy. You've been working out?"

Kit shrugged. "Just running. The usual."

"We should get going," Becky said, glancing at her watch. "It's about ten blocks from here, so we don't need to hurry, but I'd hate to lose that reservation."

As they strolled toward Frenchmen, they made a strange pair. Nearly everyone they passed looked at them, some open-mouthed. Most people stared at Becky, who, in addition to wearing a men's suit and being somewhat rotund, was also tall and imposing. Kit was slightly above average height herself, but Becky towered over her, easily topping six feet in her shoes. Becky was, Kit was amused to note, also wearing men's cologne—enough that a passersby could likely smell her. Becky, however, was oblivious to the stares she was evoking. She walked with her head held high, her eyes mostly on the balconies and the sky above them.

"It's absolutely gorgeous here," she finally said. "I'd heard about their purple sunsets but never expected to actually see one of them."

Kit looked up at the sky and caught her breath. The evening sky was a pale violet color, streaked with lines of bright green and yellow. The humidity was making the air hazy and dreamy, and this, coupled with the fairy-tale color, made the evening seem suddenly magical. She sighed and closed her eyes in pleasure.

"It is gorgeous," she finally said.

"Supposed to be a babe haven, too," Becky said, painfully elbowing Kit in the ribs for emphasis. "Lots of easy pickin's at the clubs here, if you get my drift. Warm Southern belles and all that."

Kit swatted at her arm. "You're a letch."

"Oh, and you're not? Need I remind you which one of us slept with *four* separate women at this conference last year in DC? I was lucky to sleep with one the whole time we were there. Talk about an ice-town."

It was dark enough now that no one could see her blush, but Kit's face grew hot with embarrassment. "That was an anomaly."

"Sure it was." Becky rolled her eyes skeptically. "Don't tell me you couldn't do that every night if you wanted to. You're one hot little ticket, and you know it."

Embarrassed and hoping to change the topic, Kit told her about her unfortunate adventure with the wrong hotels this afternoon, getting Becky to laugh so hard they had to pause in the street so she could catch her breath. It was funny to Kit now, too, and she giggled along with her. Still, she regretted the way she'd treated the woman from the hotel lobby. She hoped she'd meet someone else who was at least half as interesting.

As if sensing the change in her thoughts, Becky asked, "So how were the women in London and Dublin this time around? I remember you had some juicy stories after you were across the pond the last time."

Kit shrugged. "I was on a tight timetable, and most of the archives I visited were in remote places. It was a no-go from day one."

Becky stopped and stared, her eyes wide. "Are you telling me what I think I'm hearing?"

"What?"

"That you haven't had sex in, what, eight weeks?"

Kit sighed dramatically. "Even worse than that, if you can believe it. Spring semester was dry, too. I had three chapter proofs on my new book. Too busy."

Becky's humor actually seemed to fade. "Christ. So what's it been? Five-six months?"

"Eight," Kit said, her humor gone now, too.

They continued walking in silence for another block. This end of the Quarter was primarily residential, many of the balconies lush with plants and flowers. Here and there they saw a house or balcony festooned with beads and masks, even this long after Mardi Gras. Houses and buildings in the Quarter are required to use the paint colors available when each building was originally built, and Kit saw several beautiful lilacs and yellows mixed in with pale ivories and blues.

Becky suddenly punched her arm.

"Ow!" Kit yelled.

"Don't be such a baby," Becky said, chuckling. "Anyway, I was knocking you out of your funk. This is one of the wildest cities in America, and we're going to have fun every night we're here. I know some other ladies of our persuasion at the conference, and we're all going to go out every night and get laid."

Kit laughed. "Sounds like a plan."

They finally reached Frenchmen Street, and as they rounded the corner, a wave of music hit their ears. Bars and nightclubs up and down the street had musicians blasting out an interesting and lively mix of music. One place featured a huge brass band. The next had a collection of rag-tag singers belting out what sounded like a strange version of bluegrass. Must be Zydeco, Kit thought. In another, they could hear the sultry tones of a blues singer bemoaning a lost love.

Becky and Kit shared an excited glance and continued through the crowds toward the restaurant. Becky pointed out an independent used bookstore as they walked, and Kit was pleased to see a rainbow flag above its door. They decided to drop by after dinner once they saw that it was open all night.

The restaurant's location was obvious from a block away, as a long line stretched around an adjoining block. It was also well-lit compared to the nightclubs around it and shone in the darkening night like a beacon. A wave of mouth-watering scents greeted them as they approached, and a stab of desperate hunger hit Kate's stomach. She thought back, trying to remember her last meal, and couldn't even begin to do the math. It had been at least twenty-four hours ago, somewhere in an airport.

Becky ignored the line and dragged Kit to the front door, opening the exit and pulling her in with her. They went right to the podium, and a bedraggled, hassled hostess watched them approach with wariness.

"Reservation for two under Rebecca Lee," Becky said.

The hostess glanced briefly at her computer and nodded at the male attendant, who held some menus. "This way, ladies," the man said, leading them through a curtain toward the tables behind it. Kit heard the murmurs and grumbles of the hungry, angry people in line and smiled at Becky's boldness. Had Kit been here by herself, she would have waited in the line and likely lost her reservation.

The interior of the restaurant was spare and warmly lit, designed in a farmhouse style of stark-white boards and simple linens with bright-yellow Edison bulbs strung up around the room. The chairs, however, were well-designed, and instead of being as hard and unyielding as they looked, were comfortable and cushioned. They were seated in a small alcove that partially shielded them from the rest of the room, and both received a food menu and a drink list.

"Seems like a date," Becky said, raising her eyebrows up and down suggestively.

"Maybe it is," Kit said, raising one eyebrow in response.

Becky chuckled. "Now I *know* you're desperate."

"Hey!" Kit said, swatting her arm. "You're pretty hot, you know."

Becky shrugged modestly. "I do okay. I just know that I'm not exactly your type."

"Which is?" Kit asked, curious to know how obvious she was.

"You like those strong, dangerous types. Tight jeans and boots, no conversational skills, that kind of thing."

Kit agreed, remembering once again the woman from the hotel lobby. "That doesn't mean I don't, uh, go against the grain now and again."

"You *did* manage to get that femme fashion model in DC. Every dyke in the club was gunning for that one, and you just innocently swooped in and snatched her. I think I still owe you a drink on that bet."

Kit turned her eyes to her menu and grinned, self-satisfied. The model had been causing a lot of chaos that night. Kit had watched Becky and several other butch women get turned down and had decided to give it a go when Becky had dared her. She'd been surprised when the woman immediately agreed to leave with her. The sex had been a little different, as it had forced Kit to be the top, but she'd enjoyed the role change for one night.

"What's supposed to be good here?" Kit asked, trying to change the topic. Becky was a funny woman, but all she ever wanted to do was talk about sex.

"Everything," Becky said, opening her own menu. "Like I said—celebrity chef. She was on one of those cooking shows on the Food Network. I never saw the show, but my friend who recommended this place says that she kicked everyone's ass and was voted off on a technicality. Otherwise, she would have won."

Kit wasn't interested in television and usually ate whatever was put in front of her with easy indifference, but she pretended to be interested for the sake of conversation. "Oh yeah?"

Becky launched into the story of the chef—all apparently heard secondhand—but Kit was relieved to have the topic change for as long as it took them to order and begin waiting for the food. The restaurant was small enough that she didn't think it would be a long wait, but Kit was so hungry she could barely stand it. When the bread was set down in front of them, she pounced on it like a hungry dog, stuffing most of a roll into her mouth before making herself slow down and chew. She nearly guzzled her first glass of wine, and Becky laughed at her lack of restraint.

"I'm sorry," Kit said through a mouthful of bread. She forced herself to swallow and nearly choked. "I'm starving."

"You don't say?"

"This bread is amazing." Kit made herself put down a third roll.

Before the entrées appeared, Kit was actually salivating and had found it necessary to drink another glass of wine to avoid drooling on herself. The food, however, when it finally came, was worth the wait. On her first bite of the chicken, her mouth seemed to sing out in ecstasy. Rolling her eyes in pleasure with each bite, Kit wasn't able to resist actually moaning once or twice as she ate, her table manners completely forgotten as she crammed as much as she could into each bite. She shoveled in bite after bite, exclaiming over each new thing on her plate. When she was done, she set her silverware down and stared sadly at her empty plate.

"If that wasn't the best compliment my food has ever received, I don't know what is," a voice said next to their table.

Kit looked up and saw a woman in a dark-blue chef's uniform standing next to her. She was smiling down at Kit, her eyes alive with merriment.

It was the woman she'd yelled at earlier in the wrong hotel.

Chapter Three

B ecky leveraged herself up to her feet, extending a hand. "The food is incredible," she said, shaking the chef's hand.

Kit's mouth was dry, and all she could do was nod, mutely, in agreement.

"Thank you," the woman said, her eyes still rooted on Kit. They continued to stare at each other for a long moment before the woman finally glanced away and over at Becky. "Are you in town for business?"

"Is it that obvious we're not locals?" Becky asked, smiling.

The chef smiled back. "Not exactly." She was looking at Kit again.

Becky threw Kit a confused glance. "We're here for the Irish Literary Association conference."

"So that makes you what, librarians? Teachers?" the chef asked.

"Professors," Becky said. She glanced over at Kit again, who was sitting, red-faced, staring straight ahead. "I'm at Duke, and she's at San Francisco State."

"Ah," said the chef, still staring at Kit. "Brains, beauty, and a temper."

Kit looked up at her finally, surprised at her boldness. "What?"

The chef smiled but didn't respond. "Anyway, ladies," she finally said, touching both of their arms, "enjoy the rest of your stay in New Orleans."

She walked away toward the next table, and Kit stared after her, mouth open.

"What the hell was that?" Becky asked. "She was looking at you like an ingredient for her next entrée. Do you know each other?"

"Not exactly," Kit said, flushing. In her embarrassment over the incident in the hotel lobby, she'd left out that part of her story.

Becky was smiling at her slyly. "Looks like you already have a possibility for a fun night."

Trying to appear casual, Kit shrugged again. "Maybe. What did you say her name is?"

"Theodora something," Becky said, appearing amused.

Kit stored that nugget of information away for later.

The dinner continued with the rest of their wine and a scrumptious crème brûlée. Kit pictured the chef's hands crafting it the entire time she was eating it. She was so caught up in her fantasy, she didn't notice that Becky had fallen silent for a long time. She shook her head as if to clear it of cobwebs.

Becky was grinning. "You've got it bad for that hot chef."

"I do not!" Kit said, flushing with embarrassment.

Becky continued to look smug. "Why don't we come back here in a couple of hours and see if you can catch her at the end of her shift. They're only open until ten tonight."

"Seems kind of desperate," Kit said.

Becky rolled her eyes. "Always playing hard-to-get."

"If I run into her again, I'll say something. Otherwise— whatever."

Becky leaned forward. "That woman is hot, Kit. You should go for it."

"Maybe." Kit decided to change the topic again. "Anyway. What do you want to do tonight?"

"I thought we could go get some drinks and listen to some music somewhere. I also heard about this women's club not far from here. We could get a taxi."

Kit yawned. "I'm not up for a club tonight. Maybe tomorrow. How about we hit that bookstore first and see how we feel after?"

Becky agreed and then grabbed the check, pulling out her wallet.

"Let me go in on this, too," Kit said, reaching for her purse.

"No," Becky said. "I invited you, so I'm paying. This isn't exactly conference fare."

"Fine," Kit said, "but just this once. You don't have to play the strong butch type with me, you know."

"It makes me feel better about myself," Becky said. "Anyway, you're only an associate professor. I make more money than you do."

Kit laughed. "Well, that's true."

After they'd paid, they started walking toward the bookstore but were distracted by music blaring out of a club. Inside, a small jazz band was playing to a tiny room of rapt listeners. The singer, a cute little blonde, was belting a song out with a surprising resonance, and they were drawn inside almost before they'd realized it. They sat down at a small table near the back, ordering two beers a moment later. The room was packed, but the tables were arranged well, and even from the back they could see the entire stage. The crowd was attentive and receptive, with very little talking to distract from the music. The band played jazz standards mainly, with an occasional jazzed-up contemporary song, which everyone seemed to enjoy.

After a long set, Kit started to relax after her long ordeal. Normally when she came back from Europe, she had a day or two to get her head on straight. This time, it had seemed like nothing but one long, anxious, fifty-hour day. She closed her eyes for a moment, letting the music sweep over her.

Suddenly Becky was elbowing her, roughly, to get her attention.

"What?" Kit said, opening her eyes and rubbing her arm. Becky pointed, and when Kit followed the direction of her finger, her stomach dropped.

The chef was standing in the doorway, looking her way. She'd changed out of her uniform and was back in the all-black ensemble Kit had seen her wearing earlier today. She looked dangerous and scorching hot. She glanced around, spotted them, and a moment later she was walking their way.

Becky swung her feet off to the side of her stool and stood up. "I'll just make myself scarce, then. Catch you tomorrow!"

"Don't leave me!" Kit said, desperate, but Becky ignored her, disappearing into the crowd.

A moment later, the chef stood next to her table. "I watched you come in here earlier," she explained, sitting down on Becky's empty chair.

"You-you're following me?" Kit stuttered.

"Not exactly. I just happened to look out the window when you two came in here. I left early and thought I'd see if you were still here. And here you are." The woman looked pleased, satisfied with herself and the situation.

"And what did you hope to accomplish by coming here?" Kit asked, her temper rising.

The woman leaned forward. "First, I want an apology. After that, we can talk about what comes next."

Kit flushed in embarrassment and looked away, her anger instantly dying. "I'm sorry," she said. "I was a complete bitch. I regretted talking that way to you almost the moment I did it."

The woman smiled. "I could tell. I just wanted to hear you say it."

"How did you, I mean, how do you—?"

"How do I know you're interested in me?" the woman asked.

Kit nodded.

"I could feel your eyes on my ass when I was walking away from the hotel," she said. "Anyway, it's obvious you're gay."

Kit looked down at herself. "How?" she asked. She'd always managed to pass before.

The woman leaned closer again. "Sometimes I think I can see it in a woman's eyes."

Kit's stomach did a funny flip at her expression, which was dark and hungry. Up close, Kit could see into the depths of woman's gorgeous eyes, a dark-brown amber flecked with hints of gold. Her lashes and brows were dark like her hair, and her skin was olive and clear. She seemed exotic somehow, and, sitting this close, she gave off the faint odor of vanilla. Kit swallowed, visibly, and the woman laughed.

She extended a hand. "I'm Teddy. Teddy Rose."

"Kit," she replied, her voice quiet, and they shook hands. She found the woman intoxicating and overwhelming.

"So you're a professor?" Teddy asked.

Kit picked up her beer to give herself a moment to calm down and took a shaky sip before setting it down. "Yes. I teach literature in San Francisco."

"Great town," Teddy said, grinning. "And you already know what I do for a living." She suddenly stood, dropping a twenty on the table. "Well. Now that we have the niceties out of the way, do you want to get out of here?"

Kit was stunned. "What?"

"I thought we'd go back to your hotel room. At the Holiday Inn," Teddy said, smiling wolfishly. "That is where you're staying, isn't it?" Seeing Kit's dumbfounded expression, Teddy grinned. "Or we could go to my place. That is, if you're not afraid of dogs."

Numbly, Kit climbed to her feet, picking up her purse almost absently. While she'd hooked up like this before in a lesbian bar, she found the whole situation unsettling. Ten minutes ago she'd been watching the band, and now she was leaving with a complete stranger. Teddy grabbed her arm and steered her outside. They paused next to the door, soaking in the cool air spilling from inside for a moment before turning and walking toward Dauphine, the night air still heavy and hot with the day's humidity.

"So," Teddy said, "your place or mine?"

"Mine." Kit suddenly felt a thrill of anticipation.

"Sounds good to me."

They walked down the block a little, and then Teddy stopped in front of a motorcycle. Kit didn't know a lot about motorcycles, but she knew this was the Harley type, if not an actual one. Teddy unlocked a small box and brought out two helmets, handing one to her. She pulled the other one on and turned to look at Kit, who was standing nearby, confused.

"Put it on," Teddy said, gesturing at the helmet. She held Kit's purse for her as she fumbled with the buckles. Eventually, Teddy set the purse down and helped Kit with the strap, and the brush of Teddy's fingers on her chin and neck made Kit flush with heat.

Teddy climbed onto her bike, pushing it off its kickstands, and waited. Kit looked around, slung the strap of her purse over her neck, and, after hiking up her skirt, climbed up on the back of the bike with difficulty.

"Hold on tight," Teddy said, leading Kit's hands to her stomach.

She need hardly have told her that, as Kit clutched at her, terrified. Teddy stood up to start the bike, which rumbled to life beneath them a moment later. Closing her eyes, Kit held on as the bike took off. A block or two later, she finally had the courage to open her eyes, and after another block, she started to relax a little, finally enjoying the ride. She'd never been on a motorcycle before, and the open air blowing on her face and the thrill of feeling every bump in the road was exhilarating. Teddy drove through the Quarter quickly but, from what Kit could tell anyway, safely. They were at the hotel in minutes.

They pulled into the parking lot, and the valet drivers seemed surprised to see a motorcycle.

"Where can I put this for the night?" Teddy asked them.

The valets shared a look and pointed to a small area out of the way of traffic. Teddy drove over there and motioned for Kit to climb off before setting the bike on its rests. She stood up and put the helmets back in the lockbox.

"Did you like the ride?" she asked, indicating the bike.

"I loved it," Kit said, looking at the bike with appreciation.

"You were really nervous there at the beginning. First time?"

Kit shrugged, trying to downplay her inexperience.

Teddy stepped closer to her. "The ride made your cheeks red. You look even prettier than before."

Kit couldn't help but blush darker, and Teddy laughed. She came close enough to draw Kit into her arms. She was taller than Kit, but only just, and her arms were strong and solid around her. Kit looked up into Teddy's eyes and saw that same hunger from before. Her stomach clenched with desire.

"Let's go upstairs," Kit said, finally waking up from the daze she'd been in the last twenty minutes.

"By all means," Teddy said.

CHAPTER FOUR

They barely made it upstairs to her room in their haste and desire, tearing at each other's clothes the moment they were in the elevator. They stumbled out into Kit's hallway, lips locked, breaking apart only long enough for Kit to throw open the door.

Teddy slammed it behind them, and they stared at one another before crashing into each other in a wild frenzy of heat. To Kit, it seemed as if Teddy's hands were suddenly everywhere on her body—unbuttoning, unzipping, and flinging off every bit of clothing she found. Kit's hands were shaking too badly to reciprocate, so, once Kit was down to her underwear, Teddy took a step back and stripped off her jeans and T-shirt, revealing her magnificent, sculpted body. Teddy wore no bra and stood clad now only in black, nondescript underwear. It was clear that Teddy worked out. Muscles rippled beneath her olive skin, and her stomach looked firm enough to eat off. Kit had noticed some of her tattoos from beneath her clothes, but now she could see that Teddy's body had several—on her arms, back, and legs. Her dark hair, normally slicked back, had come a little loose from the helmet and the elevator, and several curls had fallen across her forehead. Kit had mere seconds to take in this glorious sight before Teddy was pushing her onto the bed and climbing on top of her.

When Teddy kissed her neck, Kit groaned, rising to meet the heat of Teddy's lips. Teddy's hands, hot and strong, were on Kit's hip and her left breast. Kit hissed, and Teddy squeezed her through the material of her bra. Teddy paused her ministrations long enough to unhook Kit's bra and throw it onto the floor. She began kissing her way down toward Kit's breast, and Kit's breath caught in her lungs. It seemed long, agonizing minutes before Teddy finally found her nipple, and Kit let out a sigh of pleasure. As Teddy continued to kiss and suck her nipples and breasts, Kit nearly seized up with pleasure and anticipation. Normally more responsive than this, she was too overwhelmed to do much more than moan with pleasure. Her body, so tense with expectation, was trembling lightly in suspense. Teddy ran her hands up and down Kit's body, leaving shock waves of enjoyment in their wake. Finally, as if suddenly unfettered, Kit let herself go, returning Teddy's embraces and drawing her close with hungry desperation. They kissed again, and as Teddy's tongue plunged into her mouth, Kit was momentarily dazed, her ears almost ringing with the intensity of the feeling.

Kit traced her hands along Teddy's strong, ripped body, sensing a barely contained strength under the surface. Teddy's breasts, small and tight, were wonderful in Kit's hands, and she was pleased that Teddy's nipples were rock-hard. Her passion now beginning to overwhelm her, Kit clutched desperately at Teddy, wanting more. She was panting, and her body, once gently shaking, was now quaking with suppressed longing.

"Please," she moaned. "Teddy, please."

Teddy grinned against her breast, and suddenly the hot weight of her fingers was on the outside of her underwear.

"My God, you're wet," Teddy whispered, rubbing her underwear slightly.

Kit moaned again, rising to meet Teddy's hand. Louder now, she began to beg, "Teddy, please. I can't wait any longer."

Teddy chuckled and then finally levered herself up, looking down at Kit. Their eyes met, and Kit saw the same dark need in Teddy's eyes that had convinced her to leave the bar with her. Once again, she held her breath in anticipation of what was coming, but their eyes remained locked. She felt, rather than saw, Teddy's hands on her hips, slipping off her underwear. When they finally broke eye contact, Kit had to close her eyes. The waiting, already difficult, was becoming intolerable.

After a long pause, Teddy's fingers traced up and down the inside of her thighs. Teddy's fingers would come closer and closer to touching her where she desperately wanted—no, *needed*—them, and then they would move away again. Kit moaned, throwing an arm over her eyes. It was all taking too long. She couldn't remember ever being this aroused before. So desperate she could feel her own heat, she trembled as she waited.

Finally, Teddy's fingers brushed between her legs. Kit almost shouted again in pleasure, but Teddy moved her fingers away again. On the verge of screaming with rage, Kit lifted her arm and looked up at Teddy, who appeared sly and satisfied, clearly aware of what she was doing to Kit.

"Do you want something?" Teddy asked playfully.

"Christ, yes!" Kit shouted.

"There's that temper I like again," Teddy said, her eyes hooded and dark.

Kit groaned again and threw her head back onto the bed. "Please!" she shouted.

Teddy's fingers slid into her, and Kit howled with relief. So keyed up it almost hurt, she gave a great shudder of relief and finally relaxed a little. She raised her hips to meet Teddy's hand, and Teddy pushed her back down. "Slowly," Teddy said. "It's better if you slow down."

"I don't care if it's better," Kit said between clenched teeth.

Teddy chuckled in response and plunged in deeper, and Kit sighed again, first with something like pain and then with mounting pleasure. Teddy's thumb was tracing circles closer and closer to Kit's clit, and impatiently she hitched her hips toward the hand, hoping to maneuver Teddy's thumb nearer. Teddy paused, and Kit tried to calm down a little. She opened her eyes again and met Teddy's smiling face. Teddy continued to inch in and out of her, and then, finally, Kit saw her move down and almost cried with relief.

Teddy kissed her stomach and then the inside of her thighs, nibbling both lightly before kissing her way up toward Kit's center. Once again, Kit tightened with anticipation, and when the gentle touch of Teddy's lips finally kissed her down there, she trembled with relief.

Kit's passion, already built up by Teddy's continued delays, began to come to a head almost immediately. As if sensing her situation, Teddy removed her lips again, and Kit moaned in frustration. Teddy plunged in and out of Kit, and the pleasure Kit received from this, while intense, wasn't enough.

"Please," she moaned again. "Please, Teddy," she said, her voice now cracking.

Finally, Teddy's tongue was on her, and a great, shuddering bolt of pleasure streaked through Kit. Teddy picked up intensity with both her mouth and hands, and soon Kit was screaming incoherently as her first orgasm crashed through her. She shuddered several times afterward, and Teddy paused just long enough for Kit to catch her breath before beginning again with just her hand. Kit's next orgasm, though not as intense as the first, was even faster to crest and break, and she moaned, tears of pleasure and relief streaming from the corners of her eyes.

❖

When Kit woke the next morning, Teddy was long gone. She hadn't expected anything else, but she couldn't help but feel a pang of disappointment. While they'd barely said a word to each other all night, Teddy had taken control of her body in the most delicious, incredible way. They'd been at each other all night, over and over again. Kit sighed, knowing that anyone else she slept with this trip would be a letdown. While she enjoyed one-night stands (in fact, she rarely had anything but), the sex was not often so satisfying. While she might have a shallow orgasm or two, she couldn't remember having the kind of toe-curling, screaming-out-loud experience she'd had last night in the near past, if ever. Teddy had seemed to simply *know* what she wanted without asking, as if she intuitively understood Kit's body. Kit shuddered with at the memory again and then grinned at herself. If she weren't careful, she was going to have to take care of things again on her own.

Someone knocked on her door, startling her before she remembered ordering breakfast yesterday. She grabbed a robe and opened the door, letting the attendant enter with a large tray. He set it on the bed and she tipped him, closing the door after he'd left. She poured herself a cup of coffee and walked over to the window, enjoying the bustle down on the street below. This early in the morning, the people out there were almost exclusively locals. She pictured tourists in beds all over the city, sleeping off the excesses of last night.

She glanced at the clock and sighed. She was supposed to help at the reception desk for the conference in an hour, and she was presenting later today. If she didn't get moving, she'd be running late and would end up feeling hassled and harried all morning. She flipped on the TV to the Weather Channel and then lifted a suitcase onto the bed to decide what to wear. The anchors were discussing a tropical storm about to hit Florida, but she was more interested in the bottom of the screen, waiting for the New Orleans forecast to appear among the list of US cities. When it did, she saw that, although it would be scorching hot all day, it was likely to rain later. She decided on slacks so she could wear more protective shoes.

Dressed and showered, she wolfed down her breakfast before checking her reflection in the mirror one last time. She had inherited delicate features and light skin from her mother's side of the family, her pale-red hair and blond body hair from her father. If she didn't wear makeup, she usually looked tired and washed out, but in her line of work, people generally overlooked such superficialities. If she'd had more time, she might have put on some makeup, but she looked fine for a day at a conference. If she went out with Becky tonight, she would spend more time on her appearance later.

As she walked the blocks over to the conference, she contemplated a night out with Becky. While she was excited to see more of the city, she wasn't interested in going to bed with someone again—or at least not yet. She wanted to savor the memory of last night a little longer. Lightning rarely strikes twice, certainly not so soon, so the next partner she slept with would be a disappointment no matter what.

She could see fellow attendees long before she reached the conference hotel. Academics always stand out among normal people. Most of the men were disheveled and unshaven, with untucked shirts and wrinkled pants. In the main, the woman wore bad dresses or unflattering pantsuits. Kit sighed. The entire academic profession needed a makeover.

She found the reception desk a few minutes later, and after putting on her nametag, she spent the next two hours helping conference attendees get their tags and programs. She'd agreed to work the desk in the hope of someday being asked to sit on the board of the association. This kind of volunteer work was both dreadfully boring and infuriating. So many academics, normally some of the most brilliant people in the world, were utterly helpless when it came to day-to-day activities. She must have explained how to plug in at the various kiosks around the lobby in order to use the Internet fifty times during her shift, and she also pointed out the very clear map printed on the back of the program at least that many times. Most of the men and women she spoke with looked just as confused leaving as they'd been when they approached her, and she chided herself for her lack of customer-service skills. She rarely could appear patient when she was annoyed—something her students were always quick to point out on her teaching evaluations.

As she finished her shift, she spotted Becky standing next to a few women in another part of the lobby. Feeling worn out and pissed off from her shift, she wanted to avoid them, but Becky spotted her.

"Hey, Kit!" she yelled across the lobby. "Get your skinny little ass over here."

Likely as red as her hair, Kit obeyed, walking over quickly but feeling every eye in the lobby on her as she did.

"Everyone, this is Kit, from San Francisco State. Kit, this is Charley, Mia, and Jackie. Charley's at Duke, with me, and Mia and Jackie are at Columbia."

Kit shook everyone's hand. Like Becky, Charley and Jackie were wearing men's suits. Both were strikingly tall and impressively built. Mia was pretty and small, wearing a delicate pink lacy affair.

"We were just about to go get some lunch," Becky explained. "Want to join us?"

Kit looked down at her watch and shook her head. "I don't think I have time. My presentation is in an hour."

"Just something quick," Becky said, linking her arm in Kit's. "There's a little lunch place right down the street."

Kit acquiesced, letting Becky lead them a little ahead of the others as they walked.

"So?" Becky asked once they were out of earshot.

"So what?" Kit asked. She knew exactly what Becky wanted to talk about. Her face was hot under the other woman's attention.

Becky snorted and elbowed her, lightly. "You know what I want to hear, woman. Spill it."

Kit's face must have told Becky all she wanted, as a second later she laughed out loud. "That good?" Becky asked.

"It was amazing."

"I want details."

Kit shook her head. "I-I don't want to tell you. Not right now, anyway."

Becky looked nonplussed. "That's different. Usually you're the first to give me every dirty tidbit. She must be something special."

Kit shrugged. It had been special. Besides being among the best sex in her life, after the initial awkwardness of being picked up, she and Teddy had been comfortable with each other. She was usually incredibly awkward with lovers during the first few times she slept with them, but something about Teddy had inspired her to relax and enjoy herself. The results spoke for themselves—she almost never orgasmed like that with a new lover. It helped that she liked Teddy, personally. Teddy's utter lack of bullshit or pretension was refreshing. They were attracted to each other—no need to pretend anything else.

"Are you going to see her again?" Becky asked.

"I don't think it would be a good idea," Kit said, shaking her head firmly. "It might...confuse things."

"Meaning you might actually feel something about her if you did."

Kit shook her head. "I don't know if that's it...more like, I wouldn't want to spoil things. It was just so perfect, just as it was. Sometimes once is enough."

Becky looked suitably impressed and thankfully let the conversation drop. Kit didn't know why she was reluctant to see Teddy again. If nothing else, she knew the sex would be fantastic. Was Becky right? Was she worried she might start to feel something for Teddy if it happened again? Kit wasn't sure, that much was true, but either way, sometimes once *was* enough. If they kept seeing each other it might be difficult to avoid some kind of emotional entanglement. It wasn't as if they would ever see each other again after Kit went home.

By this time, they had reached the little café, situated next to the Louisiana Supreme Court. This early, it was still fairly empty, and the five of them had their pick of seating. Kit ended up next to Mia, and they spent most of lunch discussing their research. Mia was on her panel at the conference this afternoon, and Kit was pleased to find that their research was complementary.

After lunch, everyone agreed to meet up for dinner and drinks on the town, and Mia and Kit walked back to the conference together in order to find their presentation room. While Mia was certainly not her type, Kit was drawn and attracted to her. Something about Mia—perhaps her smallness, or perhaps her shy demeanor—made Kit feel almost protective of her, almost wanting to wrap Mia in her arms and watch over her to shield her from the world. While not planning anything specific tonight, Kit thought she might follow up on this feeling over the next few days to see if it went anywhere. Mia was clearly interested in her, and they could share a night if nothing else.

Kit's presentation was a success, and as Kit had hoped, the room was filled with other Queer Theory scholars, all interested in her presentation on author Elizabeth Bowen. She successfully fielded several interesting questions, most of which gave her a few good ideas on how to proceed with the article she was planning based on her presentation. While she'd originally agreed to come to the conference only at her chair's insistence, now she was glad she had.

Mia's paper had fallen flat, and she seemed defeated and beaten by the experience. Rather than feeling as if she should reassure her, Kit was mostly annoyed. The paper had been poorly written, and her argument had been unclear and badly formulated. The fault was hers, Kit thought. She knew she was being a little uncharitable and certainly would never say what she thought of the paper to Mia, but watching Mia fail in front of a room of their peers had instantly destroyed any quasi-romantic feelings Kit had for her. In fact, the feelings had likely come from a vague attempt to look for a contrast to Teddy, and Mia was exactly that. Quite likely, Kit realized, Mia would have been a contrast in bed, too, which was not, at this moment, remotely appealing. Kit left the presentation room as quickly as she could to avoid having to comfort Mia or lie about her paper, and she almost ran as she dodged through the crowd milling by the door.

Out in the hallway, she decided to find some coffee and see if the snacks from this morning were still available. She followed the corridor back to the lobby, nearly colliding with several academics milling around absent-mindedly. She finally spotted the coffee urns set out for the conference and headed that way, greeting a couple of the attendees she'd helped that morning, many of whom still looked lost and confused. She was just about to grab a cup when she spotted Teddy a few feet away on the other side of the snack table. She was taking pastries off a platter and putting them into a basket on a cart. She wore black chef's clothes, and several other people in similar uniforms were removing food and trash around the room. Kit froze, staring at her, and it wasn't long before Teddy looked up and smiled.

"Fancy meeting you here," Teddy said.

"What—"

"What am I doing here?" Teddy indicated the food. "I'm the caterer."

"Oh," Kit said, still nearly speechless.

Teddy glanced around the room and then came around the edge of the table, grabbing Kit's arm. "Come over here for a minute," she whispered. She dragged Kit over behind a pillar in the lobby. From this position, they were effectively hidden from everyone else in the room. Teddy pushed her against the pillar, kissing her, hard. Her tongue darted into Kit's mouth, and a flash of desire rushed through Kit with burning heat. Their tongues met and wrapped around each other, and Kit groaned into Teddy's mouth. One of Teddy's hands was suddenly on her breast, squeezing, and Kit's legs began to weaken.

Teddy suddenly broke the kiss and leaned back a little, her eyes slightly unfocused. "I could fuck you right here and you'd let me," she whispered. She moved her face a little closer again. "I can tell how much you want me." She licked her lips, and Kit melted with the words. "I bet if I put my hand in your pants, you'd be completely soaked."

Kit nodded.

Teddy look satisfied and released her, taking a step back. "That's good." She raised her eyebrows and then walked away, leaving Kit without another word.

Kit stood there, her back braced against the pillar, unable to do anything for a long, long time. Finally, when her legs were strong enough to hold her up, she straightened her clothes and rejoined the conference.

CHAPTER FIVE

For Kit, the rest of the day at the conference passed in something of a blur. She attended several panels related to her research and also sat in on Becky's panel for support. While she tried to take notes and pay attention, her mind kept wandering. Often she caught herself daydreaming about Teddy. Sometimes she would remember the night before, and other times she would imagine what would have happened if Teddy had gone further in the hotel lobby.

Would she have let her go all the way, as she'd suggested? Kit was somewhat ashamed to realize that she would have. In fact, if Teddy walked into one of these panels, Kit would follow her anywhere at any time, whatever the consequences. Sitting demurely, legs crossed, seeming attentive to what she was supposed to be listening to, she warmed at the idea of any of the other scholars in here reading her mind. She shuddered once or twice with the heat, covered in a cold sweat almost all day.

After the presentations finally ended for the day, she intended to race back to her hotel to take a cold shower. Once again, Becky stopped her before she could escape.

"Where are you off to? I thought we were going to get dinner."

"Sure," Kit said, "but I need to freshen up. I don't want to go out looking like this."

Becky winked wolfishly and raised her eyebrows up and down. "Hoping to bag another catch tonight?"

Kit smiled mysteriously and took her leave, speed-walking the blocks over to her hotel. Finally back, with the door shut safely behind her, she took a long, deep breath and held it before letting it out, trying to calm down. In her haste this morning, she'd left the TV on, and she looked at it blankly for a moment, not registering what she was seeing beyond the shot of a weatherman being blown around by wind and driving rain on a beach somewhere.

In the bathroom, she set the water in her shower as cold as she could and jumped in before she lost her nerve, letting out a little yelp as the icy water hit her hot skin. She rubbed her entire body, briskly, trying to cool the burning she'd felt almost all day. She squeezed one of her breasts and twisted her nipple, the fingers of her other hand dancing lightly over her clit for a moment. She almost gave in to temptation, her body calling out for relief, but she moved her hands quickly away. She carefully avoided touching certain parts of her body after that, knowing from experience that if she touched herself, she would only make things worse. She would have to go to bed with someone if she did that, and she wanted to savor the memory of Teddy for at least one more night.

Back in the bedroom, she grabbed her hairbrush and sat down on the edge of the bed, watching the weather again, trying to get herself to relax a little. As she did her deep-breathing exercises, she watched the TV. The tropical storm had now turned into a hurricane and was about to hit Florida. She shook her head. Why would anyone choose to live there? It seemed like a hurricane hit Florida nearly every week during the summer.

Standing up, she surveyed her clothing choices. She'd unpacked one of her suitcases this morning—the one with her business attire, and her tired dresses and slacks hung limply in the closet. She had other suitcases with more casual clothes, and she opened a few before finding the dress she wanted to wear tonight. She managed to get it on and zip it herself, and she chose a pair of her sexiest heels to wear with it. A part of her was aware that she was dressing up for Teddy, but she dismissed the idea as ridiculous. While they'd run into each other several times now, and she was starting to realize that this part of the city was incredibly small, the chances of bumping into her again were fairly slim, particularly as Teddy would likely be working until much later. Still, as she carefully applied her makeup and styled her hair, she imagined encountering her again and letting her rip this flimsy dress off.

"Stop it," she told herself, shaking her head wryly. If she kept this up, she would have to take another cold shower.

She used the hotel phone to call Becky, who explained where to go to meet her and the others. She sighed, knowing that she was going to have to flatter Mia's paper just to make the evening run a little smoother. She had made one or two good points during her presentation, and Kit could focus on those. She put her wallet and lipstick in her purse and headed out, walking the short blocks over to the sports bar where the others were waiting. As she approached, her heart lifted in pleasure at the rainbow flags festooning the bar and other nearby establishments, knowing that they'd likely spend most of their time in the city in one of these places.

When she entered, she heard a wolf whistle and turned toward it to see Becky, Charley, and Jackie sitting at a small table near the open window. She walked over and sat down on an empty stool.

"You're awfully dressed up tonight," Becky said.

Kit shrugged.

"Hoping to see someone special?"

Kit colored again but didn't respond.

Becky threw her a knowing wink. "That's what I thought."

"Where's Mia?" Kit asked, trying to change the topic.

"Probably crying in her room," Charley said. "I guess her paper didn't go very well. I think you're the only one who heard it, Kit. How did it go?"

Kit hated to talk badly about another scholar's work, especially someone she knew. She always imagined that people discussed her work that way behind her back and tried to avoid that kind of gossip.

"It could have been better," Kit said after a pause. "She had a couple of good ideas, but…" She raised her hands.

"But her writing sucks," Jackie said.

"I don't know if I'd go that far—" Kit responded.

"But it would be true." Jackie wouldn't drop the subject. "I've worked with her for three years, and we're in the same writing group. I've probably read almost everything the woman has produced, and most of it's jargon-filled crap. With enough work—we're talking months and months of revision—she can produce something decent, but it takes a *lot* of work. She's up for her three-year review this fall, and I'm afraid she'll get turned down because of her research output."

While it was a little different at every school, tenure committees expected a certain amount of published research to accompany teaching portfolios in order to pass the tenure review. At a school like Columbia, where Mia and Jackie taught, the research component was strict and significant. A junior professor anywhere without enough published work could easily be let go if he or she didn't have enough publications.

As if to shake off the ghost of this shared anxiety, Becky suddenly slapped the table, startling everyone. "How about a round of shots?"

Groaning, Kit and the others agreed to do *one* shot, but, as usual, that quickly turned into more as the bartender plied them with several of his new inventions, almost as if sensing their desperation to have as much fun as possible.

Kit threw down her fourth shot—something red and sweet—and almost gagged. She held up her hands in defeat. "That's enough for now," she said, trying to sound decisive. "I think we should all eat something before we keep going."

"Wimp!" Becky yelled.

"Spoilsport!" Jackie added.

They all laughed and turned their attention to the bar menu. It had the usual American pub fare, and Kit frowned. She'd been in Europe for the last couple of months and missed the food already. She hated the traditional hamburgers and chicken wings that seemed to be par for the course in most American bars. Though pub food over there was hardly health food, she generally found at least a couple of lighter, usually vegetarian options beyond salads in Irish and British pubs. She decided on grilled chicken, and the others ordered burgers. As they waited for their food, she turned her eyes to one of the televisions and saw that the hurricane in Florida had made the local news.

"That hurricane's supposed to head up to the Florida panhandle after this," Jackie said.

"Really?" Kit asked. "I thought they broke up when they went over land. I think it's about to hit Miami."

"I was looking at the track, or whatever, and I guess it's going to get back over the water in the Gulf tonight or tomorrow and then head north."

Kit shook her head. "I can't imagine living down there."

"Not far from here, really," Jackie said.

The food arrived, and Kit picked at it, a little disgusted by the grease and mayonnaise. Further, the liquor wasn't sitting very well in her stomach, and she was afraid if she ate too much, she'd just end up in the bathroom all night. The idea made her stomach turn fitfully, and she finally stopped trying, sliding her dinner away almost uneaten.

"So," Becky said, setting aside her empty plate away and wiping her chin. "What do you gals want to do tonight? There's a ladies' night at a gay club down the street, but that doesn't start until ten. We could go get a hurricane at Pat O'Brien's first or check out some music somewhere."

"Music," Jackie said. "My liver needs a break for a while."

The four of them paid their bills and walked from St. Ann down Bourbon Street, amused by the crowds of rowdy drunks, most of whom were about the age of their students. Charley had heard of a good blues bar tucked away on Bourbon, and when they finally found it, Kit was relieved to find it relatively quiet and dark. She ordered a club soda and lime before sitting down with the others, closing her eyes as she listened to the music. She never really played jazz or blues on the stereo at home, so she was surprised how much she liked it. The guitarist and pianist were excellent, and the singer crooned in a deep bass, singing of lost loves and lost opportunities. She tapped her foot absently, eyes closed, trying to steady her whirling head, still a little woozy from the drinks.

Becky moved closer so she could speak quietly. "You are not going to fucking believe this."

"What?" Kit asked, opening one eye.

Becky's expression was excited and mischievous, and Kit sat forward, shaking her head to clear the cobwebs.

"What?" she asked again.

Becky lifted her chin at something behind her, and even before Kit turned to look that way, she knew what she was going to see.

Teddy was sitting at a little table nearby with another woman.

Kit turned her face away, quickly, blushing furiously. While it didn't appear that Teddy had seen her, she couldn't be sure. Kit had been sitting here for a long time. Either Teddy had come in when her eyes were shut, or she'd been here all along. Either way, she probably knew that Kit was here. It was also fairly telling that if she did know that Kit was here and hadn't said or done anything about it, she was probably avoiding her on purpose. The woman with her was probably her girlfriend.

Kit's stomach seemed to sink into the ground, and the dizziness from earlier returned tenfold. Unable to stop herself, she glanced over her shoulder at Teddy and the other woman. Their eyes were moony, and they appeared to be completely wrapped up in each other. Teddy suddenly leaned closer to the woman next to her as if to kiss her, and Kit's stomach gave a sickening lurch. She jumped to her feet, almost running across the bar to the bathroom. Once inside, she flung open the stall door and just managed to get her face over the toilet before she started heaving up the drinks and her tiny dinner. Several long minutes later, when she finally began to feel human again, she came out of the stall and went to the sink to wash her face. As she was bending down to wash out her mouth, the door opened, and Teddy walked inside. She glanced around to make sure they were alone and came over to Kit.

"I'm sorry I didn't say hello before," she said.

Kit, trying to look unconcerned, raised her eyebrows. "Why should you?"

Teddy looked puzzled, and then her face cleared up. "Are you jealous? Of Mary out there? Don't worry about her."

"It's no concern of mine." Kit tried to maneuver past her and out of the bathroom.

Teddy grabbed her arm and brought her closer. "Even now, after puking your guts out, you're hotter than any woman in this bar."

Kit flushed, but she managed to gather enough dignity to wrench her arm out of Teddy's hand. "Just who the hell do you think you are? It's obvious you're used to getting your own way, but I have a mind of my own."

Teddy only grinned in response, and Kit's temper rose several degrees. Nearly shaking with fury, she stormed out of the bathroom and headed directly for the street. She heard Becky call after her, but she was only concerned with leaving as quickly as possible. Out on the street, she paused to get her bearings, which was just long enough for Teddy to catch up with her and grab her arm again.

"Don't be this way," Teddy said, clearly trying not to laugh. "I like a hot temper, but it's misplaced here."

Kit wrenched her arm free again but didn't leave. She looked around and motioned for Teddy to follow her, off to the side and away from some of the milling crowds on the street.

"Listen," she told Teddy, "you might get to move from woman to woman most of the time, but I don't want to see it. You get me?"

A wry smile pulled up one corner of Teddy's mouth.

Kit suddenly realized how ridiculous she was being, and she flushed from head to toe. Teddy's clear lack of guile didn't help her feel any better. After all, what right did Kit have to be upset? None. But that didn't stop her from feeling angry.

Trying to recover, Kit said, "Look, I know we're not dating, and I know I'll never see you again when I leave. You're free to do whatever you want in your own time."

Teddy continued to listen, so clearly unperturbed by the whole situation she might have been watching television. Kit sighed, her face hot with embarrassment. She needed to wrap up before she said more stupid things.

She touched Teddy's arm. "Anyway, I don't have to know about the other women. Okay?"

Teddy snapped off a quick salute. "Yes, ma'am."

Kit's temper died down a little, but she was still angry, mostly out of mortification now. She didn't know why, exactly, she'd reacted the way she had. She could give a damn about the other woman, but something about seeing Teddy with her had bothered her. Deciding it was a self-reflective inquiry best left for a time when she was alone, she pushed the question aside for the time being.

"So what are you going to do about Mary?" Kit asked, trying to keep her voice as casual as possible. She wanted to make it appear as if she didn't care, even if she wasn't fooling anyone after her recent outburst.

"Screw her," Teddy said, waving her hand vaguely in the direction of the door. "I only went out with her so I could catch up with you later tonight. She insisted on coming here before the club, and I agreed. I never thought we'd run into you."

They'd started walking down the street, and Kit stopped completely. "You're just going to leave her in there? Alone?"

"She was already talking to one of your friends when I left. The big one," Teddy explained. "She'll be fine."

"You're an asshole, you know that?" Kit asked, smiling.

"Yes, I do."

They walked in silence for a while longer, neither one of them needing to ask the other where they were headed. A few minutes later they made it to Kit's hotel and headed up to her room.

CHAPTER SIX

Despite the blasting air conditioner, Kit was soaked with sweat. She lay on her back, breathing heavily and fanning her body with a magazine. Teddy was standing by the window, her naked back to the bed. Her body was also bathed in sweat, and Kit could see rivulets of liquid dripping down her skin and sliding off the cheeks of her muscular ass.

This was the first time Kit had had a chance to look at the tattoos on her back. An outline of leaves and vines on her right shoulder wrapped onto her right arm and extended up onto her neck. On her left shoulder blade was a large flower, but from her spot on the bed, Kit couldn't quite make out what kind it was. All of Teddy's tattoos were black or black outlines, with no coloring other than a lighter gray shading here and there. On her olive skin, they stood out in dark relief, almost appearing to rise off her body. Kit sat up to get a closer look, and her movement made Teddy turn to look at her. Her dark nipples were erect from the cool air coming from the air conditioner, and Kit swallowed hard, her desire rising as she stared at her.

"See something you like?" Teddy whispered.

"Everything," Kit said, looking her up and down. Teddy's body was tight and strong, and she moved with a lithe grace when she walked. Everything about her suggested a dangerous, predatory animal.

Teddy beamed as if she could read Kit's thoughts and walked over to the edge of the bed, grabbing Kit's hands. "What say we go out and cause some trouble tonight?"

"Now?" Kit asked, still looking at Teddy's nipples.

Teddy used one hand to tilt Kit's head up, looking into her eyes. "Now. There will be more time for that later."

Kit smiled at her, embarrassed to be so obvious. "Okay."

Teddy yanked her up off the bed and slapped her ass playfully. "Get some clothes on. What you had on earlier would work—something fun."

"Do I have time to take a shower?" She wrinkled her nose. "I stink."

Teddy leaned closer and kissed her neck, causing shivers to run up and down Kit's back. Teddy inhaled strongly, right next to Kit's ear, and then pulled back, meeting her gaze. "You smell delicious."

Kit swallowed again and Teddy laughed. "Anyway—everyone else will stink, too. It's summer in New Orleans. There's not a lot anyone can do about it."

"Where are we going?" Kit asked, picking up the dress she'd been wearing. A couple of buttons had been torn off, and she frowned at them.

"Dancing," Teddy said. "I need to blow off some steam before the weekend. Tomorrow's Friday, and we have solid reservations at the restaurant from lunch tomorrow until dinner Sunday. Tonight is my only night off this week."

Kit walked over to her suitcases and opened the one with her casual clothes. "Does that mean I won't see you this weekend?"

"I get off at eleven every night. I might be tired after a fourteen-hour shift, but I won't be dead."

Satisfied with the response, Kit tugged out another dress, this one made of a lighter material and more revealing than the one she'd worn earlier. Normally she wouldn't even think of leaving the house in it. While the dress wasn't designed for it, she almost considered it lingerie. Slipping it on, she turned her back so Teddy could zip her up. In a moment, Teddy's warm hands were on her back again, but before she pulled up the zipper, she snaked her hands around

Kit's front and squeezed her breasts once, hard. Kit moaned and then turned around, slowly, pleasurable warmth washing through her when she saw Teddy's eyes light up with appreciation.

"You look good enough to eat," Teddy said, looking down at her exposed legs.

"Later," Kit said playfully, echoing Teddy's own dictum back to her.

Teddy grinned back before turning around to find her own clothes. They were strewn all over the room, and it took the two of them some time to find all of them. The last sock was hiding on the top of one of the lamps, and her wallet was under the bed.

"If you want to take my money, next time just ask," Teddy said as she tucked it in a pocket.

"Don't worry—you're paying for everything tonight. My salary can't take a night out very often."

They gathered their things and left the room, heading for the bank of elevators down the hallway.

"So the ivory tower isn't all it's cracked up to be?" Teddy asked.

Kit shrugged. "The work is great, but I don't get paid much. Lots of time off but little money—the usual contradiction."

Downstairs now, Teddy grabbed her elbow, leading her out onto the street, the pavement wet from a recent downpour. "I know what you mean," Teddy said. "I used to work in a kitchen with flexible hours, but I was broke all the time. Now I work nonstop, and I don't have time to spend the money I make. I haven't had a vacation since we opened."

"When was that?" Kit asked, genuinely interested.

Teddy looked up and down the street before crossing and leading them to the left.

"Almost a year now," Teddy finally answered. "We're having our anniversary party in a couple of months." She was silent for a moment and then looked over at Kit, smiling almost shyly. "You should come back to New Orleans for it. Going to be wild."

Kit smiled without responding, her heart leaping into her throat. She had, for a moment, almost replied enthusiastically until she remembered the reality of their situation. She was here for a conference and wouldn't likely return to New Orleans any time soon. The recognition of this fact was, however, not as welcome as it would be usually. Normally she was happy to leave someone behind, even a woman she'd slept with several times. It meant no messiness—no complications. Something was different with Teddy—something she couldn't quite put her finger on. It was partly that she was so easy to be around, but, if Kit was honest with herself, she was also simply drawn to her. Her first impulse had been to agree to go to the party because she *wanted* to come back—not for some party, but so she could see Teddy again. Once more, she decided to put off thinking about it for now and changed the subject.

"So, are you from here? Is that why you decided to open a restaurant here?"

"Yes, I am," Teddy said, looking away quickly. "I lived in New York for a while, but I came back last year to open the restaurant. You know what they say: 'You can take a girl out of New Orleans—'"

"'But you can't take New Orleans out of a girl,'" Kit said, smiling. "There's a version of that for a lot of places."

"Well, in my case it was true. I had worked in restaurants here in the city for years, and I was getting tired of the scene. My family and I…Well, anyway—we weren't talking. Aren't talking still, really. A friend of mine offered me a spot in a kitchen in New York at a place she was opening. I jumped at the chance. I couldn't wait to leave." She smiled. "It wasn't even a week later when I realized I'd made a mistake, but it took me almost five years to get back here. I knew if I came back, I wanted my own restaurant, so I set out to get a lot of experience in different kinds of kitchens up there and started working on my own things on the side. I auditioned for the Food Network Challenge just to get some money to open a restaurant, but it didn't work out. So I took some small-business classes and finally had enough money saved and the credentials to get a business loan." She raised her shoulders. "It's such a relief to be back here—I can't even tell you."

Almost without realizing she was going to say it, Kit asked, "So you wouldn't ever want to leave again?"

Teddy looked at her, quickly, obviously confused, and Kit flushed with heat.

"No," Teddy said, shaking her head firmly. "I'm here for good."

They walked in silence for a while, neither of them wanting to add to the already palpable awkwardness of their conversation. Kit felt nervous and confused. What on earth was that about? she asked herself. She never talked this way to her lovers. What was the point? It was clear she and Teddy would never see each other again, so why make the time they had uncomfortable? Did she actually think for a moment that Teddy would leave, move to San Francisco? Schooling herself harshly to keep the conversation light for the rest of night, she squeezed the arm linked with hers.

"So where are we going?"

"There's an eighties night at a club I go to nearby," Teddy said. "We're almost there."

They could hear the music before they arrived and saw a long line wrapping around the block. Teddy led them past the line and directly to the bouncer, who, seeing her, waved them both inside. The room was a large converted theater, with a stage up front with go-go dancers writhing to the beat. One girl and one boy were up there, both young, college-aged kids. Teddy led them to a bar in the center of the room and motioned at a bartender who recognized her and stopped what she was doing to tend to them. The music was loud enough that Kit had to pass her request through Teddy, who leaned far over the bar to tell the bartender what they wanted.

In another moment, Kit was sipping her cocktail, watching the people on the dance floor. It was an unusual crowd, composed of a broad mix of people. Both younger and older dancers were out there, companionable and dancing, at times, together. The music faded from one eighties hit to the next, several people on the floor cheering as each song started as if they'd been waiting for it all night. Teddy touched her elbow and lifted her chin, indicating an empty table on the side of the room. Fighting the crowd, they made their way over there, sitting down so close to each other that Kit was almost in Teddy's lap. A small reserved sign sat on the table.

"I take it you come here often?" Kit asked, almost yelling over the music.

"Like I said, Thursday is my only night off. And I tip well."

"My friend told me there's a ladies' night at a gay club tonight, too," Kit said.

Teddy laughed. "There is, and good luck to her. Mostly assholes from the suburbs. Those of us that live here call them the Metairie Weekend Warriors—all of them straight every day of the week but Thursday. All of them married, all of them bitches."

Kit raised her eyebrows, startled at the language. "You sound pretty bitter about it."

"There used to be a great women's club in the city when I was younger. Had all sorts of people there, great vibe, good music." She shook her head regretfully. "Closed a while back. The scene hasn't been the same since."

They watched the dancers for a while in silence, sipping their drinks. Kit understood Teddy's disappointment. While San Francisco was indeed a gay Mecca, it was much easier to meet people if you were a man. Most of the clubs catered to men, with the occasional women's night thrown in almost out of pity. When a good place for women opened up, it was inevitably closed down, and it always seemed as if all the hot women Kit saw there just disappeared into the ether. A couple of bars and coffee shops were exclusively dedicated to women, but that was about it.

Drinks finished, Teddy hauled Kit to her feet and over to the dance floor, edging them into the crowd gracefully. She drew Kit toward her, and their hips connected to the slow beat of a Prince ballad. Teddy linked her hands around Kit's ass and squeezed, making Kit close her eyes with the sudden heat that swept through her. The front of Teddy's jeans pressed so hard into Kit's middle, she could feel the buttons on the front rubbing her under her dress. She shifted her hips a little, hoping to ease some of the aching want building between her legs, but Teddy pulled her close again. Kit opened her eyes, looking up slightly into Teddy's, which were hungry and dark. Kit's hands were on Teddy's back, and she dug her fingers into the hard muscles she found there. The two of them paused for a moment to kiss and received a wolf whistle from a nearby group of twenty-somethings. Their lips broke apart at the sound, and they grinned at each other, both amused.

A moment later the beat picked up with a pop song, and the spell was momentarily broken. Teddy released her strong grip, and the two of them started dancing, separate but next to each other. Kit let herself get lost in the song, enjoying the euphoria of dancing. She'd always loved to dance and had gone to clubs like this for most of her youth, but it had been a long time since she'd gone dancing just to dance. In the last decade she had rarely gone to clubs, but when she did, she was there to find someone for the night. She usually danced one or two songs, if that, before leaving with her next conquest.

Tonight, however, was different. She was already here with someone, which meant that she could enjoy the music and the movement for as long as they stayed. Unsurprisingly, Teddy danced with the same grace with which she moved normally—a supple series of undulations, her muscles flexed and flashing. In her tight jeans and T-shirt, she was a gorgeous combination of strength and grace—a combination Kit could never resist. Like Kit, she was covered in a thin sheen of perspiration, and Kit fought a wild yearning to grab her and lick the sweat off her neck. She continued to watch, Teddy seemingly oblivious to her gaze. Others around them, men and women, were watching her, clearly interested. Kit suddenly felt a kind of fierce pride that Teddy was hers, at least for the night. The more she watched Teddy dance, however, the more that pride seemed to turn into something melancholy—almost like longing. She would leave for home and never see this woman again.

She forced her eyes away and watched the dancers on the stage for a moment. Both of them were thin nearly to the point of emaciation, and both possessed the same kind of androgynous beauty. The girl and the boy were heavily made up, the only sex differentiation between them the slight bumps under the girl's shirt and her longer hair. Many of the people in the crowd seemed to be mimicking the dancers' clothes and style, and she also saw, to her pleasure, that the crowd in general was mixed as far as their sexual tastes. Here and there a man and woman danced together, crushed up next to each other. Over there, boy and boy and girl and girl bumped hips or caressed. In some places, small groups writhed against each other, their clear attraction suggesting group sex to follow. Unlike most of the gay clubs she'd been going to almost all her life, this club and its patrons seemed to be open to whatever came their way. With some of the best pop music ever made, the crowd was also one of the best she'd ever been in. She understood now why Teddy came here every week. She would, too, if she lived here.

She turned to see Teddy watching her with glittering, dangerous yearning in her eyes. Her body had slowed slightly, and she held out a hand, beckoning to her. Kit immediately responded, letting Teddy draw her into her body again and feeling the sticky heat of their sweaty bodies meet as they drew close.

Teddy leaned close to her ear and, whisper-shouting, asked, "Who were you looking at?"

Kit recognized that she was pretending to be jealous and played along. "That hot little number on stage." She pointed at the go-go dancer.

Teddy looked up and frowned with mock anger. "Isn't she a little young for you?"

Kit laughed and punched her arm, playfully. "Hey! Fuck you. I could take her home if I wanted to."

"Do you want to?" Teddy asked, her voice suddenly serious.

Kit shook her head.

Teddy stepped even closer, meeting her eyes. "Who do you want to go home with?"

"You know the answer to that."

Teddy's smile stretched from ear to ear, and she whirled Kit into a spin before bringing her close again, grinding their hips together. Kit gasped at the rush of heat that coursed through her body and felt momentarily giddy with need. As they danced, she clutched Teddy, curling her fingers into the other woman's strong back. The buttons of Teddy's pants were rubbing her in a delicious spot again, but the sensation was beginning to become overwhelming, almost painful in its intensity.

As if sensing her growing desperation, Teddy suddenly pulled back a little, looking into her eyes. "I need to get out of here," she said, her voice rough and choked.

Kit simply nodded and let Teddy lead her back through the crowd and out the front door of the club. The hot night air offered no relief, and they quickly walked back in the direction of the hotel. A block away from the crowds of Bourbon Street, Teddy paused, looking up and down the street. While a few people were passing on perpendicular streets on their way to the bars, they were essentially alone. Before Kit could prepare herself, Teddy was leading her into a small, arched alleyway between two buildings and pushing her up against a wall. The alley was completely dark, the light from the street barely penetrating the gloom. Teddy's kiss was intense, and, lips locked, she hiked up the skirt of Kit's dress before sliding her hand inside Kit's underwear. Her fingers slid into Kit's folds and stayed there, moving slightly but not offering any relief.

"You're soaking wet," Teddy said right next to her ear, her voice hoarse.

Kit was unable to respond, her entire body rigid with yearning.

"We're going to fuck each other here—fast. I can't wait any longer," Teddy commanded her.

This time Kit managed to nod, though whether she could be seen in the darkness of the alley was uncertain.

"Then I'm going to take you back to your hotel, and we're going to fuck all night," Teddy purred.

Kit began unbuttoning Teddy's pants, the distracting presence of Teddy's fingers in her underwear making the process much slower than usual. Her shaking fingers finally finding purchase, she slid her hand inside Teddy's underwear, finding a slick fire of heat between her legs. Seconds later, Teddy was slamming her fingers inside Kit, and, momentarily stunned, Kit was paralyzed with pleasure. Teddy suddenly paused, and Kit thought she just might die from frustration.

"At the same time, baby, or you get nothing," Teddy whispered.

Kit moved her fingers back into the slippery wetness between Teddy's legs. Teddy quickly replied in kind, thrusting her fingers inside Kit, and it was all Kit could do to keep touching Teddy as her pleasure quickly mounted. The ball of Teddy's palm was rubbing Kit's clit, and she writhed against it, her desperation for release now nearly intolerable. Teddy's fingers increased their inward and outward motion, and Kit, nearly overwhelmed with the sensation, made her fingers and hand respond. Both of them were now panting and groaning, the moment of release drawing closer every second.

Kit could detect the faint flutter of an orgasm building inside of Teddy, and the sensation of her inner walls trembling against her fingers sent Kit over the edge. They clenched, almost in unison, as they came, clasping each other closer. They stood there a long while, still pinned together, both with their hands still in the other's underwear. Teddy finally moved her hand away, and Kit almost groaned with disappointment.

Kit's knees were weak, and as she set her clothes back in order, her hands still trembled. Almost before she was ready, Teddy was steering her back into the street by an elbow, nearly dragging her toward the hotel. Teddy's face was flushed and sweaty, set with grim determination, and her T-shirt was clinging to her sweaty body.

Teddy looked over and forced a smile. "I'm sorry to rush you," she said, "but if I don't get you naked and in bed very soon, I'm going to fuck you right here in the street all night."

Kit picked up her pace as well, desperately trying to mask the frantic need surely painted all over her face.

Chapter Seven

K it arrived at the conference the next morning almost two hours late. She and Teddy had stayed up the whole night together, taking turns with each other's bodies until well into the early morning light. The only thing that had stopped them was pure exhaustion and the realization that they both had a very long day ahead. Rather than stay and sleep with her for a few hours, Teddy had made her excuses and left, sometime around six that morning. Kissing her in the doorway of her room, Kit had fought a crazy, almost irresistible yearning to pull Teddy back into her room for one more go-around, and when Teddy had disappeared into the bank of elevators, she'd felt bereft and depressed by the lonely room she was left with. She'd collapsed in bed, too stupid with fatigue to do anything more, waking up, by pure chance, to the sound of a garbage truck just outside her window. Seeing the clock, she'd raced through her shower and nearly ran the few short blocks to the conference.

She spied Becky almost immediately upon walking into the lobby of the conference center. Still somewhat embarrassed by her disappearing act the previous night, she attempted once again to avoid her but was spotted almost immediately.

"Hey!" Becky yelled from behind her. "Where do you think you're going, Professor Kelly?"

Kit turned, unable to keep the guilt from her face. Becky walked quickly over to her. "What the hell?" she asked when she came closer.

Kit decided to play stupid. "What?"

"You just disappeared last night. You didn't even say good-bye."

"I was…distracted." She greeted a fellow conference attendee she recognized to avoid looking at Becky.

"I saw what you were distracted by." Becky was still frowning. "Or should I say *who* you were distracted by."

"So what's the problem?" Kit asked, now confused. "I wasn't going to, well, stop what we were doing to call you."

"That's not the problem," Becky said, her face red. "The problem is, you and your little playmate left someone behind."

"Oh," Kit said, remembering the woman Teddy had been in the bar with.

"That's right 'Oh,'" Becky replied. "After your 'friend' abandoned her, I spent the next hour comforting her. She was very upset."

"I'm sorry," Kit said, after a pause.

Becky's serious expression suddenly broke, and she laughed out loud. Kit, perplexed, watched her for a while before finally joining in her mirth, the two of them laughing so hard together they managed to cause a small scene. Several people walking by them gave them curious looks, which only sent them into further gales. Becky put a hand on Kit's shoulder to steady herself, but it took a long time before they could calm down.

"Seriously, though, thank you. I've never had an easier time getting a woman into bed," Becky said, wiping her eyes. "If I thought you were a better person, I would think you did it on purpose."

"Hey!" said Kit, actually offended.

Becky held up her hands. "Oh, come on. You know you were only thinking of yourself."

Kit shrugged in defeat.

"Anyway," Becky said, "I'm going to see her—that is, Mary—again tonight. You and your new lady friend should join us."

"I was thinking of staying in tonight. Teddy doesn't get off until after eleven."

"Please? It's Friday. Live a little."

"I'm so tired right now, I can't even think about it. Ask me again later, when I've had a chance to rest this afternoon."

"You do look like a tired pile of shit," Becky said, looking her up and down.

"Gee, thanks." Kit rolled her eyes.

"Well, it's true. And you're walking kind of funny."

Kit slapped her arm. "Perv."

"Takes one to know one," Becky responded.

After attending another round of panels, they met Jackie, Charley, and Mia for lunch again. Mia was still subdued after her disastrous presentation the day before, but Kit managed to cheer her up by talking about a mutual scholar they both respected and admired. Mia was excited to listen to the scholar's plenary presentation that afternoon, but Kit wasn't sure she would make it. She couldn't run on four hours of sleep very well anymore. The late thirties weren't like the late twenties—she'd realized that often enough in the last couple of years.

Already, her eyes were struggling to stay open, and her body was stiff and sore from the night's activities. As Mia gushed about the scholar's research, Kit drifted into a kind of fugue state, half-aware, half-daydreaming about Teddy. The memory of her body above her in the dim light of the hotel room sent shivers through her. She could almost feel the strength of her fingers on her breasts, inside her, coaxing her body toward another orgasm despite her growing fatigue.

Mia had fallen silent as she drifted into her fantasy, and Kit smiled apologetically at her. "I'm sorry. I haven't been sleeping well," she explained.

"No problem," Mia said, though obviously miffed.

Kit raised her eyebrows and turned to the others at the table, lacking the patience to apologize with real feeling. She could give a damn about Mia's feelings at this point—the woman was a wet blanket.

"So," said Becky, slapping the table in her usual signal to pay attention. "What are we planning for this evening? I don't meet Mary until ten."

"There's belly dancing at some hookah place this evening," Charley said, her brow furrowed. "I don't remember what it's called, but I could ask around. They serve Indian, and the women are supposed to be super hot."

"That sounds fun," Mia said, her face suggesting otherwise.

"And after?" Becky asked, looking at each of them.

"Dancing again, maybe," Jackie said, shrugging. She looked at Kit. "You and Becky missed out on it last night. It's not ladies' night tonight, but I heard Oz is fairly mixed on Fridays anyway."

"Sounds like a plan," Becky said.

"Maybe, but first I'm going back to my hotel for a while to sleep," Kit said. "I wanted to go to another panel, but I can barely keep my eyes open."

"The plenary is at four," Mia said.

"I'll try to go. Otherwise, I guess I can talk to you about it later," Kit said.

Mia looked a little disgusted with her, but once again, Kit didn't really care.

"Can you call and tell me about the hookah place?" Kit asked Charley.

"Sure. I'll leave a message if you're still asleep."

"Thanks. I'll see you guys a little later, then."

Kit stumbled the few blocks back to her hotel, looking as drunk as most of the tourists she passed. By the time she was back at her door, she could barely make sense of the keycard she held, and it took her a long time to get into her room. After dropping her bag and kicking off her shoes as she walked, she fell down, face-first, onto the bed, and she was out almost before her head hit the pillow.

❖

When she woke, the evening light coming in through the windows was confusing. Pushing herself up awkwardly with her hands, she looked over at the clock. It was now almost six. She'd slept without moving for nearly five hours. Turning around and sitting up, she groaned at the stiffness in her neck and then rubbed it, hoping to relieve a little of the pain. Her clothes were completely rumpled and creased, and she realized she had a little dried spit on the side of her mouth. Climbing awkwardly to her feet, she stood there a moment, trying to decide what to do. She'd hardly had time between Europe and this trip to get over her jet lag, and this bout of afternoon sleep was not going to help her readjust. If she stayed up again tonight, she'd never get back on schedule. Still, she wanted to see Teddy again for a couple of hours. Maybe if she took it easy this evening and stayed in, she'd start to feel like a human being again tomorrow.

She took a long shower, scrubbing away sleep sweat and rubbing her sore muscles. Wrapping herself in a bathrobe, she went back into her room and saw that the message light was blinking on her phone. She punched the button to listen to her messages.

Hey, Kit, this is Charley. The hookah place is called the Dragon's Den, at the corner of Esplanade and Decatur. We're all going to try to get over there about seven. They're having some kind of party there tonight, but I managed to get us a reservation. Hope to see you there.

Kit erased the message and stood there, trying to decide. If she joined them, she'd have another night like last night. They'd end up drinking too much, and by the time Teddy was off work, she wouldn't have the wherewithal to end things early. If she stayed in, Teddy would come over here, and she could make things wrap up at a decent hour. But this was probably wishful thinking. More than likely Teddy would stay all night, and she'd walk around like a zombie again all day tomorrow. She grinned, self-satisfied, wishing she didn't have to wait until later to see her again. Going out with her friends would help pass the time, but staying in would help build anticipation. She shivered at this delicious idea and decided to wait here. Decision made, she sat down on the armchair in the room, not bothering to get dressed. Teddy would just take her clothes off later anyway.

She turned the TV on again, her robe open to let her body dry. While the hot shower had felt wonderful on her aching body, she was now overly hot. The cool air refreshed her hot skin, and it made her nipples pucker. Her nipples and her breasts were sore and tender from the attention they'd received, and she rubbed at them absently as she watched the TV.

Several officials had been on the screen when she first turned it on, and the screen flashed back and forth between them and the image of the Gulf Coast. There was a little red hurricane icon in the Gulf now, and the drawing of its projected path now stretched all along the Gulf, including the Louisiana coast. Kit sat forward a little, frowning, then turned up the volume.

The cone of uncertainty now includes the Gulf cities of Florida, Alabama, Mississippi, as well as those of Louisiana. This includes the metropolitan areas of Pensacola, Mobile, Biloxi, and the City of New Orleans, among others. Forecasters will not have a more accurate prediction for landfall until the next update, which we will share with you at eleven pm tonight. The governors of Louisiana and Mississippi have declared a state of emergency. It is vital that viewers continue to monitor the situation as it develops.

Hurricane Katrina is now a dangerous Category 2 hurricane, verging on a Category 3, and forecasters predict that it will become a Category 3 within the hour. Warm waters in the Gulf are fueling this storm, and there is no reason to suggest that it will become weaker before it makes landfall. In fact, some weather indicators have suggested that it could develop into a Category 4 or higher as it gets closer to land.

The information began to repeat after this, and Kit sat forward in her chair, looking at the screen closely. The cone of uncertainty, which she took to be the name of the possible projected path, was much different than the last time she'd seen it. Now, instead of Florida, it had tracked farther west. The coastline of Louisiana, just south of where she sat now, was now outlined in dark red. She frowned. She'd grown up in Colorado, and before moving to California, she had experienced very little weather beyond the occasional blizzard. Where she lived now, she had endured, at worst, a bad rainy week here and there, constant fog, and the ever-impending threat of the next big earthquake. She didn't really know anyone who lived along the Gulf Coast and paid very little attention when a hurricane blew through down here. How dangerous is this? she wondered. Clearly a Category 3 was worse than a Category 2—that much she could tell from the tone of the voices on screen, but what would that mean if it actually came this way? Also, how likely was it to actually hit New Orleans? The projected path was still very wide. The chances of it coming here seemed extremely slim. Still, if it hit nearby, would it be dangerous? Kit had no idea.

Knowing she could catch Teddy at the restaurant, she picked up the phone and called the front desk, asking them to connect her. The hostess at Teddy's picked up, and after she was put on hold, Kit waited impatiently for Teddy to pick up. It was right in the middle of dinner, so she knew she would be waiting for a while, but as the minutes ticked by, she started to feel foolish and more than a little desperate. Even if she could convey her genuine anxiety to Teddy, it would seem like she couldn't wait to talk to her. She waited through one more Muzak rendition of "The Girl from Ipanema" before hanging up, fighting off a pang of true longing to hear Teddy's voice. It's for the best, anyway, she told herself. No need to seem like a stalker.

She remembered, then, that Becky had done a postdoc in Tampa, and Kit decided she'd call her to ask about it. She searched her room for a while, looking for the slip of paper she'd written the number on, only to realize that the maid had likely picked it up as trash. Sighing, she looked at the TV screen again, reading suppressed fear and anxiety on the face of every official on-screen. If they're worried, that's a bad sign, right? she thought.

After debating with herself for a few minutes, she decided to track down the others after all. She dressed quickly, glanced at the map of the Quarter provided by the hotel, and realized she could walk over to the restaurant in time for dinner if she left right away. Grabbing her wallet and keycard, she took one more look at the TV before leaving, the red outline of the coast making her stomach clench in fear.

CHAPTER EIGHT

Despite the crowd, Kit spotted Becky and Charley right away. Both were putting dollar bills in a belly dancer's dress, and Kit rolled her eyes before walking over to them. They had clearly been here for a while. Their table boasted an empty bottle of wine, several empty shot glasses, and a hookah that was mostly smoked. They greeted her with a little too much enthusiasm, yelling their cheer. Becky got up and hugged her a little too roughly before manhandling her into an empty chair.

"The others bailed on us," Charley explained, pointing at their empty chairs.

"Just us hooligans tonight," Becky added, her voice slurring slightly. "I'm meeting Mary at the club later."

Kit glanced around the room. Five belly dancers were making their way around the crowded room, each pausing long enough at most of the tables to get tips. The nearest dancer was taking a rest with a glass of water, and she smiled at Kit when they made eye contact. Blushing, Kit looked away. Balloons were tied up around the room, and a sign over the bar touted several drink specials. Images of officials and screenshots of the hurricane dominated all three of the TV screens above the bar, but everyone sitting there seemed oblivious to them.

"Is it a bachelorette party?" Kit asked.

Becky, draining the last of her current drink, shook her head and set down her glass, swallowing with a wince. "No. Hurricane party."

"What's that?" Kit asked, her stomach clenching in fear again.

"Everyone drinks to the hurricane, toasting in its honor," Becky explained. "It's supposed to send it somewhere else or something. I went to a couple of them in Florida when I lived there."

"Did it work?" Charley asked.

"Nope!" Becky said, laughing. "We were hit both times."

Trying to sound casual, but desperate for information, Kit asked, "So, what do you think of the one they're talking about now?" She motioned toward the TVs.

"What, Katrina?" Becky asked. She shook her head dismissively. "It probably won't end up coming here, and anyway, it's only a Category 2."

Charley agreed. "They always hit Florida."

"And the Quarter is supposed to be safe anyway. Highest part of town and all that," Becky added, waving her hand vaguely around them.

"So there's nothing to worry about?" Kit asked.

"Not yet," Becky said, frowning up at the screens. Her eyes were clearly having a hard time focusing. "But probably not. A Category 2 isn't really that bad. Just a lot of rain and wind."

"I heard it was going to turn into a Category 3 later," Kit said, still nervous but feeling a little better now.

"Well, a 3 is a something else," Becky said, nodding sagely, "but they almost never stay that strong. It'll probably go up to a 3 and then go back down again before it makes landfall."

"And we should know the path better later tonight," Charley added. "I bet you twenty dollars it'll head for Pensacola at the last minute."

"I'll take that bet," Becky said, holding out her hand. They shook on it.

Kit was relieved. Until now, she hadn't recognized how frightened she'd been since she heard the news. Now as she watched the TV screens, she almost laughed at herself. The likelihood of it heading here seemed very remote given the length of the coast it could hit, and a Category 2 didn't sound that bad either. She took Becky's offer for a drink and decided to relax a little. She'd make her excuses in a couple of hours and go back to the hotel to wait for Teddy.

One drink quickly turned into three, and before she knew it, Kit was pretty tipsy again. It didn't help that she'd barely eaten all day. One upshot, however, was that her earlier fears about the hurricane now seemed silly. During trips to the bar, she'd heard several locals scoffing at the news and figured that, given how often the threats of hurricanes hung over the city, they must know better than most people how dangerous this particular storm was. She let a man buy her fifth drink and sniggered with the others when it arrived, giving him a little toast with her glass before chugging it down.

"What time is it?" she slurred, the drink sloshing around in her empty stomach.

Becky squinted at her watch and then tried again, pulling her arm farther from her face. "I don't know," she finally said. "I seem to have lost the…lost the…" She just sat there, dumbly, for a moment. Finally, she snapped her fingers. "The ability to read!" She looked incredibly pleased with herself.

"Give me that, you lightweight," Charley said, grabbing Becky's arm with a sneer. She peered at the watch for a long time and then shook her head, dropping the arm. "I don't know either."

Kit looked around for a clock. She didn't see one, but there was some movement up front. Almost everyone, about fifty people, was on their feet, standing close to the bar, the three of them the only ones in their chairs. They shrugged at each other and rose before making their way unsteadily over to the bar. Kit managed to kick someone's purse along the way, almost tumbling headlong into a burning hookah. Becky dragged her to her feet again, and she brushed herself off and made her way toward the bar with the others.

Everyone was silent, staring at the TVs. Kit looked around, noticing expressions of deep concern and fright on nearly every face. Confused, she remembered she should be looking at the TVs and turned her attention there.

The cone of uncertainty has now been adjusted. The storm, as we feared, is tracking west from its original path. While there are some variations in the models, most of the computer models now suggest that the path will bring Katrina directly toward either the Louisiana coast or the far western coast of Mississippi. One or two models show it moving slightly east of these projections, but the majority of the models predict that Katrina will either hit or hit near the Louisiana coast, which puts the City of New Orleans in danger. There will be updates every seven hours, and the next projection will give us a better understanding of what to expect.

The hurricane is now a strong Category 2, and predictions also suggest that it will strengthen radically in the next twenty-four to forty-eight hours before it makes landfall. Warm Gulf waters are fueling the hurricane and will continue to give it strength and power as it draws closer to land.

Again, the information began to repeat itself, with state officials and weather experts weighing in on the projected path and possible outcomes of a direct hit at various locations. Regardless of whether the hurricane came directly at them, it appeared now that New Orleans would likely be affected.

Kit instantly sobered, and every face around her reflected her mood. All of the belly dancers, standing together, looked terrified, and the bartender and other wait staff were stricken dumb. This reaction affected her even more than the news she was watching. News anchors were, after all, notorious for fear-mongering, but these people, who had grown up with hurricanes, who watched the news every summer as they drew close to the city, were frightened. That scared the shit out of her. Looking over at Becky and Charley, she could see that they were similarly affected. The earlier cheer and jolliness was no longer there in their faces. Instead, both looked incredibly lessened somehow, as if the news had physically deflated them.

Becky turned and tried to smile at her. "Well, this is the shits." Her voice was clear and focused. True terror has a way of sobering you up.

"Yeah," Kit said lamely.

The three of them made their way back to their table, not saying anything, and sat down again. Many of the bar patrons were likewise regaining their seats, but several people were already leaving, many of them looking rushed.

"When did it say it would hit?" Charley asked, her voice more subdued than Kit had ever heard it.

"Monday," Becky said, finishing her last drink.

"When are you flying out?" Kit asked.

"Tuesday," Becky said. "What about you guys?"

"Wednesday," Charley said, her face bleak.

"Monday," Kit whispered.

Becky set her glass down and stood up. "I guess I have some calls to make, ladies."

Charley also got to her feet. "I guess I do, too."

Kit remained seated, staring at the TV screens. Becky touched her shoulder, and Kit jumped, startled. Becky was looking at her, her eyes warm and sympathetic.

"It's going be okay, Kit. Even if it hits, we're in the safest part of town here."

"Are we?" Kit asked.

Her voice must have betrayed her terror, as Becky squeezed her shoulder in response. "Yes. Go back to your hotel and start making some calls. We might be able to get out of here if we start trying now. We have the advantage since we're hearing about it now instead of tomorrow morning. See you later."

Kit watched them walk out the door. She was rooted to her chair, overwhelmed not only by the information, but also by the idea of all she would need to do to help herself out of this mess. She had to try to get on a new flight—tomorrow, if possible. If she couldn't do that, she would have to figure out how to leave the city another way—renting a car, maybe. She sat there long enough, paralyzed, that a belly dancer returned to their table, asking for her next order. She shook her head mutely and finally managed to get to her feet. Though she was almost completely sober now, the alcohol and adrenaline had worn her out. She felt drained and exhausted. Nearly staggering with fatigue, she walked outside into the hot night air and stood on the corner for a long time, trying to decide what to do first.

She should get back to her hotel as quickly as possible. She should already be on the phone with her airline or a car-rental agency. She should be thinking about what she would do with her mountains of luggage, but all she wanted to do was to go find Teddy. She'd wanted to see Teddy since the moment she heard about Katrina earlier today, and now that it was definitely headed this way, she had a deep pang of yearning for her. Seeing her, she sensed, would solve everything. Teddy would know what to do.

Looking around to get her bearings, she realized she was very near Frenchmen Street, and, if she was lucky, she might be able to catch Teddy at work. She crossed Esplanade and then started dodging through the crowds spilling out onto the sidewalk of Frenchmen as she made her way toward the restaurant. Most of the people on the street were either oblivious to the news or unconcerned about it. From the few conversations she overheard, almost everyone was still interested in talking about the music they were listening to or the men and women they'd seen in the bars they'd been in. No one was talking about the hurricane. She took some comfort in this ignorance, wondering again how frightened she should be. Back in the Dragon's Den, as she looked at the TVs, she'd experienced an almost supernatural sense of foreboding, as if she was looking at death coming for her. Now, out here in the warm summer night, her fear was fading. She should be frightened, should be making decisions, making plans, but none of that mattered as much as what she needed to do right now: see Teddy.

The lights were still on at the restaurant, but the doors were locked. She spotted a few staff members inside, moving furniture around to clean under the tables and wiping down surfaces with rags and sanitizer. She knocked on the window long enough to get someone's attention, and his annoyed expression almost made her leave. However, she managed to hold her ground and stood there until he finally came over.

Without unlocking the door, he yelled, "We're closed!" through the window. He pointed at the little sign with the restaurant's hours.

"I'm here for Teddy!" she yelled back.

He looked surprised and then annoyed again. "Go around to the back!" he yelled, indicating the side of the building.

She followed the direction he'd pointed to the edge of the building and then around to the back. The back door was open and several workers were standing by the door, smoking. Teddy was near them, smiling as they laughed and joked, listening quietly. A small part of Kit had convinced herself she'd never see Teddy again—that she'd already left. The sight of her made Kit sag with relief.

Teddy looked up, and when she spotted Kit, her face lit up from within. "You tracked me down!" Teddy walked over to her. "Sorry I missed your call earlier. We were slammed." The happiness in her expression faltered a little when she came closer. "What is it? What's the matter?"

"Did you see the news?" Kit asked, almost breathless.

"What news? What are you talking about?"

"The hurricane. Katrina. It's coming." Kit's voice was shaking so badly she could hardly get the words out of her mouth.

"What do you mean? The one that hit Florida?"

"Yes," Kit said, heart hammering.

Teddy put an arm around her shoulders and steered her toward the back door, helping her up the little steps into a brightly lit kitchen. Other employees looked over at them curiously, and Teddy nodded at them, waving away their concern. Teddy led her to a small office, opening the door for her and helping her into a chair behind a tiny desk. She sat down on the edge of the desk and grabbed Kit's shaking hands.

"Start from the beginning," Teddy said. "What did you hear?"

"The hurricane is coming this way. We'll be hit on Sunday… no, Monday. I don't remember when. It's supposed to be really bad."

Teddy smiled. "It's probably just the anchors trying to get ratings. They always make it sound worse than it is."

Kit shook her head. "I don't think so."

Teddy considered her for a moment and then seemed to finally accept that Kit was genuinely worried. "Okay. Even if it is as bad as you've heard, it's very unlikely to flood here. A lot of things would have to happen for us to get water here. The stars would have to align in just a certain way."

"But what if they do?" Kit could hear the pleading in her voice and felt a little disgusted by her own neediness. Still, she desperately needed reassurance.

"Even if they do, you're in the safest part of town. It never floods here. We're above sea level here along the river."

"Can you get me out of town? On your motorcycle?" Kit asked.

Teddy shook her head. "It's in the shop. I took it in yesterday."

"You can't go get it?"

"No," Teddy said. "The mechanic is out of town, actually. I don't trust the local one. It's ten miles away."

"You don't have another car?"

"No," Teddy said. She thought for a moment. "I might be able to borrow one, though, if it came to it."

"Can you borrow it now?"

"Right now? Right this minute?"

"Yes," Kit said, actually pleading now.

Teddy laughed. "It's almost midnight. I wouldn't call anyone this late unless it was an emergency."

"Teddy, this is an emergency."

Teddy looked at her a long time and finally sighed. "Okay. I'll do it. For you." She stood up and made her way around the desk before picking up her phone and dialing. She waited for a long time and then shrugged and hung up.

"No one's home or they're not answering. I can try again in the morning."

"Would you? Please?"

Teddy walked back over to Kit and grabbed her hands, squeezing them. "Don't worry about it too much, okay? If you need it, I'll get you out of town. I promise."

Something about the certainty in Teddy's voice made Kit finally relax a little, which also made her recognize her exhaustion once again. Teddy, as if sensing this, patted her shoulder. "Let me get you a glass of wine. You can drink it while I finish up here, and then I'll walk you back to your hotel."

"Thank you," Kit said weakly.

She spent the next thirty minutes staring into space, clutching a glass of wine in her fingers, untouched. Through the open door to the kitchen, she could see Teddy bustling around, helping with various closing tasks. Her staff clearly respected and appreciated her, most of them still smiling despite the late hour, all of them joking around and bantering with clear warmth between them.

When Teddy finally returned, she had taken off the top of her chef's uniform to reveal a dark undershirt, damp with perspiration. She smiled wryly and wrinkled her nose.

"I'm sorry," she said. "I stink, and I forgot to bring a change of clothes."

"It's okay," Kit said, setting down her glass of wine.

"Are you ready?"

"Yes." Kit got to her feet, wobbling slightly, and Teddy grabbed her arm.

"Steady there," she said. "Have you been drinking?"

"I was. A while ago," Kit admitted.

Teddy looked a little annoyed, but the expression passed. "Why don't I take you to my place? It's closer."

"Are you sure? I don't want to put you out."

"It's fine. I have three dogs, though. I hope you don't mind."

Kit felt the same relief she had when she'd seen Teddy standing behind the restaurant. She wasn't being sent away or abandoned. Teddy was here for her.

"No. I don't mind dogs."

"Okay. Let's go."

Chapter Nine

Teddy's house was a short walk away in the Marigny. Her place was half of a double shotgun house, and it shared a porch with the neighbor in the other half. Flowers and herbs were growing in the boxes on the porch, and even in the dark night, Kit could tell that the house was nicely painted and maintained. Before she unlocked the door, Teddy knocked on it, loudly, three times. Kit assumed this was a ritual with a roommate she hadn't mentioned, but when Teddy opened the door, Kit saw three dogs sitting with preternatural stillness a few feet away. They stared at Teddy with rapt attention. She beckoned Kit in, closed and locked the door, and set down her belongings and keys.

"Meet Jingo, Bingo, and Dot," Teddy said, indicating the three dogs. They were sitting in order of size from left to right. Kit didn't know many dog breeds, and the middle- and smallest-sized dogs were clearly mutts. The largest she recognized as a Great Dane.

"Did you train them to do that when you knock?" Kit asked.

"Yes," Teddy said, smiling proudly. "I hate for dogs to jump all over you when you come in."

"Impressive."

"Come here, Jingo," Teddy said, and the giant Great Dane loped over to them before sitting down again right next to Teddy. Seeing Kit's apprehension, Teddy laughed. "I know he's huge, but he's very sweet."

Kit petted him, tentatively, and the giant animal seemed to smile up at her, his enormous pink tongue lolling out with a trail of drool. His head was massive, and the teeth that showed as he panted happily looked fierce enough to rip off an arm.

"Okay, you two," Teddy said to the other dogs, who, released from their imprisonment, leapt to their feet and ran over, nails clicking on the hardwood floor. They reluctantly sat down again with barely contained eagerness. Teddy knelt to pet them both, and Kit bent over to give each a quick pat on the head

"They're cute," Kit said, just to say something.

"I take it you're not a dog person?" Teddy asked, clearly amused.

"Oh, I like dogs," Kit said. Teddy raised her eyebrows with disbelief. Kit colored and tried to make herself sound more genuine. "No, really! I'm just not very familiar with them. I've never had one before."

Teddy stood up. "Okay, y'all," she said in a deep voice, making eye contact with each dog. "Go get your leashes."

They scampered away to a small basket, each animal retrieving a separate leash before bringing it back to Teddy. She clipped one onto each of their collars.

"I'm going to take them over to the neutral ground for a few minutes," Teddy said. "Why don't you sit down and make yourself comfortable? You can help yourself to anything in the kitchen."

Kit watched the four of them leave, all of the dogs patiently waiting as Teddy walked out first before following her outside. While Kit had never been comfortable around animals, she did appreciate that Teddy's dogs were clearly well-trained. She supposed, given enough exposure, she could become comfortable with a dog that didn't jump all over her. She'd always wanted dogs growing up, but her mom and brother were allergic. If she could start with Teddy's well-trained dogs, maybe she could be a dog lady after all. She grinned at the idea of walking all three of them, knowing that she'd look completely ridiculous. The grin slowly faded and she shook her head. Why imagine what's not going to happen? she thought. Once she left New Orleans, she would never see Teddy or her dogs again. Why worry about getting comfortable with them?

She turned to survey the living room. Three differently sized dog beds sat in one corner of the room, but that was the only indication that the animals lived here. The rest of the room was immaculately clean, and the house overall smelled lightly of lemon oil. A brown, worn leather couch hugged one wall, and a comfortable-looking armchair sat next to it, a small reading table nearby. Curious, Kit walked over to see what Teddy was reading and was pleasantly surprised to see three classic novels: *Madame Bovary*, *Jude the Obscure*, and *The Ambassadors*. It almost looked like the book selection for a college course. Underneath these was a French cookbook, written in French. After seeing this, Kit opened *Madame Bovary* and saw that it too was in the original French.

Feeling like an ass for underestimating her new lover, Kit put everything back the way she'd found it and walked around the living room, peering at the framed photographs and artwork. In the photos, she saw Teddy at various ages with various women in various cities, and one of a much-younger Teddy and a young woman who strongly resembled her. She and the woman were sitting on a bench by the Mississippi River, at a park Kit had visited just days before here in town. The framed artwork on the walls was almost entirely Impressionistic, as if in keeping with the time period Teddy clearly favored reading.

She went through an open doorway into a bedroom, walked through another and passed the bathroom, and then found a smaller sitting room with a television. Sitting down on a lavishly cushioned loveseat, she grabbed the remote and turned on the TV. She found the news and became absorbed in it again. She was only dimly aware when Teddy and the dogs returned some time later and didn't even look up when Teddy came back to find her.

"More bad news?" Teddy asked. She was holding the smallest dog in her arms.

Kit looked up, startled to see her there. "Yes."

Teddy's mouth hardened into a grim line, and she stared at the TV screen. She watched it for a couple of seconds before setting the little dog down. Then she walked over to the coffee table, picked up the remote, and turned it off.

"Hey!" Kit yelled. "I was watching that!"

Teddy shook her head. "There's nothing we can do about it right now. Watching that shit will only make you more anxious than you already are. You need sleep. We'll take another look in the morning and make some plans."

"But—but—" Kit sputtered.

Teddy shook her head again, firmly. "I'm serious." She held out a hand. "Why don't I put you in a warm bath, and then we'll go to bed." Seeing Kit's surprise, she smiled. "I mean—we'll go to bed to sleep."

Kit took one more desperate look at the TV and then made herself let it go. Teddy's argument was sound. They couldn't do anything right now, and really, there was nowhere she wanted to go. Right here, right now, she was safe. She took Teddy's hand and followed her into the bathroom.

❖

Kit was sitting in the backyard watching the dogs, the morning sunlight so bright it was painful. Her hangover made her head tight and hot, but considering how much she'd had to drink, she knew she should feel much worse. She'd woken up this morning, curled around Teddy's warm, sleeping body, and had a moment of tender affection for her so deep and strong she'd almost sobbed. Here in the beautiful sunshine in Teddy's backyard, she felt embarrassed about last night. Her terror about the hurricane seemed silly and needy. She should have gone back to her hotel and gotten her shit together. In fact, she should be there now, but she couldn't make herself leave. Not yet.

Teddy shared the backyard with her neighbor. The lush plants back here were well-manicured, the fishpond was sparkling and fresh, and the small green space for the dogs was clearly cleaned every day. The larger dogs were wrestling with each other while the smallest, Dot, stood by, watching anxiously, a ball in her mouth. Dot apparently wanted to play with them, but, wrapped up in their own antics, they were ignoring her. Her little body was quivering with impatience, and she occasionally let out a low moaning growl of displeasure.

Teddy and her neighbor had placed a large canopied table out here near the house. The chairs were comfortable and cushioned, and a gas grill stood nearby, well-used but clean. Several bug-catchers were set up around the yard, but the frogs and dragonflies also helped, as Kit found that, for the first time since arriving in the city, no flying pests were around to bother her. She was sitting in a chair in Teddy's bathrobe, but, hidden from the street and other neighbors, the backyard sheltered her from passersby. The heat was crushingly oppressive, but lounging here and soaking in it lulled Kit into a heavy, languid relaxation. This kind of heat seemed to dissuade action, and she relished the fantasy of just staying here and not moving for the rest of her day. Every time she tried to make a plan, her mind revolted in a panicky haze of inaction. She wished someone else would make the necessary decisions for her.

Teddy appeared a couple of minutes later, carrying a large coffee pot and a small pitcher of cream. She set them down on the table, went back inside, and brought out a tray with two plates of eggs, fresh fruit, and bread.

"Sorry it's not very fancy," Teddy said, setting the food down. "I haven't had time to go shopping in the last couple of days."

Kit couldn't help but feel some small manner of triumph at this, silly as it was. "Someone taking up your time?"

Teddy grinned back at her. "Something like that."

They ate in companionable silence for a few minutes, Kit closing her eyes in pleasure after the first bite and then attacking the food with ravenous intensity. The eggs were delicately seasoned and expertly prepared, and the bread was freshly baked and warm. She was eating her fifth slice, sopping up the last remaining egg yolk, when she looked up to see Teddy smiling at her.

"You're easy to please," Teddy said.

Kit shook her head and then made herself swallow her huge mouthful of food. "It's incredible. You baked the bread yourself?"

Teddy colored slightly with pride and nodded.

"It's amazing. Really, it is. When I was at the restaurant the other night, I assumed you brought the bread in from an outside bakery."

"A lot of restaurants do that," Teddy said, "but I've always wanted to do everything in-house. I'm a fair baker, so it seems to work."

"Fair," Kit said, rolling her eyes. "It's only the best bread I've ever had."

Teddy grinned, still apparently embarrassed, and her color deepened further.

Kit smiled, pleased that she'd managed to flatter her. So far, except in bed, Teddy had come off as impassive and somewhat closed off. Some of this was, perhaps, butch affectation, and some of it was likely the result of being lovers and not quite friends. Something seemed a little different this morning—as if spending a night together without having sex had made whatever this was a little more real, more serious. Kit wasn't sure if this was a good thing. She liked Teddy, and she'd wanted to be around her from the moment they'd first seen each other, but the notion of feeling something for her was dangerous and stupid. That would only lead to heartache.

They turned to watch the dogs a while longer before Kit finally sighed and stretched, her back popping pleasurably. "I guess we need to watch the news now."

Teddy agreed, looking unperturbed. "I bet it calmed down overnight. It also looked like it was headed for Mississippi last night."

"I hope so," Kit said, then blushed. "I mean, I would rather it didn't hit anywhere, but…"

"I know what you mean," Teddy said. "No one wants a hurricane headed right for them."

They stood up, each grabbing something to carry. Dot, still left out of the play between the big boys, decided to follow them in, and Kit held the door open for her with her elbow. They put the dishes in the sink and went into the TV room and sat down. Teddy sighed and turned the TV on, and they were both sucked into it.

Even before they started listening, Kit knew the news was bad. The projected path had been narrowed and more closely fixed. Now it was clearly headed for Louisiana or the far western coastline of Mississippi. The weather experts and officials suggested that there was still some margin of error, but now the options meant that it could either be a worst-case scenario, with a direct hit to New Orleans, or that it would hit nearby and still cause significant damage. The hurricane had intensified in strength to a Category 3, and there was no suggestion that it would weaken any time soon. Further, what many of the weather officials seemed to fear but wouldn't voice was the fact that it would likely strengthen before hitting land. Already evacuations of coastal parishes were underway, but the mayor of New Orleans had yet to recommend this action for the city.

After several minutes of watching, Kit glanced over at Teddy. Her face was pale, her eyes wide with disbelief. She looked scared— an expression that seemed entirely foreign to her. Kit felt a stab of tenderness, wishing she could do something to make her feel better. She grabbed Teddy's hand, squeezing it. Teddy looked over at her, and Kit's stomach dropped with dread at her somber expression.

"What should we do?" Kit asked. "Do we need to get out of here?"

Teddy shook her head. "I don't know. I mean, I don't think so. If they'd actually thought it was coming, they'd have called for an evacuation here, too. But it looks like we're going to get some major weather here, no matter what." She shook her head again, clearly confused and obviously frightened.

Kit sprang to her feet. "We have to get out of here. I need to see if we can get a car, or get on a plane, or…" Her mind was a whirl of confusion.

Teddy stood up and gave her a tight hug before holding her shoulders at arm's length. She squeezed them with her strong hands. "Calm down. There's no use getting upset. We'll leave." She looked around for a moment and then walked across the room, picking up her phone. "I'm going to call my friend—the one with the car. Go get dressed, and we'll figure out what to do next."

Kit was glad to have someone give her directions. She went back to the bathroom and searched around, finding most of her clothes and pulling them on. She was still missing her underwear and one sock, but she didn't have the patience to keep looking for them. She went back into the TV room and immediately sensed from Teddy's body language that something was wrong. She was still on the phone.

"Oh yeah? Okay, sure," she said to the other person on the line. "No, I understand. No, really, it's not your fault. I'll think of something." She waited for a moment, listening. "Okay. If it comes to that, I'll do it, but I think we'll be okay. I'll call you when I can. Good-bye." She hung up and then stood there, staring blankly at the phone for a moment before turning to Kit. She shook her head. "My friend's car is a no-go. She barely drives it. It has a flat tire she's been meaning to fix, but she didn't get to it before she left town. She also left the keys inside her place, and her house is locked."

Feeling a slight bubble of panic, Kit asked, "Now what?"

Teddy thought for a moment. "I need to go to the restaurant and tie up some loose ends. I think I'll go ahead and let the lunch crowd in, then close until this thing passes. I don't want my staff stuck here if they want to leave, but I need a couple of hours to cancel the reservations we have for today and tomorrow, call my other staff, and get the kitchen ready to be closed for a few days."

Kit remained quiet, waiting for direction.

Teddy looked at her, thinking. "You should go back to your hotel and make some calls. See if your conference is arranging anything for your group. See if you can get a rental car or a flight. At the very least, you'll want to get your things or put them in storage. Who knows if the hotel will close."

Their eyes met. Both of them knew where this conversation was going, but Kit didn't want to be the one to acknowledge the situation. Rather than her usual stoic grace, Teddy looked crestfallen. Then, almost as if it had never been there, Teddy's expression cleared.

"If you can get a ride out of town, take it," Teddy said. "Don't worry about me."

"But—"

"I mean it." Teddy cut her off with a gesture. "I have friends and places I can go to—you don't."

"When will I…" For a moment, Kit had been about to ask when they could see each other again, but she shook her head, as if that could banish the thought. "I mean, what if I can't get out?"

"We'll cross that bridge if it comes to it. Do you know how to get back to your hotel from here? It's a bit of a walk, but you can do it in half an hour or so."

"I believe I do," Kit said, thinking hard. "I was a little drunk when we came here."

Teddy smiled. "I'll say you were. Here—let me draw you a map." She grabbed a napkin and sketched for a moment before handing it to Kit. Kit put it in a pocket, and they stood there for a long moment, gazing at each other. Kit wanted to leave, but she wanted Teddy with her. She couldn't come up with any solution to this quandary. It made more sense to separate—even Kit could see that.

She saw her fear mirrored in Teddy's eyes, and that fleeting bubble of panic and welled up inside her again, threatening to burst. Teddy's eyes softened, and she drew Kit into another embrace before kissing her, softly.

"You'll be okay," Teddy whispered. "Call me when you can, will you? If you get out, let me know."

"I will," Kit said, subdued.

"Good luck."

CHAPTER TEN

After taking several wrong turns and wandering far into an unfamiliar neighborhood, Kit finally managed to walk into the Quarter and back to her hotel. By the time she got there, she was drenched in sweat, hot, and impatient. The mood in the lobby was tense. Several hotel patrons were at the front desk, their voices high with panic and hurry. Everyone looked upset and worried, including the staff. A middle-aged couple was standing by the front door with their luggage, peering outside apprehensively, seeming to wait for something or someone. A mother with three crying children stood by a pillar, looking stricken with fear and distress. Two hotel maids huddled together, whispering quickly and looking around conspiratorially. Everyone Kit saw appeared either frightened or angry. The room seemed about to burst with anxiety.

The only exception was an older gentleman in a lobby chair, seemingly oblivious to the chaos around him. He sat calmly playing with an unlit cigar in his hands. Kit took one look at the crowd of people by the desk and decided to go to her room first and pack up as well as she could.

Upstairs, her room had not yet been cleaned. This surprised her at first, considering that she hadn't been here all night, but as she thought about it, she realized that the hotel staff were likely beginning to leave town. She pictured the maids she'd seen downstairs, both of whom had looked as if they were planning to make a run for the door. Anyone with a brain would leave if they could, she thought.

All the more reason, she realized, to make sure she was organized and try to get the hell away from here. She spent the next twenty minutes unpacking and repacking her suitcases. She put things for immediate use in a large backpack she used for smaller day trips and everything she thought she could do without for a while in the suitcases. While she knew on some level that she might not find a way out of town today, she wanted to be able to leave quickly if she could.

Finally packed, she walked over to the hotel phone to call Becky. After waiting a long time with no answer, she hung up and sat on her bed, thinking. Next she riffled through the phone book and found the numbers for several rental-car companies. The line was busy at all of them. She kept trying, only for an answering service to finally pick up. She left her number and sat there again, staring at the phone. The panic, which she'd been suppressing on and off all morning, was starting to well up in the pit of her stomach. Standing up, she went over to her travel folder and pulled out her airline ticket, looking for a phone number. She went back to the phone and called the customer-service number and, for the first time today, managed to talk to an actual person.

"This is Timothy. How can I help you today?"

"Hi, Timothy. My name is Katriona Kelly. I wanted to see if I could arrange to change my flight. I'm willing to pay the difference."

Timothy walked her through several confirmation steps, asking for her original flight numbers and date of birth, and then he paused for a long, tense moment. He cleared his throat. "It appears from my computer, Miss Kelly, that your original flight has already been cancelled. The airport you're flying from in New Orleans is working with our airline to get passengers originally scheduled for tomorrow and Monday out on earlier flights today."

"Tomorrow, too?" Kit asked.

"All flights after ten a.m. tomorrow have been cancelled out of Louis Armstrong International," Timothy said.

Her stomach clenched with fear. "That soon?" she whispered.

Timothy paused and then cleared his throat again. "Our airline and the others are trying to avoid potential damage."

"Shouldn't you, I don't know, bring in extra airplanes? To help people get out of here?" Kit asked, her voice rising with anger and worry.

Timothy paused again before replying. "Unfortunately, ma'am, that isn't airline policy."

Kit sat still for a long moment, clenching the phone to her face painfully. While she'd been dreading and anticipating exactly this news, part of her had believed that she would still manage to book a flight out of here sometime tonight or tomorrow. The likelihood now seemed quite dim.

Kit cleared her throat, trying to remain calm. "So is there a flight I can get on today?"

"One moment, please," Timothy said. Kit could hear him typing during a long, tense pause. Finally, he spoke again. "There's one seat left today out of New Orleans. It's a flight to St. Louis in two hours. From there, I can get you a connection to your original destination in San Francisco. Should I book you on it?"

"Yes," Kit said, her heart giving a leap of triumph.

"May I have your credit-card number, please?" Timothy asked her.

She read it to him and recorded her confirmation number, scribbling it with a hand so shaky she was afraid she wouldn't be able to read it later. She hung up and looked around the room, trying to decide what to do first. If she waited too long, she'd likely miss her flight. She looked at her pile of luggage for a moment before she grabbed her backpack and one small suitcase. Then she looked over at the phone, wishing she had time to call Teddy and let her know, but, after an internal debate, she thought better of it. She'd call at the airport.

She decided to give up her other belongings as lost and simply walked out her door. She'd phone later from St. Louis to see if she could have the rest mailed to her, but getting out of here seemed more important right now. She dashed into the hall, racing to the elevator. It seemed to take forever to come, and she waited inside, impatience rising, as she rode down to the ground floor. The lobby was already far worse than it had been when she'd arrived. Now it appeared that nearly every guest was at the front desk, trying to get information or check out.

Out on the street, she spotted a row of cabs and walked over as quickly as she could. A cab driver sprang into action when he saw her, dropping his newspaper on the ground. He took her backpack and suitcase from her and put them into the trunk. He'd left his cab running, and they climbed inside the refreshingly cool car. He started driving immediately, clearly sensing her haste.

"You have a flight soon, ma'am?" he asked.

"Yes. I managed to switch my flight from Monday," she said, leaning back into the seat with relief.

"You're lucky."

Kit felt a wave of sympathy for the man. Twenty minutes ago, she'd been in the same position, facing the possibility of weathering the storm from ground zero. "What will you do?"

The driver grinned at her through the rearview mirror. "I'll probably wait until tonight and take my family in the cab. I have relatives in Houston."

"Won't you get in trouble?"

"Who knows?" he said, lifting his eyebrows. "Maybe my boss will be happy I got the cab out. The parking lot for his company is in a flood plain."

Kit's relief and happiness lasted barely two minutes longer. Once the cab attempted to turn onto the Interstate, she saw that the ramp was completely blocked. It didn't look like anyone was going anywhere. They sat in the turn lane for the ramp through several lights, not moving. The cars on the ramp were simply sitting there, almost as if in a parking lot. After a while, her driver sighed and cursed under his breath and then turned around to look at her.

"Do you want me to use a different on-ramp?" he asked. "There's one near City Park I could try."

Kit nodded, her voice caught in her throat. The driver tore out of the turn lane onto Canal and drove quickly, dodging cars and streetcars as he went. Long before they were very close to the next Interstate ramp, Kit could tell that they were going to face the same problem. Cars on the road ahead of them were backed up nearly a mile before the on-ramp. The driver cursed again and joined the line. Kit glanced at her watch. Already, the time before her flight had been significantly shortened. She'd been booked on the flight almost exactly two hours before it was scheduled to take off. Now she had an hour and thirty minutes. Even if they managed to get on the Interstate, the airport was significantly far away. She would be lucky to make it on time. The driver, impatient, honked his horn often in frustration.

"Can you call someone?" Kit finally asked him. "Maybe someone else knows a better way."

He glanced back at her, annoyed, but followed her advice. After picking up his radio, Kit heard a scratchy voice give him some directions, and the driver tore out of the line before getting in a turn lane for another road. He drove quickly, dangerously, but Kit was overjoyed simply to be moving. Even if this was a longer route, at least they were going somewhere.

Once again, a few minutes later they hit a new pocket of traffic. This time the driver didn't even bother to mutter his curses. He shouted out at the cars in front of him and actually shook his fist at them out the window. As they sat, immobile, for a long while, Kit's hopes gradually died. The window of time for escape was disappearing. In a few more minutes, she wouldn't have enough time to get through security, let alone catch the plane, and she wasn't anywhere near the airport yet. She stared at her watch and waited with growing dread until it was too late. Time passed and she sat there, staring out the window at the cars in front of her for a long moment, trying to decide what to do. Logic, perhaps, dictated that she keep going and head to the airport. While Timothy had told her it was the last seat available, perhaps people on later flights would have the same problem she was having right now. Everyone trying to get to the airport would be stuck in this traffic. If she was there waiting, she might be able to get one of those spots. That was the rational thing to do, after all, wasn't it?

Emotionally, she could barely stomach the thought of hours in a panicky airport. She'd seen the lobby of her hotel. Already, she sensed the horrible way people were going to behave as the hurricane grew closer. If one seat was available, thirty people would likely be vying to get it. She'd have to fight someone for it—not necessarily physically, but it could come to that. If someone pushed her, she would have to push back. The idea made her shudder with fear and dread. She hated crowds, let alone the idea of an angry, frightened group of people. Further, she had a place she could be instead. She could stay in her hotel room, at the very least. She highly doubted anyone would actually force her to leave. She might still be able to get a car. If she got one, she could leave tonight, in the middle of the night, when the traffic died down.

Barring that, there was always Teddy, who was the real reason she wasn't breaking down in a hot panic. Teddy would help her, she knew it. It had only been a couple of hours since breakfast, but already Kit missed her with a nagging, aching longing. She'd do just about anything to be back at her house right now.

She tapped the driver's shoulder and held up some money. "I'm sorry to put you through this. I'm missing my flight as we sit here waiting. Please just take me back to my hotel."

He looked at her, obviously incredulous. "Are you sure?" If you go to the airport, you might—"

She cut him off with a gesture. "Exactly. I *might*. And I might not. And then I'll be stuck at the airport."

He still looked doubtful, and she sighed. Now that she'd made up her mind, she was impatient to be out of this car. "Please. Just take me back."

The man stared into her eyes for a long moment, and then he pulled into the lane in the opposite direction and tore away, his wheels squealing. They were back at the hotel in minutes.

He helped her take her bags out of the trunk. "I'm sorry you didn't make your flight," he finally said. He looked guilty, as if it were his fault.

She gave him some money, which included an enormous tip. "It's okay. There was nothing you could do."

He pocketed the cash without looking at it. "Good luck to you," he said. They shook hands, the strangeness of the situation not lost on either of them.

Turning back to the front door of her hotel, Kit was grateful now that she hadn't had time to check out. There was a mass of people in the lobby, the crowd doubled from what she'd seen earlier. Everyone was attempting to leave at the same time, the lone desk clerk looking as if he'd been standing there for the last twenty-four hours. No other hotel staff was present, and Kit wondered idly if he was the last holdout. She went over to the elevator and up to her room, throwing her suitcase into the pile with the others and slinging her backpack onto her bed. Although she had left this room only two hours ago, it felt like an eternity.

She looked around, appraising her room from a new vantage point of recent events. The windows were large and faced the street. There were blinds, but she doubted that the hurricane shutters outside were anything more than decorative. If she ended up staying here, she needed to ask for a room with smaller windows, preferably ones that faced the inside courtyard. She grinned wryly as she thought this. The idea of being practical in an apocalypse was exactly the kind of thing people made fun of her for—especially impractical people like Becky.

The thought of Becky shook her out of her planning long enough to try to get her on the phone again. This time Becky answered almost immediately.

"Jesus, Kit! Where the hell have you been?" Becky shouted. "I've been trying to reach you all morning."

"It's a long story," Kit said, lying down on the bed and throwing an arm over her eyes.

"Listen to this: Mia managed to get a car."

Kit sat up so fast she almost dropped the phone. "What?" she said.

"Mia has a rental car. She's bringing it back to our hotel now. She offered to drive me, Jackie, and Charley out of town. If you get over here soon, you can ask her if you can come with us."

"You're at the conference hotel?"

"Yes, and she's going to be here any minute. She called a while ago to tell us she was on her way back. Traffic getting over to the rental place was a nightmare."

"Tell me about it," Kit said.

"Anyway—get over here. Like yesterday. And pack light."

"I'll be there right away," Kit said, and hung up. She jumped off the bed and grabbed her backpack. Before leaving, she took one more look around her room, grinning at her own foolishness. Five minutes ago, she'd been thinking about staying here. The idea now seemed absurd.

She walked quickly, forcing herself not to run. Becky would make Mia wait until she got there, but she didn't like the idea of making anyone wait any longer than necessary. The sooner they were on the road, the better.

She entered the conference hotel lobby so quickly she almost bowled over an older couple fighting with their luggage. Barely pausing to apologize, she looked around wildly before spotting Becky, who was standing by the pay phones. Becky looked strangely subdued and pale, which made Kit's stomach clench once again with dread and fear. If Becky was scared, things were definitely serious.

Becky spotted her and walked toward her.

Kit looked around, confused. "Where is everyone? Where are the others? Where's Mia?"

"I have some bad news," Becky said, and Kit's stomach lurched. "You can't come with us."

"What?" Kit said, almost shouting.

"There isn't enough room. The car is very small—just big enough for four of us and a couple of suitcases."

"A couple of suitcases?" Kit said, actually yelling now as fear and a new wave of adrenaline kicked into her bloodstream. "You'd rather take suitcases than me?"

"It's not my choice, Kit," Becky said, grabbing her hands. "I don't know what you did to Mia, but she absolutely hates you. She said something about you dismissing her presentation or something. What the hell did you say to her?"

"I didn't say anything!" Kit said, flushing scarlet. "In fact, I avoided saying anything after that debacle. I didn't want to hurt her feelings."

Becky shook her head. "I don't know, but I guess that must have been enough. She was crushed after her presentation. I think she was hoping you would say something to make her feel better about it. She really respects your scholarship."

"Are you fucking kidding me?" Kit said. "Of all the immature, misplaced academic bullshit! You mean to tell me that bitch—"

"She refused to even consider trying to get you in the car. At first it seemed logical—the car barely seats four. But the more I thought about it, the more I figured we could make it work if we had to. You could sit on my lap or something. I told her that, but she wouldn't listen. She said you should figure it out yourself."

"What the hell, Becky?" Kit said, hands out in defeat.

Becky's expression was pained. "There's nothing I can do."

"So you're okay leaving me here?"

"What else can I do? What would you do? Do you want me to stay here in protest?" Becky asked, her voice quiet.

Kit thought about this, perhaps longer than was quite politic. If their situations were reversed, she would have no problem leaving Becky behind. The realization made her flush with embarrassment and shame.

Meeting Becky's eyes, she said, "It's okay. You should go. It's not your fault."

"I feel terrible about this, Kit," Becky said, but the relief on her face was evident.

Trying to remain magnanimous, she gave Becky a quick hug. "It's okay. Get going. Get to safety."

Becky's eyes were welling with tears. "What are you going to do? Where will you go?"

"I don't know. I'll think of something."

"Maybe if you go to the airport—or the train station—or the bus station…"

"Maybe," Kit said, uncertain. Both of them knew, without discussing it further, that all of those options were rapidly closing.

Becky gave her a firm hug and then held her at arm's length, making eye contact. "You'll be okay." She riffled around in her pockets and produced a keycard. "This is the key to my room upstairs—1412. It might be safer than the Holiday Inn. I don't know. I have the room until Tuesday morning. I haven't checked out yet. Take it."

Fingers numb, Kit slipped the card into a pocket. Becky's eyes were now welling with tears, but Kit's were almost entirely dry from frustration and fear.

"Please just go," she managed to say, not looking at her any more.

"Good luck," Becky said, turning, and then she walked away.

Kit stood there for a long time—long after Becky had disappeared. The lobby was relatively empty. Clearly the guests here had made arrangements faster than those at her own hotel. The idea of moving over here, where it was calmer and relatively safer, was appealing, but Kit couldn't make up her mind. For one thing, Teddy wouldn't be able to find her if she left her room at the Holiday Inn, and who knew how long the phones would last.

The thought of Teddy made her heart surge with hope and relief. All morning, ever since she left, she'd been trying not to think about her. It had been difficult to leave and even more difficult to accept that they would likely never see each other again. The realization had hurt her far deeper than she wanted to acknowledge. But now, when it seemed as if the universe was putting them together, despite the situation, she felt relief and something akin to happiness. She would see her again and Teddy would help. Teddy would know what to do.

Straightening her shoulders in anticipation of whatever would come next, Kit walked out the door into the heat of the afternoon sun.

Chapter Eleven

When Kit was back in her room, she knew she should keep trying to get out of town, but the thought both depressed and overwhelmed her. She sat in an armchair for a long time doing nothing. Part of her was too overwhelmed to do anything, and another part of her simply didn't want to. Her life had brought her here, and here she would remain, at least for now. The idea was both terrifying and liberating.

Death, Kit thought, puts everything in perspective.

She stared at her luggage and her briefcase, reflecting on the fact that she'd brought just about everything she owned with her when she left San Francisco. She was normally a light packer, even for long trips. Besides some photographs and books, she could easily leave everything she had in San Francisco behind and never go back. Her place in California seemed vague and unreal. While she hadn't been gone very long, her apartment had never seemed farther away. It almost seemed like she didn't live there anymore.

This was, she realized, partly because she didn't exactly live there—she existed. She went from work to home to work and home again, day after day. Some weekends, she would go out to the clubs or the bars and go home with someone, but that activity had become rarer and rarer. She had been somewhat truthful when she told Becky she'd been too busy to go out last semester, but she actually hadn't really tried to make time for it. The loud music in clubs and the same old faces at every bar were starting to wear on her. She'd been doing the same thing—going to bars and clubs—since late high school, after all, so it had been, she thought, only a matter of time before she burned out on the scene and everything that went along with it.

When she'd first moved to San Francisco after graduate school, she'd been thrilled by the sheer quantity of lesbians she saw on the streets. Now, several years later, she didn't want to go back. Part of her, she realized, had been looking for a way to leave the city for a while. She had done everything to be gone for a couple of months this summer, and it still didn't seem like long enough.

Truthfully, given a little more money in her savings account, she would gladly never return. The full recognition of this truth made her smile. During the first year she'd lived there, if anyone had told her she would want to leave San Francisco, she would have laughed in their face. She had been so excited to get her first tenure-track job and had been the envy of all of her graduate-school friends. The city had thrilled her, excited her every time she walked out the door. Now her life there depressed her. She would give it all up if it meant never going home again and starting somewhere new, somewhere like here. As she contemplated the thought that she might not make it home anytime soon, she realized she was actually happy about it—certainly not with the circumstances that were keeping her here, but with the idea of not going back.

It wasn't just that her so-called life was depressing, she admitted to herself. Honestly, the biggest reason to leave San Francisco was Teddy. Kit hadn't dated anyone seriously in a long time, and she wasn't even sure she would call what she and Teddy were doing together "dating," but she was drawn to her in a way that she hadn't felt in a long, long time about a woman—certainly not any of the women she'd been seeing San Francisco.

It was silly. After all, she and Teddy had just met a few days ago. You didn't throw your whole life away for someone you'd just met, especially when you didn't know how they felt about you. Why had she worked so hard if she was just going to drop everything for a pretty face? Kit shook her head. Her common sense simply wouldn't let her leave her job. That didn't, however, make running away with Teddy less tempting to fantasize about.

Sighing, she propelled herself to her feet and walked over to the telephone again. She needed to make several phone calls and should make some others. She decided to take care of the worst of them first.

He answered on the first ring. "Hello?"

"Hi, Dad, it's me," Kit said, sitting down again on the edge of the bed. Her legs were suddenly unsteady and weak.

"Hey, sweetheart! I haven't heard from you in weeks! Last time you called me you were in, what, County Cork? How are you? How was London? Where are you?"

"I'm fine. Everything's fine." She paused. Ever since her mom had died two years ago, she'd avoided telling her father anything upsetting. When she'd had minor surgery, when she'd almost failed her tenure review, and when she'd been devastated by some bad reviews of her first book, she hadn't shared any of it with him. She didn't think of this as lying so much as holding something back for his own good. Her mom's death had sent him into a spiraling depression that he'd barely pulled out of. In fact, she'd been convinced for months afterward that he would kill himself, and he practically had, simply from self-neglect. It had taken him almost a year to regain a semblance of normality, and he still wasn't anything like his old self. The process of grief and recovery had aged him considerably. Now, he seemed much older than his actual years.

"How are you, Dad? How's Jim?" she asked. Jim was her younger brother.

"I'm fine. Jim's fine," he said, and she could hear his reluctance to say more. "At least, I think he is. I haven't heard from him in a while."

Kit had to force herself not to shout with anger. She had been sending her brother money every month so he would help out around their dad's house. He was supposed to do the heavy yard work and keep an eye on their dad—help him get to doctors' appointments and his grief-counseling sessions. Jim always had a hard time keeping a job, so the arrangement had seemed like the perfect solution to both problems—she would know that her dad was taken care of, and she could give her brother some money for actual work instead of just out of charity. Their dad wasn't aware of this agreement or the money, so Kit wasn't surprised that she hadn't heard of Jim's disappearance before now. As in every other job in his life, Jim apparently couldn't commit, even if it meant helping out his own father.

She made herself pause in order to control her emotions. "When was the last time you saw him?"

"Oh, let's see…" Her dad paused. "It was about a month ago now."

Kit flushed with white-hot anger, and once again she stopped to control herself before saying anything. "But you're okay? The house is okay?"

"Sure, I'm fine. The house is fine, sweetie."

Kit knew he would say this even if the roof had caved in. Their entire family avoided confrontation and reality. Frustration welled inside her. She couldn't do anything for him right now. She would eventually track down her brother and give him a piece of her mind. Perhaps in the meantime she could hire someone to go over and do the yard once a week, no matter what her father said.

Knowing that she had more phone calls to make, and knowing that she couldn't put off what she had to say any longer, she paused, overwhelmed with the gush of emotion that welled up inside her. Her throat felt thick and her eyes filled with tears. "Dad?"

"What is it, honey? You sound upset."

"I just wanted you to know that I love you. That's all."

"What? I love you, too, honey. What's this about?"

Her family didn't share emotions well, and she knew he was surprised to hear her words. "I'm going to try to visit soon, okay, Dad? But if I can't make it…"

"I know, honey," he replied. "I know how hard it is these days. Your career comes first. I know that."

Choking back the tears, Kit managed to say, "Thanks, Dad. I have to go."

"Are you okay, sweetie? You still sound upset."

"I'm fine. I'll call soon."

"Okay. Good-bye. Call me when you can."

"Bye," she said, and hung up, tears now streaming down her face.

She cried for a long time. The idea that she might never see him again was too much, but she cursed herself for her melodrama. It was very unlikely that she would actually die here, but then why did she feel like she'd actually told him good-bye? If she was hurt down here, he would always wonder why she hadn't explained where she was beforehand. Kit shook her head. She'd made the right decision not to tell him. No way would she worry him like that. She could be honest later when she was safe.

She went into the bathroom and washed her face with cool water before returning to make her other phone calls. First she called the English department at San Francisco State. She was scheduled to fly back on Monday before her first class for the semester on Tuesday. Even in the best circumstances, she wouldn't be back that soon, but she figured she might be there by Thursday. As it was Saturday, she had to leave a message, and she told them she'd call with news when she could.

In some ways, she thought as she hung up, this was better. If she wasn't there at the beginning of the semester, it would be easier for her to leave her job now rather than later. They would already have to cover her classes this week, and perhaps whoever covered for her could just keep teaching her courses for the rest of the term. The thought gave her a momentary feeling of buoyancy—as if she'd just set down a heavy weight. Until the last hour, she hadn't realized how much she dreaded going back to work. While she enjoyed teaching and doing research, everything else that went along with a position in the academic world was awful. She shook her head, smiling wryly. She wouldn't actually leave her job—she'd never forgive herself for giving up on her career. The thought steadied her a little. All these fantasies were a waste of time. She needed to do some things—now.

Walking over to the small desk in the corner of her room, she made a checklist for herself of the other phone calls she needed to make. She went through the list methodically, marking off each one as she made it. First was the train line. After waiting on the phone for almost an hour, she was told that the remaining trains would be evacuated from the city within the next few hours. They were no longer selling seats. The train line didn't have the staff to sell tickets, and most of them hadn't been cleaned well enough to house passengers. She called the bus lines next and received the same news. All of the car-rental agencies were out of vehicles, and her airline was unimpressed with her story about missing the plane. They seemed to think that if she couldn't make the first plane, they had no reason to believe she could make another. Moreover, they could only offer her a position as a standby passenger, which meant basically nothing. She would be fiftieth in line for a seat on the last plane flying out tonight. After thinking about their offer, Kit decided to give up. Barring a miracle, she was going to be stuck here, and the last thing she wanted to do was to wait out the hurricane at the airport.

Her last call wasn't on her checklist, but it had been in her mind the whole time, waiting for its place in line. Sensible or not, responsible or not, she'd been wanting to do this since she left this morning. First she called the restaurant, which was busy, and then she called Teddy's house. After the phone rang several times with no answer, and figuring that Teddy was still stuck at the restaurant, Kit decided to walk over there and see if she could catch her. She left without waiting to think it through.

Rationality be damned, she thought.

The streets were relatively empty. Most of the bars she passed still had a few patrons, and it appeared that most of the hotels were still open, but, considering that it was now the weekend, the strange emptiness struck her hard. The air had a tense, waiting quality—as if the city were holding its breath in anticipation. With no crowds to fight, Kit quickly made it out of the Quarter and over to Frenchmen, where the emptiness was even more apparent. The Quarter was slightly more tourist-heavy than this part of town, so it made sense that the places locals frequented would be emptier, but it was like a ghost town over here—somber and creepy. Apparently most locals were at home getting ready to leave or already gone.

Once again, Kit knocked on the restaurant's window to get the attention of the waiter inside. The same young man was cleaning the dining room. He recognized her, and this time he unlocked and opened the front door.

"She's in back," he said, his face tight with tension. The dark circles under his eyes indicated a sleepless night and significant worry.

She went through the doors from the dining room into the kitchen. Most of the employees had already left, but a lone sous-chef was mopping the floor. Every surface was cleared of food and most of the dishes had been put away. The place looked forlorn, abandoned. The chef with the mop pointed toward the door to the office, clearly recognizing her from last night. Kit walked over, seeing Teddy before she was noticed. She was on the phone and looked haggard and worn. Her hair, normally neat and styled, was mussed and knotted, as if she'd been clutching it in worry. Her clothes were soaked with perspiration, and her pants, normally the very definition of clean, were spattered with food and oil. Kit paused in the doorway, just watching, eavesdropping without necessarily meaning to.

"Listen, I know, I get it," Teddy was saying, "but there's nothing I can do about it." She paused, her face crumpled with frustration as she listened. "I know! I tried. I did. I'm not being macho." Normally so placid and calm, this angry Teddy was scary to see.

"I'm not listening to this anymore," Teddy said. "Good-bye." She slammed down the phone, the bell ringing for a moment with the force of her anger. A moment later, she saw Kit, and her face underwent a shift of emotions from rage to confusion to relief. She came over to Kit and gave her a long, hard hug. Teddy's arms, warm and strong and familiar, felt like coming home. For a moment, Kit was convinced she would start crying.

"You're still here!" Teddy said. "I wasn't sure I would see you again." She colored after she said this, looking a little guilty. "I mean, I'm sorry you couldn't get out, but I'm just so glad you're here." She blushed even harder. "I mean—"

"I know what you mean," Kit said, reveling in a rising sense of triumph. Teddy was happy to see her again.

"I take it you couldn't get out?" Teddy looked away to hide her awkward embarrassment.

Kit sighed, not wanting to go over it. It all seemed so fruitless—such a waste of time. She realized now that she should simply have gone to her hotel, packed, and waited for Teddy at her place. She shouldn't have even bothered trying to leave. Ever since she'd first seen the news about the hurricane, she'd had the strong impression that she would be here in New Orleans for it. While she didn't believe in ESP or anything like that, she should have listened to her instincts rather than worry herself with everything that had gone on today. She was limp and tired from her efforts. They were all for nothing.

"No," Kit finally said. "I almost caught a flight, and then I almost had a ride, but neither one worked out."

"Something like that happened to me, too." Teddy indicated the phone. "I was just explaining that to my sister, who's convinced I'm staying because of some kind of butch, macho thing."

Kit snorted. "That would be taking butch a little far."

Teddy laughed. "Right? I know some people in town are staying because they think nothing can hurt them, but I'm not one of them. I'd leave if I could. I tried to get a ride, a car, *anything*. It was a no-go."

They stood there a moment, staring at each other. Neither one needed to say anything at all. They were both in the same situation, and it seemed to bring them closer—a bond neither one of them needed to point out. Kit couldn't explain why she was so relieved to be here in this kitchen. By any rational standards she should be terrified. And true, she was still scared, but the feeling was distant now, and nothing like her earlier terror.

"So…" Teddy finally said. "What do you want to do? Do you want to stay at the hotel or at my place?"

Kit knew if she chose the hotel, Teddy would go with her. They were in this thing together now. A feeling of overwhelming relief swept through her, and she was nearly dizzy with it. Teddy was with her, and she was with Teddy. It didn't need to be explained beyond that right now.

"I want to stay with you. At your place," she finally said, resolved.

"I think that would best." Teddy was clearly relieved. "Let's go get your things and move you in. Then we'll come back here and get some of the candles and nonperishable food."

"Do you think it will be that bad?" Kit asked, stomach fluttering with fright.

Teddy shook her head. "I have no idea. The electricity goes out at the drop of a hat here even without a hurricane, so even if things aren't too bad, we should plan for it to be out for a day or two, at least. I have a gas-powered stove and grill we can use it to heat things up."

Kit nodded, trying to accept the inevitable. She found herself in the strange position of wondering if she were over- or underestimating their situation. Having never been through something like this, she couldn't tell. In the best-case scenario, they would be laughing at themselves in a few days. In the worst case…she made herself dismiss that thought. There was, she realized, no use dwelling on it.

"Let's go," Kit said firmly. She felt better now that she had something concrete to do. As long as she stayed busy, she would be okay. More importantly, as long as she was with Teddy, she knew she was safe.

CHAPTER TWELVE

When they reached Kit's hotel, the level of chaos had escalated exponentially. The lobby was full of shouting people, desperately talking on cell phones and pay phones, trying to get out of town. The remaining staff had apparently abandoned their posts at the desk or were, at the very least, no longer visible. No one seemed to know who to turn to or where to go. Kit saw several women simply crying as they stood or sat, their husbands and boyfriends likewise despondent or paralyzed with fear. A television was set up near the desk, and Kit heard, as they walked through the crowd, that there would be some kind of announcement soon. She and Teddy shared a look and, without discussing the situation, made their way over to the elevator, grabbing a luggage cart along the way.

Upstairs in her room they quickly loaded the cart, and Kit took one last look around her, knowing she'd never come back here again. In the bathroom, she found the lanyard with her nametag from the conference. If her chair hadn't talked her into attending, she wouldn't be in this mess. She threw the lanyard in the trash and came back out into the room.

"Do you want to watch the announcement before we leave?" Teddy asked, clearly reluctant to do just that.

Kit shrugged. "More bad news. I'm sure they'll repeat whatever they want to say several times this evening anyway." She walked over to Teddy and grabbed her hands, squeezing them. "I bet when

I yelled at you, you never thought I'd be moving in with you a few days later."

Teddy grinned weakly. "I never thought I'd live with anyone but my dogs."

Kit bent forward and kissed her. "Things change, I guess."

Teddy's face was serious. "Are you sure you want to do this? You could probably stay here. It might be better for you. You'll probably be evacuated faster if you're with the other tourists."

Kit looked around the room, her eyes lingering on the large, exposed windows. She shook her head. "No. I'll be safer with you. Actually," she paused and met Teddy's eyes, "I want to be with you. I feel better when we're together."

They stared at each other for a long time, their eyes locked. Kit meant it. All day today, when she'd tried to leave, all she'd wanted to do was go back to Teddy's place and be with her through whatever was coming. In the cab on the way to airport, and then when she got back here, all she really wanted was Teddy. While Kit couldn't be sure, Teddy's eyes were warm on hers, suggesting that she felt the same way.

Finally, Teddy squared her shoulders, as if readying herself to carry a heavy weight. "Okay. Let's go. I don't think they'll miss a luggage cart at this point. We might need it to carry the food later anyway."

The walk back to Teddy's took well over an hour. The streets and sidewalks, which were poorly maintained, made it difficult to use the cart, and the heat made their efforts that much harder. At first they took turns pushing the rickety metal cart through the streets, but in the last few blocks, they were doing it together, both using the remains of their strength to get it a few yards farther between breaks for air. Several times Kit almost suggested that they abandon it. Once they hit the halfway mark, however, it became a testament of will. To make herself feel better, Kit told herself that if they managed to do this one, small thing, they could make it through whatever was coming their way. They could do it together.

After they'd thrown her luggage up the stairs onto Teddy's porch and slung it all inside the house, they sat down on Teddy's couch, completely spent. The dogs had watched all of this, impassive, from their beds, accepting the new person in their life with no qualms. The luggage cart was left outside on the sidewalk, both of them agreeing that if someone wanted to steal it, they were welcome to it. Kit closed her eyes and rested her head on the back of the couch, the cool breeze from the air conditioner one of the best things she'd ever experienced.

"Do you want a drink?" Teddy asked. "Water?"

"Water. Please."

Teddy handed her an icy glass a moment later, and she drank the water in one long swig, almost slamming down the glass when she was done. Teddy was watching her, smiling.

"I bet you can do that with a beer, too," Teddy said. "Party trick?"

"I outdrank all the boys on my college debate team." Kit smiled proudly.

"I just bet you did." Teddy leaned closer for a kiss.

Kit kissed her back and then pulled away a second later. "My God! I can smell myself. You must think I'm disgusting."

Teddy pretended to think about it. "Nope. Not the first word that pops into my head."

"What is the first word?" Kit arched an eyebrow.

"Sexy. Cute. Hot."

"In that order?"

"Yes." Teddy was leering slightly as she said this, and Kit pushed her shoulder, snorting with amusement.

"Is that all you can think about, you sex maniac?"

Teddy reached forward, sweeping a sweaty lock of hair off Kit's forehead. "When you're around—yes."

Kit swallowed, desire suddenly rushing through her with a white heat. Teddy saw the look in her eyes and inched closer on the couch, running her hand lightly along Kit's bare leg. Goose bumps greeted her hand, and Kit shuddered slightly, the air suddenly chilly on her overly hot skin. She was about to move forward for another kiss when she seemed to feel eyes on her. She looked over and saw that all three dogs were watching them, curiosity clear in their guileless faces.

Teddy laughed when she saw them and then stood up. "Maybe we can talk about this in another room," she suggested, holding out a hand.

Kit let herself be tugged to her feet before following her back into the bedroom. She barely had time to turn around when Teddy was there, her mouth on her neck a moment later. They wrapped their arms around each other, and Kit felt the dampness of Teddy's shirt clinging to the hard muscles of her back. Kit edged her fingers under the hem of Teddy's shirt and lifted it off in one motion, exposing her small, bare chest. Teddy's nipples were slick with sweat, and Kit licked at one, sucking at the salty flavor. Teddy moaned, and Kit moved her hands to her hips, maneuvering her back toward the bed. Teddy sat down heavily, looking up at Kit with thinly veiled surprise.

"Lie down," Kit commanded, pointing.

Teddy held her hands up in defeat and obeyed, lying back but propping herself up on her elbows. Kit stood, looking at her, half naked, her dark nipples hard. She slipped her dress over her head, standing before Teddy in her bra and panties a moment before kneeling between her legs. She unbuckled Teddy's belt and jeans, then yanked them down to her ankles. Teddy yelped in surprise, and when Kit looked up and met her eyes, she could see her own heated desire reflected there. Teddy's sex exposed, Kit turned her attention there, just looking. She ran her hands along Teddy's thighs, eliciting a long moan, and then kissed her, very gently, just above the hairline on Teddy's stomach. She brushed her fingers over Teddy's curls, slick with hot wetness. Teddy squirmed, and she used her other hand to push down on Teddy's stomach.

"Don't move," she said. Teddy stilled, and she continued, kissing her way across Teddy's stomach and then farther down. Teddy's legs squeezed her slightly as she approached the top curls of the dark hair between her legs, and Kit stopped. Her fingers were resting on Teddy's thighs, and she moved them again, quickly, between her legs, making Teddy jolt again. She left her hand there, frozen, her fingers just outside the soft, fleshy folds, lying on the dark curls of her hair. As she kissed her way slowly downward, she slid her fingers, very slowly, inside the folds of skin, and Teddy moaned again, her hips rising to meet her fingers. Kit paused once more and then sank her fingers inside, Teddy arching upward to meet her. She raised her face, watching as Teddy threw her head back, her body rising and falling in rhythm with the fingers sliding in and out of her. Using her palm, Kit massaged her clit for a few moments before putting her mouth there, first licking the hood and then sucking on it until it became more and more exposed. She kept all of her fingers inside Teddy, and the dampness coated her hand as Teddy's excitement built.

The end was quick and hard, Teddy groaning with what almost sounded like pain as the orgasm shook through her body. Kit sat back for a quick breather before climbing up and lying down on Teddy's chest. Teddy was slick with sweat, her hair nearly soaked, and Kit reached up to brush it off her wet face before kissing her, slow and hard. She put her head back on Teddy's shoulder, and they lay there for a long time, not saying anything. Teddy ran her hand up and down Kit's back, and, despite the heat, Kit snuggled closer to her, putting her face into Teddy's neck.

"If that's what I have to look forward to the next few days, consider your rent paid in full," Teddy said, her voice still weak.

Kit propped up on one elbow, looking down at Teddy as she ran her hand along her stomach.

"You were going to charge me to stay here?" Kit asked.

"Not in money." Teddy looked coy.

Kit enjoyed the feeling of Teddy's tight muscles, which bunched under her fingers as she brushed across each part of her body. As her nipples hardened again, Kit paused, playing with one before changing to the other. Teddy's eyes widened a little at this and then went hazy again, her desire still there, still present, waiting to be fully awoken again. Kit had become possessive of her. That desperate longing she had for her sometimes had abated, but something else was here now: fear. Fear that this would all be over soon, that Teddy would no longer be hers and that Kit would, in fact, have to go back to living without her, all alone in San Francisco. Teddy would, of course, forget her, the next woman likely right around the corner. Chastising herself, Kit dragged herself back to the present, trying to focus on the very real sensation of her fingers on Teddy's beautiful body. Her jealousy returned anyway.

"I just thought of something," Kit said, trying to sound innocent.

"What?" Teddy asked, her eyes focusing and her brow furrowing.

"Why were you in that hotel when I first saw you? I've been meaning to ask." She continued to play with Teddy's nipples, lightly squeezing each in turn.

Teddy looked shamefaced for a second, and then she grinned widely. "I stayed with someone there the night before, but I forgot my wallet. She left it at the front desk for me, and I was picking it up."

Kit had a flash of real dread and something like anger, but she tried to suppress those feelings almost as soon as she felt them. Trying to sound lighthearted about it, she asked, "So is this the usual week for you? Going from one tourist to the next and staying in her hotel room?"

Teddy chuckled and kissed her before rolling her onto her back, slamming her onto the bed.

"I think you know the answer to that, missy," Teddy said, and kissed her, hard.

They waited until late afternoon had cooled things off a little before walking back to the restaurant with the luggage cart. They left it by the back door and made several trips between the walk-in pantry and the cart, loading up bottled water, boxed food, and cans. They took enough for a week, figuring there was no way on earth it could take longer than that to get the city back on its feet. Teddy also suggested that Kit choose some of the fresh food from the refrigerator to eat before the neighborhood and the restaurant lost electricity.

"We'll have my gas stove and the grill," Teddy told her as they stood in the refrigerator looking at the fresh meat and cheeses. "So even when the electricity goes out, I'll be able to cook as long as the gas is on and as long as there's propane in the tank for the grill. I can't imagine we'd ever get to it, but we can use my camping stove after that if we have to. The thing I'm worried about is keeping the meat and dairy fresh once the electricity goes. We can pack what's left in ice, but that won't last very long in this heat."

"I'm so sorry," Kit said looking around. "It's such a lot of food to go to waste."

Teddy's face was pained. "Almost all of it is local, too, from some of the best farm sources in the state." She shook her head. "If this place is wrecked, it won't just hurt me. It'll also hurt my suppliers."

Kit walked closer and gave her a quick hug. "It'll be open again soon. You just wait and see."

Teddy still looked troubled. Kit decided to give her a minute and took the opportunity to tour every shelf, choosing the chicken she'd had the other night, some lamb chops, and some fresh steaks. It was far more than they could eat in a couple of days, but she was having a hard time leaving so much behind. They grabbed vegetables, butter, cheeses, and fresh, prepared salads, as well as some eggs and fresh spices. The whole experience was novel for Kit. Having never worked in a restaurant, she was impressed by the scale of what she saw. She wanted to take everything she saw back with them, but Teddy told her the food would just go to waste and end up rotting at her place instead of over here. As it was, they had yet another full cart to move back to Teddy's place.

As they pushed the cart, Kit asked, "Do you think you could teach me how to bake those breads you serve? I'd love to know how to make them."

Teddy thought for a moment. "It will be a little harder in my kitchen than in the restaurant, but that should help me show you how to do it at home. I can't teach you all of the recipes, since some of them need special ovens, but we can do a few."

They struggled for a moment getting the cart around a particularly bad stretch of road.

"Do you cook at all?" Teddy asked when they were past it.

Kit shook her head. "I mean, I can do pasta, eggs, that kind of thing. I'm also very good at making pan-fried steaks. I've never really been what you would call a foodie, and I'm impatient."

"The first lesson in baking or cooking is patience. You have to break a lot of eggs and make a lot of messes before you get good at something."

Kit nodded, her face serious.

Seeing her expression, Teddy laughed. "This isn't a lecture, Kit. You don't have to memorize everything. At first, a lot of it is watching—passive learning. You start to get your hands dirty right away, but you're always watching when you learn how to do something with food."

Kit smiled. "That's almost the same way I learned my work, too. In undergrad, we're told new ways to think—passive learning at its best. In graduate school we develop those new ways and learn how to think on our own."

"Cooking is something like that," Teddy said, smiling. She looked at the road ahead. "Now come on. If I have to push this fucking thing ten more minutes, I'm going to just leave it in the road."

CHAPTER THIRTEEN

When they finally made it back, Teddy's neighbor, Mrs. Williams, was sitting on the porch in her rocking chair. She greeted both of them with a wave, her thin little arm enveloped in a cardigan despite the heat. Kit walked up to shake her hand and introduce herself. Mrs. Williams looked to be in her eighties, at least, and the chair dwarfed her small, bent body. Her hand felt bony and frail in Kit's.

"I saw you with some luggage a while ago, and now here you are again with another load of stuff. You two are working too hard!" Mrs. Williams said.

"Doesn't look you're working at all," Teddy said. "What are you still doing here? Are you getting out of town?"

"My grandson Jake is picking me up in a little while. He takes good care of me, ever since his daddy passed. I keep telling Jake there's nothing to worry about, but he insisted on taking me with him and the great-grandkids."

"When will they be here?" Teddy asked, glancing at her watch.

"Shortly. An hour or so. They were packing up, and then they have to drive in from Slidell. I guess the traffic is a nightmare. That's why we're traveling at night."

"Do you think they'd like a big, hearty meal before they hit the road?" Teddy asked.

The woman laughed. "I can't imagine there would be any objections. It would be a real treat for the kids to try that fancy stuff you cook up over there at your restaurant."

"Well, I can't promise fancy, but it should be edible, anyway. You know you have an open reservation at my restaurant anytime you want to come, Mrs. Williams. I can always get you a table."

Mrs. Williams flapped her hand dismissively. "I don't have the time to get dressed up anymore, honey. I love it when you cook here for me. You're almost as good a cook as my mama, and that's saying something."

Teddy looked flattered as she turned to Kit. "You feel up to being my assistant for the evening?"

"I can't promise I'll be very good at it, but I'll try."

It took several trips to bring the food inside. The dogs followed them like ghosts through the house when they smelled the fresh meat. They were too well trained to jump up and try to get things from Teddy or Kit, but they couldn't resist looking at the packages they carried, probably hoping that one or both of them would drop something for them. As Kit tried to make room in the freezer and fridge for everything, she could feel the three of them looking at her with hungry eyes. Teddy brought the last of the steaks in, set them on the counter, and then put the dogs in the backyard.

"I think simple grilled steaks are in order," Teddy said. "I'll serve them with fingerling potatoes and a fresh tomato salad. The kids probably wouldn't eat anything more complicated than that, anyway." She paused, looking around at her kitchen as if to determine where everything was located before starting. "I think we can also do a lemon pine-nut tart. If we get it in the oven soon, it should just be ready by the time we're done eating. It would also help me use up some of this rosemary you brought back here."

Kit smiled. "I just couldn't leave it there in the kitchen. It was too pretty."

Teddy put her on chopping and juicing duty. For each ingredient Kit had to work with, Teddy would first show her the best way to cut it before leaving her to the task. Kit prepared tomatoes, herbs, and garlic, then juiced several lemons for the tart. Teddy paused in her preparations to show her the recipe for the lemon tart and help her put the ingredients together and into a special pan. Kit was starting to feel a little nervous. While she'd had big dinners at her place in

San Francisco before, she'd almost always either had them catered or served ready-made foods. The idea of several strangers eating what she helped cook was intimidating, and she told Teddy so.

"It's almost like teaching a new class," Kit explained. "You walk in that first day, and they're judging everything about you: your clothes, the way you talk, everything. All of this before you even open your mouth or give them the syllabus."

Teddy nodded. "I remember how it was the first time I was put in charge of the line at a restaurant. I thought people would be sending their food back. I was surprised when, instead, several sent their compliments to the chef. I'm still pleasantly surprised to see people enjoy my food, and I've been cooking for almost twenty years."

The Williams family showed up just as Teddy was ready to put the steaks on the grill. Teddy had marinated each one for the last hour in a special sauce to help them stay moist and tender, but she was fretting over the short notice, afraid they would come out tough and inedible. Kit was putting the finishing touches on the salad and potatoes, unaccountably pleased with the result. It remained to be seen if anyone else liked what she'd done, but she was strangely proud of herself for getting things together on time.

The kids ranged in age from six to thirteen, the eldest a quiet, studious-looking boy with his dad's face and eyes and thick-framed, hipster-style glasses. The two middle boys were so similar they were hard to distinguish, and the youngest, a girl, trailed after her older brothers in silent reverence. All four went into the backyard to play with the dogs after politely introducing themselves. Kit watched them for a moment, seeing the oldest dictate the rules of the game and smiling in memory of her childhood. She'd always been the boss when she played with her younger brother, and she could still clearly remember the pleasure she'd gotten from being in complete control of him.

The father, Jake, was an enormous man—a famous ex-football player for a state-college team, now a lawyer. He had apparently grown up in the house they were now standing in, back before it had been divided into two apartments. He towered over Kit and Teddy, looking around the kitchen in quiet wonder.

"I've actually never been in this apartment before," he said. "My parents and I lived in this house with my grandparents until I was ten. My grandparents split the place after my family moved out so they could have some retirement income. They never expected the neighborhood to take off like it did. This apartment has never been vacant for more than a couple of days since they started renting it. My bedroom was actually right here, where this kitchen is."

The three of them stood there a moment, looking around, Kit and Teddy trying to picture it as it had been. Jake and Teddy were sipping on beers, and Kit had a glass of wine. Mrs. Williams had gone to her side of the house to change her clothes before dinner and the trip, and by the time Teddy, Jake, and Kit went into the backyard, she was already ensconced in one of the chairs by the table, a little quilt on her lap. Teddy walked immediately to the grill, which had been heating, and put the steaks on. The kids and the dogs, who had been rolling around in the grass together or playing fetch, ran over to watch, all of them mesmerized by the flames and smoke.

Kit sat down next to Mrs. Williams, Jake across from them.

Mrs. Williams patted her hand. "It's so nice to see our Teddy settling down with someone. She's been a bit of a rolling stone for a while now."

Kit blushed, not sure how to respond, and Jake, seeing her expression, laughed out loud.

"I think you're embarrassing her, Nana," he said.

"Well, you shouldn't be embarrassed, dear," Mrs. Williams said. "Love is nothing to be ashamed of—that much I can tell you." She gestured at Jake. "When Jakey was a little boy, he got a lot of lip from the other kids at school 'cause his folks were mixed race. Even me and Jake's granddad had a hard time being happy when our son brought home a white girl. But we soon realized they were in love, and love changes opinions quick."

"Come on, Nana," Jake said, clearly embarrassed. "You don't have to tell her all that."

"She should hear it!" Mrs. Williams said. "Anyway, when all this stuff about same-sex marriage starting coming up in the news, I remembered how different things used to be for couples like Jake's parents, and it made me realize that couples like you and Teddy have similar problems. Things aren't altogether better about mixed-race couples—especially down here in the South. But they're better than they were." She nodded firmly. "When Jake here married an Asian lady—Jill, God rest her—her parents were real mad for a while, but they got used to it, too. People understand love, even if they don't like what it looks like when they first see it. Love always wins."

Kit smiled at her and was surprised to feel the prick of tears in her eyes. As if sensing her emotion, Mrs. Williams patted her hand. "You and Teddy are good together. I can tell. Love is a beautiful thing."

Kit let the words sink in for a while, sitting back and watching the others. Jake and Mrs. Williams were making plans about the drive tonight, which gave her a few minutes to herself. She watched Teddy at the grill for a while, thinking about love. While it was true that Kit enjoyed being around the other woman, she wasn't sure if what she and Teddy had was love. She felt a certain kind of tenderness, possessiveness even, when she looked at Teddy, but was that love? Kit had been in love once, when she was younger, and the pain of that breakup had put her off trying to find it again. She'd always believed you loved like that only once, and so far it had been true. Still, she hadn't really tried to find love.

She continued to watch Teddy, who was now playing with the kids and the dogs as the steaks cooked. Everyone was laughing or barking happily, and Teddy's face, normally so reserved, was wide and open with simple joy. Kit's stomach dropped as she watched Teddy, the depth of her attraction and fondness washing over her with clear recognition.

This probably wasn't love—not yet, anyway. That would be silly after just a few days. But she did have feelings for Teddy. She couldn't deny it. When she'd left Teddy's this morning, it had been with a heavy heart. The thought of not seeing her again had actually hurt. And now, despite the danger they were in, despite the fact that they couldn't simply get in a car and leave, despite everything, Kit was glad she was here.

The food was ready, and Kit and Teddy couldn't have hoped for a more appreciative audience. Plate after plate disappeared in record time, and even the youngest, pickiest eater asked for seconds. By the time they were done with the main courses, the tart had cooled, and they split it into eight even pieces for each person present. Teddy gave the kids a scoop of homemade ice cream with their tart, and the little girl looked at her as if she were an angel sent from heaven.

"Don't you go making yourself ill, child," Mrs. Williams chided. "We have a long drive ahead of us tonight."

"I won't, Great-Nana," the girl said, rolling her eyes.

"Where are y'all headed?" Teddy asked, sitting down again.

"We have some family up in Shreveport that's taking us in," Jake said. "We've been there before for storms."

Mrs. Williams tsked and shook her head. "I sure hope this is all a bunch of fuss over nothing. Those news people made it sound like the end of the world—but they always do." She looked at Teddy and Kit. "I hate to think of you girls alone down here." She turned to Jake. "Don't you think we could take them with us?"

Kit's hopes momentarily rose before she saw Jake's face, which was deeply troubled. He didn't meet either Kit or Teddy's eyes. "I'm sorry," he said, "but we don't have the room. We already have to have Alex, my oldest, sit up front with us."

"Don't worry about it, Jake—it's not your problem," Teddy said. "Just some bad luck on our part. We'll be okay."

He looked relieved but was still clearly bothered by the situation. Mrs. Williams's face was dark with worry.

"They said on the news you can go to the Superdome as a last resort," she finally said. "That slick willie we have for a mayor invited anyone without another place to stay to go there. If they need it."

Kit and Teddy shared a glance. They hadn't turned on the news since this morning. "I think we'll be okay here," Teddy said. "At least for a while."

"Speaking of which," Jake said, standing up, "I brought some wood panels to cover the windows. I was hoping to do it before the sun set, but I have a spotlight in the car. There should be enough wood for the whole place, including your side. You think you could help me put them up before we leave?"

"Absolutely," Teddy said, standing. "I'll wait until tomorrow to do my windows. It'd be nice to have a little more sunshine before all of this starts."

They disappeared into the house, and Kit was left to make small talk with Mrs. Williams. Finding out that she actually lived in San Francisco, Mrs. Williams spent the next half hour trying to convince her to quit her job and move to New Orleans—this despite the fact that a hurricane was bearing down on them. Kit tried to change the subject several times, but Mrs. Williams kept coming back to it, repeating her earlier statements about love and the importance of connection between people. Jake and Teddy reappeared in the backyard, nailing up the last of the boards on Mrs. Williams's side of the house. Kit continued to listen to her and was starting to feel almost half-convinced the older woman was right.

After all, she thought, what do I have to go back to?

She pictured her tiny apartment in San Francisco and her musty office at work. She pictured another semester of teaching mired in university politics and funding problems. She pictured the desperate nights she went searching for something, someone in some bar, some club, only to find empty sex and the same desperation she knew and understood reflected back at her in the eyes of her one-time lovers. Everything she pictured from her real life seemed empty, weightless, and worthless. What's more, beyond simply leaving her empty life behind, a growing part of her actually *wanted* to stay here with Teddy.

How pathetic, she thought to herself as she watched Teddy and Jake. If Teddy knew what I was thinking she would send me packing, hurricane or no hurricane.

When Jake and Teddy were done with the last window, she stood up to see the Williams family on their way. Everyone was laughing and well-wishing, and she tried to force herself to shrug off the ghost of her future. It could wait.

The three younger kids were almost instantly asleep when Jake put them in the backseat, and Kit realized, looking at the small sedan, why he'd been so reluctant to entertain the idea of taking Teddy and herself along: there was really no room. With Jake, Alex, and Mrs. Williams up front, the car was packed to the gills. Mrs. Williams rolled down her window. She held her hands out, and Kit and Teddy each squeezed one of hers.

"Good luck, girls," she said, fighting back tears. "Get out if the getting is good. And be safe."

"We will," Teddy said.

A moment later, the car was driving away. Teddy and Kit shared another look, both of them glancing at the dark houses around them. To Kit, it seemed as if they were the last people on earth.

"I guess we should watch the news," Teddy said, her voice uncertain.

"It'll still be the same in the morning."

Teddy turned to her, smiling, her grin just visible in the dark. "That's true. We have better things to do right now than watch TV."

CHAPTER FOURTEEN

Kit woke up just as the sun was rising. Teddy was sleeping next to her, her naked body exposed to the cool air-conditioning unit next to the bed. Her dark nipples were hard from the air, and she'd thrown an arm over her head, her hand in her hair. Her body was a magnificent landscape of muscles and smooth skin. Kit had looked at most of her tattoos before, but now, as Teddy slept, Kit followed their pattern closely over her firm body. Teddy's skin was a uniform olive, suggesting that she either tanned naked or was, perhaps, that color naturally. Kit had to fight the urge to run her fingers along the smooth expanse of her exposed stomach, where the muscles stood out in firm relief.

Teddy looked worn and troubled, even in sleep. Kit knew she'd been keeping a brave face on for her and for Mrs. Williams yesterday. She'd sensed Teddy's worry several times during the evening and wondered what Teddy would have done if she hadn't needed to help her. She felt a sharp pang of guilt when she remembered Teddy saying she had friends to be with and places to go. Was she keeping her here in danger? While Kit didn't want to ask, she knew she should and promised herself to ask Teddy about it when she woke up. Maybe she could stay here if Teddy knew a way out of town—it was still better than being at the hotel. The thought of Teddy leaving gave her an empty, hollow feeling in the pit of her stomach, and a prickle of tears stung her eyes.

As quietly as she could, she climbed out of bed and went into the bathroom. She washed her hot face in cool water and then stood there for a moment, eyes closed, taking deep, slow breaths to calm down. She opened her eyes and stared at herself in the mirror for a long time. Her feelings were chaotic, unsettled. Every moment she was with Teddy, she felt better, safer. Every time she thought about where this was inevitably going, she was almost physically ill. The smart thing to do would be to hold herself back, get whatever these feelings were under control. Maybe if Teddy left, it would be better. The thought made her stomach flip-flop again, and she cursed under her breath. She was being ridiculous.

She brushed her teeth before going into the sitting room, where they'd placed all of her luggage. She dug around in her backpack for her running clothes and slipped them on. She hadn't been running since she'd been in Europe, and her body was craving the exercise. After days of heavy food and drink, and days of worry and heartache, she needed the endorphins. She scribbled a quick note to Teddy in the kitchen and took the map of the French Quarter from her purse.

The dogs looked up from their beds as she walked by in the living room, and she paused for a moment, wondering if she should let them outside in the backyard. Jingo put his head back down when he saw that she was headed for the front door, and she took that as a sign that they were used to waiting for Teddy. She saw Teddy's house keys by the door and grabbed them, locking the door behind her when she was outside. She stood stretching on the front stoop for a while, looking up and down the street. She glanced at her map. Apparently the Marigny was built on the same grid pattern as the Quarter, and the street she was standing on—Chartres—was the same as one in the Quarter. She decided that she could run in the direction of the Quarter on the Chartres and then come back on a parallel street without getting lost.

Despite the early hour, the air was already dense with humidity and heat. Kit had never spent time in a climate like this, and she found the heaviness of the air oppressive and strange. While her childhood summers in Colorado were hot, it was a dry heat. San

Francisco was humid, but never this hot. She could appreciate the idea of a warm winter, but she couldn't quite fathom how people could live here year-round. This heat, coupled with the threat of hurricanes every year, would encourage her to leave every summer. She smiled. She was once again making plans as if she intended to move here. Why bother thinking about something that wasn't going to happen?

She knew the answer to that, though: Teddy. While she still didn't think that what they had was love, there was something there between them, and the longer they were together, the more it grew, moment by moment. Already, she could feel herself changing slightly to accommodate Teddy's habits and ideas, and Teddy was doing the same thing. Though she hadn't known her before this week, Teddy had clearly changed, at least a little, for her. Even Mrs. Williams had noticed. Wasn't that, after all, one of the early stages of love? Adaptation? Once again she cursed herself for thinking this way.

She passed a surprisingly large number of people when she hit the Quarter. While the Marigny had seemed like a virtual graveyard, even last night, the Quarter was still relatively populated. The early hour meant that those remaining were mostly in bed, but there were still people bringing dollies of supplies to restaurants, elderly people walking their dogs, and a few tourists still up from the night before. A few of the locals waved at her and she waved in return, confused to see them here. She was tempted to stop and chat with some of them to get details, and when she ran by the police station, she almost went inside. She decided to ask Teddy about it. Maybe these people knew something they didn't. Maybe it was going to be okay after all.

She saw a surprising number of cars on the road and wondered if the owners planned to leave or were simply going about their regular day-to-day business. Given her panic yesterday and the mass exodus she'd assumed had taken place already, she was amazed at the quantity of people still around. While she knew the Quarter was generally full of tourists, and they, like her, might be stuck here, she couldn't understand why anyone who could leave would stay.

She hit Canal and turned around, making it back to the cross street with Teddy's place fairly quickly. Then she decided to keep running in the opposite direction, away from the Quarter, hoping that the neighborhood she was heading into was a safe one. As she ran on Royal, she wasn't surprised to see that most of the houses she passed looked empty. Out here in a more residential neighborhood, people had apparently left when they could—most of them last night, like Mrs. Williams. She passed a few people loading their cars, likely hoping to beat the traffic that would build throughout the day. Like the locals in the Quarter, almost everyone waved, and she waved and greeted them as she ran. One thing that was true of the South was the almost universal friendliness of the people here. She might pass a hundred people jogging in San Francisco, but it was rare for anyone to acknowledge her, let alone wave.

She went as far as she could on Royal, eventually hitting a large concrete wall, and turned around again, running up Chartres to Teddy's. When she finally got there, she was dripping with sweat, but she felt better than she had in days, physically and mentally. The exercise had banished some of the future for a later day.

As she struggled with the locks, Teddy opened the door for her. They smiled when their eyes met.

"You're disgusting," Teddy said. Teddy was wearing a tank top and shorts, both of them wet with her sweat.

"Thanks!" Kit replied, grinning in response. "So are you."

"I was just working out, too," Teddy said. "I have some weights here if you want to use them." Kit made a face and Teddy laughed. "Not a bodybuilder?"

"I know I should, but I hate it," Kit said. "I like going places when I exercise. I never know what to look at when I'm lifting weights."

"That's a strange excuse."

Kit told her about the people she'd seen in the Quarter and the relative emptiness of the Marigny and the adjoining neighborhood, the Bywater.

Teddy wasn't surprised. "Sounds about right. Anyone with half a brain would leave if he could. I know some people will stay even if it's coming right for us—especially in the neighborhoods along the river. We've had some false scares before. People leave town, pay for hotels, all for nothing. I think some people don't like to be fooled that way."

Kit was confused. "But it's pretty clear that this one is a real threat."

Teddy shrugged. "A lot of people won't listen to reason. They'd rather risk it."

"Have you watched the news yet?"

"No. Not yet," Teddy said. "I thought I'd wait until after breakfast."

"How long do you think we'll have power?"

"The hurricane's not supposed to hit until tomorrow morning, but we could lose it before then once the winds start. It'll probably go on and off for a while before we lose it for good. We should take advantage of having it today and cook the rest of the food that will spoil. I also want to bring over as much ice from the restaurant as we can. I turned up all the icemakers before we left yesterday, so there should be plenty."

Despite getting to bed so early last night, Teddy still looked tired and worn, and Kit frowned. Her stomach dropped with dread, but, remembering the promise she'd made to herself, she grabbed Teddy's hand and pulled her in the direction of the couch.

Seeming confused, Teddy followed. "Shouldn't we take a shower? I know I stink, and I won't tell you about your odor."

"Let's sit down for a minute," Kit said, sitting on the couch. "I want to ask you something."

Teddy sat down next to her. "What's up?"

Kit made eye contact with her, holding her hands. "Listen. I know you're trying to help me out here, and I appreciate that."

Teddy's brow furrowed.

Kit hesitated and then made herself continue. "You told me yesterday you had places you could go—people you could go stay with. Are you staying here just for me? Because if you are, I don't want you to. You should leave if you can."

Teddy drew her into an embrace, kissing her sweaty cheek. "You're adorable, you know that?"

Now Kit was confused.

Teddy sighed. "When I told you that I had places I could go, I was mostly talking out of my ass. I just didn't want you to worry about me. I was afraid if I told you I would have to stay, you wouldn't take any chance you could get to leave." She paused. "After you left yesterday morning, I called everyone I knew in town, even though I already knew what I'd hear. Almost everyone had gone already, or, if they hadn't, were planning to leave before I could go with them. Three of my closest friends are on vacation anyway—so they're already safe. The only other people I would ask…" She paused again and shook her head. "Anyway, they wouldn't help me, so I didn't call them."

"You mean your family?"

Teddy nodded. "They probably left yesterday, too." Seeing that Kit still appeared to be weighing her words, Teddy put her arm around her. "Don't worry about it, Kit, and don't feel guilty either. We're stuck with each other, and we're stuck here."

Kit managed a weak smile. "Do you think we'll be okay?"

"Of course we will. I don't know how comfortable we'll be if we lose electricity, but we'll make it."

"Mrs. Williams said something about the football stadium?"

"The Superdome?" Teddy raised her eyebrows and then shook her head. "I wouldn't go there for almost anything. I can only imagine what a shit-show that will be." She shook her head again. "No—I think we're better off here. I can't leave the dogs, anyway."

Not having thought of that, Kit was momentarily taken aback. Of course Teddy wouldn't be allowed to take her dogs to a shelter. The idea was absurd, really. If everyone took their pets, it would be that much more chaotic. Still, Kit didn't think even Teddy would risk her life for her dogs if it came to it. This suggested that Teddy was fairly certain they would be safe here. Perhaps staying here was best—Teddy wasn't simply saying what she wanted to hear. The relief that came with this recognition almost made her cry again, though she wasn't sure if it was relief that Teddy was staying with her or that they would be safe. Some of both, perhaps.

"You can't think of any other way to get a car and get out of here?" Kit asked. "No one you know has an extra one?"

Teddy sighed again and shook her head. "That friend I called—Margaret—she has a car. But like I said, it has a flat tire and the keys are in her house. Margaret said we could break in through the back and get the keys, but I don't want to do that unless we have to. Breaking her window would leave her house open for animals or worse."

With this, Kit's last hope for getting out of town died. She sat there for a long time, staring into space. Finally, she decided that she had to accept their situation, at least for now.

"Okay," she said. "If this is where we have to be, and you can't leave anyway—I'm glad to have you here with me."

"Me, too," Teddy said, squeezing her hand. "I'd hate to be alone."

"Me, too," Kit said. Their eyes met, and Kit thought she saw something of the same tenderness and relief reflected in Teddy's eyes.

As if sensing her thoughts, Teddy looked embarrassed and broke eye contact. She stood up and yanked Kit to her feet. "Let's take a shower before we stink up the place any more than we already have."

Kit grinned slyly. "I think you're just trying to get me naked again."

"Maybe I am," Teddy said, and kissed her.

They spent the rest of the morning and early afternoon bringing ice and more nonperishables over from the restaurant. By the time they were done, Kit was a little stunned by the haul they'd managed to acquire. Piles of food had basically taken over the kitchen, and the pantries and shelves were completely stuffed. Teddy explained that she didn't want to have to go back in the restaurant after the hurricane, as it was generally better to leave the first viewing for the insurance people after a storm. While she was fairly certain the restaurant would be fine, even if there was flooding, she didn't want to go back until this whole thing blew over. Anyway, the dogs would also be able to eat some of what they'd brought.

"Are they okay for regular dog food?" Kit asked. "We might be able to go get some more somewhere today if they're low."

Teddy frowned and then went over to a panty near the kitchen. Inside was a large plastic bin full of dog food. A large, unopened bag and several cans of dog food sat on a nearby shelf.

"Jingo eats a lot, but this and the stuff from the restaurant should be enough for all of us for a couple of weeks, anyway." Teddy closed the door. "They'll be fine for now. I can't imagine things will be screwed up for that long. I'll get them out of town before I let their food run out."

"We still have a ton of fresh food in the fridge, too," Kit said. "How are we going to eat it all before it goes bad?"

"I'll make a big dinner tonight for us and the dogs," Teddy said, ticking off her fingers, "and I'll help you make some bread and pastries with the rest of the eggs and milk. I could probably also cook something for tomorrow. Even if the electricity goes out, things will stay okay in the fridge for a few hours as long as we don't open the door. And we have the coolers with the ice. We'll have something fresh for a couple of days, anyway."

"When do you want to put up the paneling over the windows?" Kit said. She'd been wondering all morning but was reluctant to mention it. The last thing she wanted was to hang out in a house without a view of the outside.

Teddy shrugged, clearly as reluctant as Kit. "We should do it before it gets dark. I don't have a light to use like Jake did last night."

"Do you want to take care of it now? I'm already really sweaty from moving all that stuff."

Teddy sighed. "We should cover all the windows in the back at the very least. We could leave the front window and the one to the TV room off for now and do them right before the sun sets."

The dogs followed them outside from window to window, sitting down and cocking their heads as they watched. They seemed to sense that something strange was happening, and once or twice Kit saw Jingo staring at the sky, as if he could tell the trouble was coming from there. Dot had taken to cowering underneath the backyard chair and table, like she too knew where the danger lay. Only Bingo seemed to be relatively unaffected, but, even with her limited exposure to him, Kit knew he was the dumbest of the three dogs—sweet, but dumb.

Attaching the paneling was difficult, but Kit was thankful that they hadn't put it off any longer. The air felt strange outside, and bands of rain were already beginning to sweep through the city in uneven intervals. The hurricane was, they knew, quite large, and would cause rain and wind long before it hit town.

Kit and Teddy avoided the television all day. They both walked a little faster when they walked by the TV in the house, and neither suggested to the other that they pause in their preparations long enough to catch up with the news. Staying busy all morning and afternoon allowed them to forget about it for the most part, but as the evening drew closer, they both knew that they wouldn't be able to put it off much longer.

After they screwed in the last of the wood panels they'd planned to put up, Kit dropped into one of the chairs in the backyard, exhausted. Her arms were shaking with fatigue.

"Damn," she said. "I guess I need to start weightlifting after all."

Teddy collapsed in the chair next to hers. "It wouldn't matter. That was exhausting for me, too."

"Should we just go ahead and do the TV room and the front of the house?"

Teddy sighed. "I'd like to have some natural light a little longer, but I guess you're right—maybe we should just get it over with."

They sat there for several long moments until it started raining again, making the decision a moot point. The dogs raced inside with them, and Kit helped Teddy towel them off before they covered the kitchen in water. Dot was the most patient with this task and stood quietly shivering with anxiety and cold as Kit dried her. Jingo and Bingo seemed to think the whole thing was a game, and Jingo grabbed the towel Teddy was using and snapped it from side to side with his head, cracking it like a whip. Teddy snickered and took it from him, leaving Kit to try to dry off Bingo, who was having none of it. He danced away from her every time she approached him with the towel until she was quite literally playing chase with him. He woofed at her a couple of times, his long tongue hanging out in a stupid grin. Teddy finally helped her by making him come and sit, commands he obeyed with good-natured defeat.

The rain continued to pour down outside, and Kit and Teddy watched it for a couple of minutes before turning to each other, almost as if on cue.

"We should watch the TV," Kit said, her tone resolved.

Teddy agreed, but her face was grim. "We've put it off long enough."

Without another word, they both walked into the TV room, the dogs following, heads down, almost as if they sensed the abrupt change in their people's mood. Kit and Teddy sat down next to each other, and after a glance at Teddy, Kit turned the TV on.

A very young anchor was on the screen. Her face was pale and frightened, her hair unusually unkempt for a news program. She paused for a moment before speaking.

As of this morning, there is a mandatory evacuation in place for the City of New Orleans. If you have the means, you must leave the city. Other mandatory evacuations are in effect for the following parishes and cities…

They listened to the long list of cities, towns, and parishes in Louisiana, and cities, towns, and counties in Mississippi. Clips of official announcements from earlier in the day followed, as well as recent updates from the National Hurricane Center. The storm was now a Category 5 and was described as being "potentially catastrophic."

Much of the information they heard went in one ear and out the other as Kit listened. She would hear a phrase and focus on that, mulling it over in her mind for long minutes. "Category 5" had done this, as had "potentially catastrophic" and "potentially breached levees." Images of people stuck in traffic, weathermen standing in the wind on the coast, and the pale, scared faces of every single person that came on screen only added to the mood. Teddy had grabbed a pen and paper at one point and was making notes, something Kit watched in paralyzed fear with only vague awareness beyond her crippling panic. Rain was still battering the widow behind them, and, in her stunned perception, Kit wondered if they would get a chance to put the rest of the paneling up before the storm hit.

Almost as if it had been waiting for her to think this, the rain suddenly died down. Teddy glanced back at the window and then at Kit. Seeing her scared face, she suddenly looked concerned.

"Are you okay?" she asked. "You're white as a sheet."

"Can we turn it off for a while?" Kit said, indicating the TV.

Teddy turned it off and scooted over to hug her. "We're going to be okay, Kit."

"How can you know that?"

"I don't know, but I think we will. Anyway, what choice do we have? We're stuck here."

"We should have tried harder...we should have..." Kit knew what she was saying was pointless—all the "should haves" were in the past.

Teddy stood up. "We need to get the last of the panels up while we can. The bands of rain and wind will come more often as the storm nears the city."

Kit stood up, her legs feeling momentarily numb. As if shaking herself out of a trance, she made herself focus on the present, pushing the idea of rising water out of her mind.

When they went outside, the wind was still blowing slightly and it was still drizzling, but the sky looked momentarily clear. She spotted clouds on the horizon, but for now, Kit could still see the sun. They managed to put up the remaining panels in record time, both of them fighting through their fatigue in order to get back inside as quickly as possible. Despite the clearing skies, a sense of impending menace lurked outside now. Kit knew that most of this feeling was her imagination, brought on by the fright of what she'd seen watching TV, but she could sense that Teddy felt the same way. She too seemed to be in a rush to go inside, where it was relatively safe.

They stood for a while in the dark kitchen, both breathing heavily from the strain of their recent activity. Finally, Teddy flicked on the light. They looked at each other for a long pause, both of them drenched in rain and sweat.

Finally, Teddy grinned. "You looked like a drowned rat."

"Fuck you!" Kit said, laughing harder than the joke deserved. Exhaustion made her punch-drunk.

Teddy looked around the kitchen. "Okay. We're going to start cooking, and we're going to cook until we run out of fresh food. You're getting a crash course in bread-making and pastries. I'll start dinner while you're working on the first batch of bread."

"What if I screw it up?"

"It's fine. We have plenty of flour, milk, eggs, and butter. You can't make an omelet without breaking some eggs."

"We're making omelets?" Kit asked, confused.

Teddy shook her head, grinning. "No. You're making bread. First, let me show you how to do a simple French baguette, and then we'll move on to something harder."

They spent the rest of the evening baking and cooking. Kit managed to completely ruin her first three baguettes, but Teddy was a patient teacher. She would examine each loaf of bread and know exactly what had gone wrong during the preparation. The fourth loaf had the right consistency, but it was tasteless. The fifth showed a great deal of improvement, and Teddy instructed her to make three more just like it. They didn't turn out exactly as the fifth had, but they were still decent. While the bread was baking, Teddy showed her how to make puff pastry and pie shells, and they made several turnovers and pies with different ingredients, knowing that even without refrigeration, they could eat these for days. Teddy showed her a cake recipe as well as one for chocolate butter-cream frosting, and, by the time she got around to it, Kit found that she was comfortable enough to try making it on her own despite the complex instructions.

While Kit whisked and beat ingredients together, Teddy was preparing a feast on the stove top: chicken paprikash, bacon Brussels sprouts, and spaetzle. They paused their baking long enough to eat the enormous meal, wrapping up what they couldn't finish in hopes that it would last long enough for lunch the next day. They put the food in the fridge on top of a bag of ice to help it last longer. The dogs were given ground-beef patties with carrots, all of them eating largely and quickly. Dot looked up first to see if there was more for her to wolf down. Like they'd done with the human food, they wrapped the leftovers carefully and put them on ice, then did the same to the rest of the fresh food in the fridge. Some of it they moved to a large cooler full of ice. If they kept the doors to the fridge and cooler closed for the most part, Teddy explained, they could have fresh food for at least for a couple of days.

They left the cakes, pies, pastries, and bread cooling and, completely satiated, went into the front room, avoiding the TV room. Teddy took a bottle of white wine, two glasses, and a corkscrew and opened it without asking, as if sensing that Kit could use a drink. She poured them each a large serving, and they sat there, sipping the cool, tart wine for a long, quiet moment.

"That was fun," Kit said, smiling.

Teddy looked pleased. "I'm glad you liked it."

"I've never done a lot of cooking like that all at once. Is that how working in a restaurant feels?"

Teddy shrugged. "Sometimes. On good nights. Other nights, it gets so busy, you feel like you'll never finish. You end a shift still in motion, looking around for the next task, the next disaster."

"Thanks for helping me forget about everything for a while," Kit said. "I know that was part of what that was all about."

Teddy looked at her and nodded. "It helped me, too."

As if hearing them acknowledge their situation, the lights flickered on and off. Kit and Teddy shared a glance, both of them wondering how long the electricity would last.

Teddy stood up. "I need to see if I can find my battery-powered radio. Do you want to watch a little more TV? Get the most-recent update?"

Kit shook her head. "I've had enough for one day. I'll listen to the radio, though, if you find it."

Teddy disappeared into the back, and Kit could hear her rustling around in different closets and drawers, moving things and cursing as they fell off shelves. Standing up, Kit shucked off her T-shirt. She unhooked her bra and slipped out of her shorts and underwear. Then she sat back down on the couch, picking up her wine, and faced the hallway, waiting.

Teddy reappeared a moment later, a radio in her hand. "I found it!" she said, then trailed off when she saw Kit sitting there, completely naked.

Kit pointed at the coffee table. "Put it there and take your clothes off. Then we can turn off the lights and go to bed. I don't want to watch them flicker on and off all night."

Teddy visibly swallowed and obeyed.

Once again, Kit took the lead. This didn't surprise either of them. Sometime in the last few days, either because of circumstance or growing comfort, the need for a leader had died away. The position of instigator could shift from one of them to the next with ease and current need. Kit, without really recognizing her reasons, needed to be in charge tonight. She needed to feel like she could control something in a chaotic situation. What she could do with Teddy was, she knew, something she was good at, something she could manage. In the middle of a day—a situation—that she could do nothing about, there was something to be said for knowing exactly what to do.

They were uninhibited with each other, perhaps rougher than they'd ever been before, even when they hadn't started caring for each other yet. Something like desperation gripped them—a violent need to feel wanted, connected to something warm and alive. Kit ripped Teddy's clothes off her body, her nails actually making two scratches on Teddy's arms in her haste. Their mouths met and broke apart, Kit kissing Teddy's neck and shoulder before moving down as if she were consuming her. They were still standing, both naked, Teddy's head thrown back as Kit found her breasts and then knelt before her, first kissing her stomach and then forcing her legs apart before setting her face between them, licking and sucking.

Kit stuck her tongue in as far as she could and noticed Teddy's knees buckle slightly. She put her hands on Teddy's legs to steady her and continued, drinking in the salty taste of her. After a while, she stood and shoved Teddy onto the bed. Teddy lay there, panting. In the light drifting weakly in from the living room, Kit could see the look of dark desperation there, but she made her wait a moment and stood there, taking in the magnificence of the woman on the bed for a long moment before climbing on top of her.

The sex went on and on into the night, control shifting from Kit to Teddy and back again long into the early morning hours. Their passion managed to keep the darkness away, and for a while, their desire and the contact of their bodies distracted them from the sound of the rain and wind outside.

CHAPTER FIFTEEN

A loud rumble of thunder made Kit's eyes snap open. When she finally woke up enough to recognize what it was, she realized she'd been hearing it in her dreams for a long time. She looked at the window, and a brilliant purple flash of light followed the sound seconds later. Another roll of thunder followed, the sound so deep and low she felt rather than heard it. Through a small gap in the boards, Kit could see that the window was streaked with rain. The rain was falling so strong and fast it almost looked like a hose was pointed at the house.

In the next flash of lightning, she looked up at Teddy, whose eyes were still closed. Kit had been sleeping on Teddy's chest, and their lower bodies were still tangled beneath the sheets. Teddy's mouth was open slightly. Kit listened to her heavy breathing for a while, trying to let the sound soothe her. Teddy's naked body, limp with exhaustion, was splayed out, her breasts visible in the flashes of light. As Kit continued to stare at her, Teddy's brow furrowed slightly, as if she could feel eyes upon her. She frowned a little and pulled Kit closer. Kit put her head back down on Teddy's chest and tried to relax. She didn't think she'd be able to get back to sleep, but she started to doze a few seconds later.

When she woke again later, it was light enough to see most of the room, but the rain was still pummeling the house. The wind was louder now as well, and the shadows and branches outside were whipping around. Stretching a little, she looked up to see Teddy's eyes rooted to the gap at the window, a worried expression on her face.

"What time is it?" Kit asked.

Teddy looked down at her and shook her head. "I don't know. Six maybe?"

They both stared out the gap long enough to see another flash of lightning, and then they looked back at each other. Seeing her expression, Teddy squeezed her, hard.

"Don't worry too much, okay? We'll be all right."

Kit nodded, but her heart was racing. Should they be here in bed? Shouldn't they be listening to the radio? What if there was news they needed to hear? Was this the hurricane they were seeing or just outer bands of rain?

As if sensing her thoughts, Teddy grabbed her chin and made eye contact with her. "Hey. We can't do a lot now but sit and wait for this to blow over."

Kit agreed, but her nerves were like a knife in her gut.

"How about we get up and dress?" Teddy suggested, as if sensing her worry. "Then we can eat and listen to the storm blow in."

Kit was happy to have a task. They both scooted out of bed, and Teddy did a few jumping jacks to stretch out. Kit watched her naked body moving around, and a smile rose to her lips despite her worry. Teddy caught her watching and they both laughed.

"Can't keep your eyes off of me, can ya?" she said.

Kit threw a pillow at her. "Pervert."

"Takes one to know one," Teddy said and stuck out her tongue.

Kit dug around in her backpack, finding an easy outfit of jeans and a T-shirt. Before she went into the bathroom, she noticed that Teddy was putting on a raincoat and galoshes.

"I have to take the dogs out," Teddy explained. "Who knows how bad it'll be later."

Kit threw a wary glance outside and shivered in sympathy.

The electricity was out, as expected, and the bathroom, with no windows, was completely dark. Kit set her clothes down and went out through the TV room into the kitchen, where they'd put all of their lighting supplies. They had three flashlights and two oil lamps, as well as several boxes of candles. They'd agreed yesterday to use the candles only as a last resort. Keeping lighted fires in an old wooden house seemed like a bad idea. Kit grabbed a flashlight.

Back in the bathroom, the water was still running, but cold. Kit, however, decided that she would take a shower anyway in case they lost water pressure later. Already nervous and strangely excited, she let the water erase the rest of her sleepiness and emerged from the bathroom completely alert—ready to face whatever was coming.

Teddy and the dogs were just returning from the backyard, all of them dripping with water. Teddy made the dogs wait and then toweled dry each of them as well as she could. She grabbed Jingo's collar and led him into the TV room before she let him shake off, then did the same with the other dogs.

"Can't imagine we'll be in there very much," she explained, "and now the kitchen won't smell like a wet dog." Teddy carefully removed her rain jacket and hung it next to the door, trying not to drip everywhere. She used a small kitchen towel to help dry her hair and face before hanging it next to the three damp dog towels on a small coat rack.

Kit turned her eyes to the open door. Although the screen door was closed, she could see the backyard already flooding. Flashes of lightning lit up the pools of water in various spots in it, and the large drops falling out of the sky made ripples across them and the frog pond. The rain was falling so fast and so hard it was difficult to see almost anything but water between the flashes of lightning. The trees were blowing around in the wind, branches slapping each other and the fence, the clatter adding to the white noise of the wind. The idea that this was only the beginning—that things would actually be worse before they were better—made her stomach clench with terror.

Teddy put her arms around her from behind, making her jump. She squeezed Kit lightly and kissed the side of her head.

"Let's close the door," she said. "It's not safe to have it open right now."

Kit nodded, all too happy to block the view. Seeing all of the water and wind made everything real to her once more. Her strange elation from the shower had turned back to fear, and her racing heart beat painfully.

Teddy lit an oil lamp and then, after closing the back door, she grabbed Kit's hands and kissed her palms. "Try not to worry, Kit. We're as safe as we can be right now. Let's eat something and listen to the radio."

Almost on autopilot, Kit took out two plates from the cabinet and set them and some silverware on the small breakfast table. Teddy lit the stove with a match and put a kettle on to boil.

"We can only use the French press for coffee, I'm afraid," Teddy said, frowning slightly.

Kit laughed. "Considering the circumstances, it sounds like heaven. I like French press, anyway. It's what I use at home."

Teddy raised an eyebrow. "One of the things I hate about Europe is not being able to get drip coffee."

"I think you'll survive." Kit shook her head.

Teddy grinned and brought one of the pies over to the table. "Blueberry pie okay?"

"Breakfast pie sounds absolutely decadent," Kit said.

Almost as if the weather sensed that they'd forgotten about it for a moment, a loud clap of thunder sounded, and all of the dishes and glasses rattled. Kit ducked, as if attacked from above, and all the dogs yelped in surprise from the next room.

"Jesus," Teddy said, eyes wide.

"Sounded like a bomb." Kit was still cringing.

The light from the oil lamp was fairly strong, but the room seemed darker, more ominous now. The wind, which had been a constant low drone outside, also seemed to pick up, and they could hear the lashing of branches and debris flying around.

Kit made herself sit down, her legs rubbery and weak, her self-control slipping away in her panic. Watching Teddy bustle around making coffee helped, but Kit remained tense. Teddy smiled at her a couple of times as she gathered mugs and the last of the cream, and then she finally sat down across from her. The drone of the wind and rain seemed to have died down for a moment, and Kit forced herself to eat her pie and drink a strong cup of coffee. Just as she was finishing it, a loud slam next to the kitchen made her and Teddy jump in surprise.

Teddy grabbed her hand, squeezing it lightly. "It was the screen door. I must have forgotten to lock it."

They both looked over at the back door just as the screen door slammed again. Kit couldn't help but jump in surprise once more.

"I'll lock it now," Teddy said, getting to her feet.

"Don't!" Terrified, Kit grabbed Teddy's hand again and pulled her closer.

Teddy looked confused. "Why not?"

"Don't open the door," Kit said. "What if you can't get it closed again?"

"It's okay, Kit. It's not a tornado. It'll just take a second."

Kit wasn't sure why she was so terrified now. Opening the door for a couple of seconds wouldn't do anything, but somehow it seemed that if Teddy did that, the storm would come inside and sweep them away. She was being silly but couldn't dismiss the idea that, should the door open, the house would blow apart around them.

Powerless to stop her, Kit watched Teddy walk over to the back door and quickly open it, letting in a rush of wind and the smell of wet and damp decay. Kit cringed in panic as Teddy wrestled with the screen door. Teddy finally managed to lock it after a moment's battle, and then she closed and locked the back door. The few seconds she'd been outside had soaked her to the skin, and she stood there for a moment, dripping wet and panting.

"Jesus," she finally said.

Another loud gust of wind was followed by an earth-shaking peal of thunder. Kit clapped her hands over her ears, screaming. She kept her eyes squeezed shut, trying not to hear or see what was going on.

Teddy suddenly had her in her arms, squeezing her. She held Kit for a long time, running her hand up and down her back until Kit, almost against her will, began to relax a little. Despite the cold wetness of Teddy's soaked clothing now seeping into her own clothes, Kit was comforted. She opened her eyes to meet Teddy's. Teddy's concerned expression was clearly for her and her alone. Teddy wasn't worried about herself—only Kit.

Kit felt embarrassed. Teddy didn't need any hysteria right now. Kit made herself square her shoulders and then rolled her head, trying to release some of her tension.

"I'm sorry," she finally said, still attempting to relax. "You must think I'm a complete fruitcake."

"It's fine, baby. It's okay to be scared."

"I'll try to keep it together. I lost it there for a second."

Teddy's expression was still wary, as if she was waiting for Kit to start screaming again.

"I promise I'll try harder to stay calm," Kit said.

"It's okay, really. We'll be okay."

Kit made herself nod in agreement.

"Let's go in the bathroom." Teddy got to her feet. "That's the safest room in the house. We can wait out the storm in there."

"Won't that be incredibly uncomfortable?"

Teddy shook her head. "We can take some blankets and pillows. It'll be fine." She looked around, as if debating. "I'll take some water and food, too, just in case we're in there for a while. Let's change first, though."

Kit, still shaking, followed Teddy to the bedroom, where both of them changed into warm, dry clothes. After that, Kit sat down on the bed, almost as if to catch her breath. Teddy, meanwhile, kept busy, disappearing into the other rooms, obviously getting things ready for them. She finally came back, holding out a hand.

"Our chamber awaits us," Teddy said, smiling.

Kit grabbed her hand and let Teddy lead her into the bathroom. An oil lamp lit the room, and it was considerably brighter than her flashlight earlier. The glow from the lamp was warm and welcoming, bathing the room in a mellow, golden light. Teddy had filled the bathtub with pillows and blankets, and it looked like a cozy nest. She helped Kit climb into the tub and then disappeared again. Kit looked around the room, smiling despite her fear. It was comfortable, and, as Teddy had suggested, it felt very safe here. While she could still hear the rain and wind outside, it was considerably muffled in this inner room. Because the room had no windows and no access to the outside, the storm seemed very far away.

Teddy reappeared a moment later, leading the dogs. She made each of them lie down on the ground, then climbed into the tub behind Kit, wrapping her in her arms and pulling her into an embrace.

"See?" Teddy said. "Safe as houses."

"Thanks," Kit muttered, still embarrassed by her earlier hysterics.

"You're welcome. It's better this way anyway. Some of the windows might break, even with the boards over them. It's safer in here until the storm passes."

Kit inched back into her, snuggling closer, and closed her eyes. If only I could sleep through the next few hours, she thought. I just want it over with already.

As if reading her mind, Teddy suddenly leaned forward and grabbed a small book off the toilet seat. "I brought this to read while we wait," she said, showing Kit the title. It was William Goldman's *The Princess Bride*. "It was one of my favorites when I was a kid."

Kit was touched and had to blink away tears. "It's perfect," she whispered.

Teddy began to read, and her voice quickly lulled Kit, who wasn't exactly listening, into a deep sense of relaxation. Teddy was a good reader, using different voices and reading the rest with clear precision. Her slight accent came through here and there as she spoke, and Kit smiled as she listened, loving the way she pronounced certain words. She closed her eyes and turned a little, wrapping her arms around Teddy's body and laying her head in her lap. Teddy continued to read, and, feeling herself slipping into exhausted sleep, Kit didn't fight the urge.

Kit wasn't sure how long she was asleep, but once again the storm woke her. Teddy had apparently turned the lamp down to conserve oil, and the warm glow from before had turned into a dim, creepy haze. The dogs were whining softly, and Teddy's tension was apparent in the arms wrapped around her.

"What is it?" Kit asked. "What's happening?"

Before Teddy could answer, the storm did it for her. The wind, which had been muffled, and constant, ratcheted up again, blowing so hard against the house that the boards creaked around them. Too scared to scream, Kit buried her face against Teddy's stomach and squeezed her. Instead of quieting again, the wind continued to blow and wail against the house. Everything around them seemed to shake. The howling wind sounded almost like a train coming through the room. The sound would pause just for a second before continuing, its volume loud enough to make her clap her hands over her ears. In the dim light, she saw Teddy do the same. She could see the dogs barking but couldn't hear them, despite their nearness and the closeness of the room. Kit realized she was screaming—could feel the scream coming out of her mouth, but she couldn't hear it. Everything was lost in the deafening howl of the wind.

Finally, for the first time in what seemed like hours, Kit could hear herself breathing again. Her throat was sore and scratchy from screaming, though she didn't know when she stopped. While she'd been able to feel Teddy next to her, she could hear her now, too. The dogs had also stopped barking and whining. They were cowering on the floor, but, straining, she could hear them breathing, too. Everyone in the room seemed to be waiting, listening for what was next. Kit could hear the muffled moan of the wind and the patter of rain on the roof, but it was quieter, calmer. The storm was beginning to pass.

Jingo suddenly got to his feet and then sat down heavily, yawning before panting, staring at the two of them in the bathtub as if expecting something from them. The other dogs, taking their cue from him, stood up, both of them standing there next to the bigger dog, waiting.

Teddy laughed, and some of the tension seemed to leave her body. Releasing her death grip on Teddy, Kit sat up in the tub, turning back to meet Teddy's eyes.

"Is that it?" she asked. "Was that the end of storm?"

"I think so. I believe it's over. It will probably rain on and off all day, but we probably just heard the worst of it."

"I thought we were going to die," Kit said simply.

"So did I. For a moment there, anyway."

"How long have we been in here?"

Teddy shrugged. "Three, maybe four hours. I don't have a watch."

Kit looked around. "The house is still here. At least this room is."

Teddy climbed out of the tub and stretched before petting all three dogs. "Let's go see if the rest of the house is here, too."

Kit was reluctant to leave the safety of the bathroom, but a prickle of curiosity and restlessness encouraged her to get moving. She let Teddy help her up and out of the tub and followed her out of the bathroom and into the rest of the house.

CHAPTER SIXTEEN

The rain and wind were louder outside of the bathroom, and they both felt a breeze before they found the broken windowpane in the TV room. One board had somehow slipped off outside, and rain and wind were blowing into the room. They glanced into the other rooms and found no damage beyond this. Inexperienced as she was with hurricanes, Kit couldn't help but feel that the little house had done remarkably well.

"One window isn't too bad at all," Teddy said, clearly pleased.

"Can we do anything about it now? I wouldn't want the water to ruin your furniture."

Teddy agreed, and they spent the next few minutes covering the broken pane with duct tape and cardboard.

"That's okay for now," Teddy said. "We can do something more permanent about it when the rain stops for a while. Shouldn't be long now."

"Should we go look at the backyard?" Kit asked.

They took the dogs outside with them. The rain had let up significantly, and the wind was only gusting occasionally. The dogs ran around the yard chasing each other and kicking up water as they raced through the puddles. The only damage the two of them spotted was the significant number of branches and leaves scattered throughout the yard. Most of it was minor, but one large branch had broken off a neighbor's tree and was resting on the fence, making it lean precariously. The fence was still standing upright, however, and again Teddy suggested that they wait for the rain to stop before doing anything about it. The dogs would still be safe back here for now.

Kit stood on the small stoop by the door in order to stay out of the rain as much as possible and smiled as she watched Teddy and the dogs play in the yard, all four—Teddy and the dogs—getting soaked with falling rain and splashing puddles. Kit hugged herself anxiously at first, but gradually, without realizing it, she began to relax as she watched them, her arms dropping into a natural position after a few minutes. Little Dot was having a hard time keeping up with the others and continued to bark in frustration as they all galloped away from her. At one point Jingo, who was in the lead, stopped quickly in order to avoid running into a chair, and Bingo, Teddy, and Dot crashed into him and the chair from behind. All four ended up on the ground in a large, muddy puddle, and Kit laughed harder than she had in a long time.

Teddy brushed some mud off her face and, covered in filth and leaves, smiled sheepishly up at Kit. "Wanna join us?"

"No, you go ahead," Kit said, still chuckling. "I'm going inside to make some coffee."

The kitchen was warm and dark, the boards still secured over the windows. Kit lit the oil lamp and the kitchen stove and set the kettle on to boil. She was happy to see that the water was still running and promised herself another shower in a little while. Despite her shower a few hours ago, she was damp and dirty. Her T-shirt was stuck to her with sweat, and she could smell her dirty hair. In a few hours, she had lived a whole week's worth of worries. She was also completely famished, so she cut another large slice of pie for herself and Teddy. She hadn't seen the dogs eat today, either, but she didn't know how much they ate. She would ask Teddy when they came back inside.

As she waited for the water to boil, she remembered that they'd left the radio in the living room. She took the lamp with her to light her way, picked up the radio, and took it back to the kitchen. She set it on the counter with the lamp and then fiddled with the dials until she found a station.

When Teddy came in a few minutes later, she looked relaxed and happy. Seeing Kit's face, her smile died a little.

"What's the matter?"

Kit indicated the radio, and Teddy came closer to listen. The news was grim. While the storm had hit to the east of the city, several of the levees in town had failed. No one was sure which levees had been breached and which of them were still standing—it was impossible to get around town right now to check. Flooding was, however, visible in some parts of town, including the Ninth Ward and the Bywater. If the levees had completely failed, the city would continue to flood until it filled up like a big bowl.

"Will it flood here?" Kit asked.

Teddy shook her head and then set down her empty coffee mug. "No, I don't think so. We're very close to the river. The rest of the city is below sea level, so it makes sense that other places would get the worst of the flooding, but I guess it could happen here, too. I don't know. I wouldn't have thought the Bywater could flood. That's near us here."

"How near?" Kit asked, trying to keep her voice calm.

"It depends on where it flooded. Parts of the Bywater are only a couple of blocks away. I assume they mean closer to the canal, though, and that's about a mile away. No one seems to know anything for sure."

"What will we do if it floods?"

Teddy looked uncertain, and for the first time in this whole experience, Kit realized with dawning clarity that Teddy didn't know anything more than she did. She was just as scared and confused by all of this as Kit was. Having a little more experience didn't make her an expert—it had simply helped her prepare a little better. Kit wasn't sure if this realization made her feel better or worse, but it did make her understand that Teddy was scared, too. Kit stood and walked over to Teddy, hugging her.

"You're going to get filthy," Teddy said, brushing at the mud on Kit's shirt.

"I don't care." Kit hugged her again. "I just want a hug."

Teddy hugged her back fiercely and then gave her a solid kiss. "Okay," she said, her voice firmer. "Here's what we're going to do. First, I'm going to find some rain stuff for you. I know I have another raincoat, and I think I have an extra pair of galoshes. It's barely drizzling now, and it might stop soon, but we'll wear it just in case. Then we're going for a little walk. I don't know what the streets are like. There might be a lot of trees down and things. But if we can, we'll check out the flooding or see if we can meet someone who's seen it. Once we know if it's going to get worse, we'll make another plan. How's that sound?"

"Okay. Sounds good."

They spent the next few minutes gathering clothes and boots for the journey. After a short debate, they decided to leave the dogs at the house. Although they needed a walk, Teddy wasn't sure what they would encounter outside in the neighborhood. While her fence had stayed up, that might not be the case with everyone, which could mean wandering, scared animals. Also, Teddy was hoping they could be as discreet as possible. While she was fairly certain no one would follow them home, they didn't need to attract any extra attention, either, and the dogs always attracted attention.

They brought the dogs in, and Teddy showed her how much they were fed. The animals seemed perfectly happy to stay behind, settling into their beds the moment they were done eating. They, too, were apparently exhausted by the morning's anxiety.

"Lazy beasts," Teddy said, grinning at them.

Kit finished donning her rain gear—all of which was ridiculously large on her—and Teddy looked her up and down, nodding approvingly.

"Even in rubber clothes, you're super hot," she said.

Kit snorted. "Sure I am."

Teddy smiled, and then her face became serious. "When we're out there, if we see people, let me talk to them first, okay?"

"Sure, I guess so," Kit said, a little miffed.

Teddy grabbed her shoulders and made her look at her. "I'm not trying to be an asshole here, or macho, or whatever. I just have a better idea who we should avoid and who we can talk to. I'm trying to keep us safe."

Kit relented, but she was still a little angry. Kit was, after all, a fairly good judge of character.

When they finally made their way out the front door, Kit was shocked by what she saw. Branches and garbage littered the street. Several larger branches had landed on parked cars, crushing them or breaking out windows. Power lines hung down from poles everywhere, making it seem as if they were trapped on all sides by black wires. The rain was now a light mist, but the sky was still dark and foreboding above them.

"Should we be out here?" Kit asked.

Teddy looked at her and shook her head. "I don't know. It doesn't look very good, that's for sure."

"I don't want to get electrocuted," Kit said.

Teddy looked at the power lines. "They don't look safe, do they?"

Kit saw one stretch on the sidewalk to their right that looked fairly open and pointed at it. "I guess we could get through there."

Teddy agreed reluctantly. "It's the wrong direction, but we should try."

It was extremely slow going. They would walk half a block only to have to turn around. Teddy was trying to get them pointed in the direction of the levee on the canal, away from downtown, but they were continually forced to travel in the wrong direction. Finally she suggested walking down to the road closest to the river, North Peters, and they had better luck there. The view along the river, however, was terrifying. A large barge had been swept ashore, and a fire was burning uncontrollably in a large industrial complex. Only the light rain kept the air breathable, and the heat from the fire was palpable even from nearly half a mile away. As North Peters had houses along only one side, however, there was less debris, and much easier to walk there. At the end of North Peters, they went back onto Chartres, but once again, they were forced to backtrack half a block for nearly every block as they went. They saw no one and heard nothing but the light patter of rain on their hoods and the occasional gust of wind. The emptiness was eerie, and Kit couldn't help but continually look over her shoulder, constantly feeling watched and followed.

"I think this is as far as we're going to get," Teddy said after nearly an hour of walking and backtracking. "Why don't we sit down and rest for a minute?"

After they sat on the curb on a stretch of sidewalk clear of debris, Kit realized she was exhausted. The idea of having to trudge all the way back to where they'd started was daunting. She would happily stay there on the curb forever.

"I don't understand," Teddy said, shaking her head. "So were all those rumors wrong? I don't see any flooding here, and we're only a few blocks from the levee at this point."

"Maybe we don't have to worry about it," Kit suggested. "I guess there are always a lot of rumors after a storm."

Teddy shook her head. "I wish I could believe that. I think we're missing the flooding somehow. Maybe the water is lakeside from here. I want to go that way a couple of blocks just to see. If we don't spot any water, then maybe you're right." She shook her head in obvious frustration and then turned to Kit expectantly. "You ready?"

Kit sighed and reluctantly agreed. The only thing she wanted to do right now was take a nap.

They met the edge of the water a few blocks north of Chartres. It stretched out in front of them in an unending swath of dark, muddy gray. At the edge they approached, it was only a few inches deep, but they could see that even a block from where they stood, it was much deeper, as it hit higher on the houses farther away. Teddy, still curious, insisted on continuing north, and they sloshed another two blocks, the water lapping over the edges of their galoshes. As expected, the water continued to get deeper the longer they walked, and the debris floating around them became more and more difficult to move through.

Besides branches, leaves, and trash, Kit was starting to see other things floating by—personal items from the houses around them. At one point, she saw a photograph of a little girl. A few feet later, several books blocked her way. Peering up the block, Kit could tell that some houses had water up to their doorways, and she imagined that beyond that, the water was hitting the windows. Kit knew that Teddy would likely continue moving in that direction, just to see how deep it actually got, perhaps to the point of swimming. Kit, however, stopped completely when the water hit her thighs.

"It's far enough, Teddy. We should turn back."

Teddy's lips were a thin line of disgust and hurt. She shook her head angrily. "Goddamn it," she said. Then louder, "Goddamn it!" She slapped the water, sending up chutes of it into the air and splashing Kit in the face.

Kit, however, didn't chide her for her actions, wiping it off her face without comment. She put a hand on Teddy's shoulder. "We need to go back, Teddy."

Teddy's face, a mask of rage, crumpled into pain when she finally met Kit's eyes. "I can't believe it," she said, sobbing.

Kit pulled her into her arms. "I'm so sorry."

Teddy hugged her back, crying into her shoulder. "I can't fucking believe it."

Kit looked around them. Even the house near where they stood now had taken extensive water damage. Houses deeper in the water would likely be completely ruined. This whole neighborhood would have to be gutted to recover, and who knew how bad it would be elsewhere in the city if the flooding was as bad or worse.

"Let's go home," Kit said. "We can't do anything here." It felt strange, in that moment, to realize that she was now the voice of reason.

Teddy nodded, and they turned around, sloshing their way back to higher ground.

Once out of the water, they stood there, gazing back. The water seemed threatening, somehow, as if it were waiting for them to wade back in. Kit glanced nervously over at Teddy. Her face was blank. Instead of looking angry or upset, she simply looked deflated, as if all the fight had gone out of her.

"Do you think it will continue to rise?" Kit asked. She was no longer as nervous about it as she had been. Instead of a flash flood, the water, if it came, would likely creep up on them. So long as they kept an eye on it, they would probably be okay.

Teddy shrugged. "I don't know. I don't know anything anymore."

The emptiness in her voice gave Kit a chill, and she shuddered. "Let's go home." Kit grabbed Teddy's arm, steering her away and back in the direction they had come from. Teddy gave no resistance, following Kit with sluggish compliance. Kit wanted to get her back home and quickly, if only to remove that terrible, bleak look from her eyes.

The walk home was much faster. Kit remembered several of the blocks that were impassable, which saved them from having to backtrack there. They would likely have made it even faster if Teddy had participated in the navigation, but she didn't. Kit simply walked as fast as she could lead them, her arm linked in Teddy's. Teddy was walking, but she said nothing, did nothing. Her face continued to be expressionless and blank, and the longer Kit saw that look, the more frightened she became. Teddy seemed to be slipping into some kind of shock, and Kit wasn't sure what to do about it. She needed to get her inside, quickly.

When they finally made it back to Teddy's house, Kit was thoroughly chilled. While the air outside was warming up considerably, her damp clothes and hair were cold inside the insulated rainwear. She stripped down to her underwear as fast as she could, drying off a little with a hand towel. She was shivering, still, and yearned for a warm shower.

Teddy was silent, standing just inside the doorway nearly motionless, dripping in her soaked clothes.

"Honey, you need to get out of those wet things," Kit said, more than scared now.

Teddy looked down at herself, her expression vague and confused. She did nothing.

Her fear escalating with every passing moment, Kit helped Teddy take off her raingear and get out of the sodden clothes she had on underneath. Teddy let her do this, not helping beyond moving her arms and legs as Kit directed. Once Teddy was naked, Kit led her into the bathroom and lit the lamp, setting the wick as high as possible to cast the most light. Teddy was pale, her eyes sunken and her lips bluish-white. Altogether, with her paleness and blank expression, she looked like a different person. Kit made Teddy sit down on the toilet seat. Teddy complied with all of her directives wordlessly, blankly. What Teddy really needs right now, Kit thought, is to get warm. She was, Kit knew, very cold, but she wasn't shivering or reacting to the cold in any way. Is this shock? Is this what shock looks like? Kit wondered.

Kit grabbed her chin and tried to make eye contact with her. "Teddy? Are you in there? What's happening? Talk to me, goddamn it."

Teddy's eyes didn't focus on her, and her breathing sounded strangely labored and quick. Hearing it, Kit's heart rate picked up further. Standing upright again, Kit looked around desperately, wondering what to do. The water coming out of the faucet was cold, she knew, but she could always heat water in the kettle. Grabbing the blankets they'd left in the tub, Kit wrapped Teddy in them, tucking in the corners as best as she could.

"Stay here for a few minutes, okay?" she asked.

Teddy didn't respond, but, as she didn't move either, Kit decided she could leave her there. Racing into the kitchen, she set a full kettle on to boil and waited impatiently. The dogs were watching her. Dot seemed to sense her anxiety, as she whined a few times. Kit raced back and forth from the bathroom to the kitchen as she waited for the kettle, checking on Teddy, but she was in exactly the same spot Kit had left her in, staring dully in front of her and not responding. Kit had no idea what to do beyond getting her warm.

The kettle finally boiled, and Kit took it, a large bowl, and a dishrag back to the bathroom. She poured the boiling water into the bowl and then added a little cold water from the tap before putting in the rag to soak. She moved the blankets off Teddy's shoulders, and then, after wringing out the rag, she began to give her a rubdown with it. Kit scrubbed hard, warming the rag every few seconds. Eventually, Teddy's skin began to turn pink with heat, and the color in her face looked a little more normal. Kit continued to wash Teddy's shoulders, back, and chest with the hot rag until the water was almost completely gone from the bowl.

Teddy blinked a couple of times, and Kit realized she hadn't seen her eyes move for a long time. Kit moved in front of her trying to make eye contact, and Teddy finally looked up at her voluntarily. Her movements were slow and labored, as if she were mired in molasses.

"Teddy?" Kit finally asked.

Teddy nodded slightly, and a rush of relief sweep through Kit.

"We need to get you into bed, honey," she said. "Can you walk?"

Teddy seemed to think about it for a moment and then nodded, very slightly. Kit helped her stand, and then they nearly fell to the ground when Teddy's legs buckled. Bracing herself and Teddy with all of her strength, Kit helped Teddy leave the bathroom, and after a long struggle, they finally made it into the bedroom. Kit got her near the bed and Teddy fell on it heavily, horizontally, her legs hanging off the edge. Kit picked up Teddy's legs and swung her body around until she was lying across the bed the right way, then went back to the bathroom for the blankets and pillows. When she returned, Jingo had jumped up on the bed with Teddy, resting his body along hers to keep her warm. Dot and Bingo were watching from the foot of the bed, their eyes dark.

"Good dogs," Kit said.

She covered Jingo and Teddy as well as she could with the blankets and then remembered something about elevating someone's feet if they were in shock. She slipped the pillows underneath Teddy's feet and left her head down on the bed, hoping that was enough.

Then she stood there, watching, for a long time, her heart in her throat. She was distantly aware that she was wringing her hands, but her worry had dampened self-awareness. Her terror for Teddy was the only thing within the realm of her awareness. She knew she'd done everything she could, that all she could do now was wait, but that didn't make her alarm any less terrifying. She continued to fight back the idea that Teddy would get worse, that she would slip into some kind of coma and there would be nothing, absolutely nothing she could do about it. Tears were falling down her face, but she hardly noticed. She sat down on the edge of the bed and squeezed Teddy's hand.

Things stayed the same for an interminable length of time. Teddy's breathing sounded better, but she was still ghastly pale. Kit heated another kettle of water and washed her face and shoulders again, massaging and rubbing her skin. Once or twice Teddy's eyelids flickered, and Kit's heart lifted in triumph and relief, but her eyes remained closed. After a long, terrifying length of time, more color returned to Teddy's cheeks, and her breathing became even and natural sounding, as if she were sleeping. Bingo and Dot, as if sensing the end of the emergency, stopped their vigil, lying down at the foot of the bed to sleep.

Kit sobbed, once, and then swallowed, hard. Leaning close to Teddy's prone body, she whispered in her ear, almost unaware of what she was saying. "Come back to me, Teddy. Please. I can't live without you."

Exhaustion overtaking her, Kit sank down on the bed and fell asleep almost instantly.

Teddy shook her awake, and Kit blinked at the bright light coming in from the crack between the boards nailed over the windows. Teddy looked confused, and Kit sat up quickly and hugged her, hard, her relief a tight, piercing pain in her stomach.

"You scared the shit out of me," Kit said, choking back tears.

"What happened? The last thing I remember is seeing all that water..." Teddy shook her head. "Then I was here suddenly, in bed. Naked."

"You went into some kind of shock," Kit explained, wiping her cheeks. "At first you were quiet but able to walk around. I brought you back here and warmed you up, and then you were unconscious."

Teddy shook her head. "I can't believe it. That's never happened to me before." She reached out and wiped away some of the tears on Kit's face.

"I've never seen it, either," Kit said. "I didn't know what to do." She took Teddy's hand and kissed it before holding it in both of hers.

"Seems like you did a pretty good job for not knowing what to do," Teddy said, smiling weakly. "I'm still here."

"I had first aid in high school. I remembered something about keeping the victim warm and raising their feet above their head."

"'The victim?'" Teddy repeated, smiling. She flexed her arms and rolled her neck, as if experimenting with her body. "I seem okay. I'm kind of sore and my head hurts like hell, but that's about it. How long was I out?"

"I don't know. It took all my strength to get you in bed, and then I watched you until I knew you were okay."

"I'm sorry," Teddy said, clearly ashamed. "I don't know what happened."

"Me either," Kit said. "Maybe you were repressing too much or something."

Teddy grinned. "Are you a psychiatrist now or something?"

Kit smiled back. "Well, I am a doctor."

Teddy kissed her. "Thanks."

"For what?"

"For saving my life." Teddy's face was completely serious now. "If I'd been by myself, I probably would have died out there from the shock."

Kit felt the blood drain from her face at the realization. Even before her shock, Teddy had been dead set on exploring farther into the water. She might have drowned. As for the shock, it had been very serious when it was happening. Teddy was right.

Teddy gave her a quick squeeze. "Don't look so scared. It's over now. We're safe."

They stared at each other for a while longer, Kit still frightened by Teddy's brush with death. For the first time, their situation seemed as perilous as she'd feared it would be. They could die out here and no one would know about it, possibly for days or even weeks. She shuddered at the idea and hugged herself, suddenly cold.

Teddy grabbed her shoulder and squeezed it. "So," she said.

"So," Kit repeated.

"The city is flooded. We have no electricity, and it seems that we're stuck here for now. Alone."

Kit nodded.

"What do you want to do now?" Teddy asked.

Kit thought about it for a long moment and then laughed. "I'm really hungry. Let's eat something and then we can decide."

Teddy smiled. "Sounds perfect to me."

Chapter Seventeen

The next few days passed in relative peace. Occasionally, Kit would hear or think she heard people, and the two of them would run outside and rush toward the sound, only to find nothing and no one. Finally, on Wednesday, they saw several people pass their house, dragging belongings toward the Quarter. Teddy was reluctant to go outside and meet them when they were in large groups, but the few smaller groups they talked to were evacuees from the flooded areas. Search-and-rescue and good Samaritans had picked them up in boats only to drop them off, stranded, at the edge of the water. The evacuees usually knew less about what was happening than Teddy and Kit. Most of them had the look of refugees: worn, defeated, and filthy. Distant rescue helicopters caused a constant buzz in the air for the first few days, but one morning they didn't hear them anymore, and both Kit and Teddy breathed a sigh of relief. Perhaps it meant that the rest of the stranded people were safe again.

The day after the hurricane they removed the boards from the side and back windows and finally had natural light in most of the house again. They moved one of the boards over the front windows slightly to give themselves a better view of the street but left those in the front up for safety. Teddy wanted protection from the street in case they needed it. Some of the groups of people that had passed the house had been intimidating and could easily break in if they felt so inclined. Teddy explained that she wanted Kit and Teddy to be the ones to decide whether to approach anyone outside, not the other way around, and Kit agreed. They were safe for now, and unless authorities showed up, they had no motivation to take risks with strangers on the street.

The local public radio station had gone off the air, but Kit and Teddy were able to listen to news from a feed in Mississippi. It reported that some parts of New Orleans were chaotic and dangerous. From the sound of it, the Superdome and the Convention Center were filled with desperate, angry people, and Kit was glad Teddy hadn't even considered going there. Here in the Marigny, in their peaceful stretch of emptiness, they were lonely but safe.

Kit and Teddy decided to stay put for a week. Listening to the radio for an hour every afternoon, they heard that the city was still essentially isolated because of the floodwaters and roads, and the airports, train stations, and bus stations were not yet functional. Until they heard otherwise, it made no sense to try any of these places in order to leave town. If, by Monday—a week after the hurricane—mass transportation out of town was still inoperable, they agreed to go to Teddy's friend's house, break in, and retrieve her car.

At first they would walk the blocks over to the water every morning to check the level of the flood. After their first disastrous visit, Kit was reluctant to let Teddy see the flooding again, but, as it was unsafe to be out on the streets alone, she finally allowed it. Teddy's eyes welled up with tears the second time they saw the water level, but the earlier shock didn't return. The water level remained about equal to what it had been before, so Teddy decided after their third visit that they could forgo checking on it every day.

Their food held out well. The ice kept the fresh food edible for a couple of days, and the pies, bread, and pastries they'd baked fed them otherwise. Several days in they'd barely needed to touch the canned food, making their elaborate collection of nonperishables seem a little silly. The dogs were getting the leftovers and stale bread from Kit's experiments on Sunday as well as their regular kibble, and with the water still on and the toilets still flushing, the whole household was doing fine.

Kit found that, after the initial awkwardness of living together had worn off, it was incredibly easy to be around Teddy, in part because they complemented each other. Kit was somewhat high-strung, but Teddy was composed, methodical, and easygoing, and her calmness was contagious. After a while, Kit quit worrying so much. Despite the strangeness and initial terror of their situation, they spent their time together in warm and easy companionship.

They both began to wake up with the dawn, which meant their days started and ended far earlier than either of them was used to. Without electricity, they seemed to naturally revert to waking and sleeping with the rise and set of the sun. Their lives quickly fell into a pattern. They would wake, take the dogs on a quick walk, eat breakfast together, and then clean up or repair something in the house or yard. Late mornings and early afternoons they spent reading outside or in the TV room. Teddy loaned Kit books from her extensive collection, and Kit shared the few she had with her. Although Kit's research focused primarily on the early twentieth century, she also loved the late-nineteenth-century literature Teddy read. Their conversations about the books were fun and lighthearted and generally focused on plot and characters. One afternoon they got into a lively debate about the merits and strengths of French versus American Naturalism. Teddy became so worked up about the superiority of the French that she was almost yelling. When Kit revealed that she'd taken the side of the Americans just to play the devil's advocate, Teddy had looked murderous for a moment and then burst out laughing, embarrassed by her earlier fervor.

In the afternoons, they would take another walk with the dogs, always careful to check around corners for people and police. They ran into a few other holdouts in the neighborhood, but, like themselves, most of these people didn't want to be bothered. They seemed wary of being found and forced to leave, and neither Kit nor Teddy felt the need to make connections with them. It was enough to realize that they weren't completely alone in the city and leave it at that. For Kit it was also a relief to know that should something happen to one of them, the other would have at least a few people to ask for help.

During these walks or afterward, during dinner, they began to open up. Their first deep conversation covered the usual subject with a new lover—old lovers. Teddy's past was checkered primarily with short-term girlfriends, though some had lasted a few weeks or months. Kit's recent past was similar, but she finally decided to share something that had happened long ago.

"I mean, I think I knew I was gay in high school," Kit explained. "I didn't come out or anything, but I also didn't date guys—I wasn't interested in them. I think my friends, if they thought about it, just considered me a prude. I don't believe I even knew what I wanted on a conscious level yet, but I was sure I didn't want men."

Teddy smiled and nodded, clearly understanding what she meant.

"Anyway, when I met Bridgette, my first semester in college, it was all over for me. For both of us, I think. It was like a mystery was finally solved—I finally had the answer: I'm gay. We managed to get our room assignments changed at the end of the semester and basically spent the next year and a half joined at the hip."

"What happened?"

Kit couldn't help a bitter laugh. "Her parents finally figured it out. They'd been in serious denial the whole time. I think they'd genuinely convinced themselves that we were just close friends. Finally, when I was visiting her at their place in the summer after our sophomore year, they walked in on us in bed together."

Teddy grimaced.

"Exactly," Kit said, shaking her head. "They were hysterical. Her dad physically forced me out of the house and threatened to call the police. He was screaming at me, and her mom was screaming at me. The neighbors came out of their houses to watch, like it was an episode of *Cops*. Her dad had a baseball bat the whole time and actually took a swing at me before I drove away."

Kit was quiet for a while, the memory suddenly fresh and painful. She shook her head again and met Teddy's eyes. "I never saw or heard from Bridgette again. Her parents made her withdraw from college, and she never tried to call or write or anything. I was devastated."

They were quiet for a long time, and Kit sensed that Teddy wanted to share something with her, but she didn't pry. She'd started to suspect that some of Teddy's reserve was a defense mechanism, a way to avoid being hurt. And there was hurt there, Kit could sense it, but she knew better than to force it out.

The next night they were eating the last of Teddy's homemade pasta. Kit had heard that homemade was better, but she'd never had it before. Now she knew what all the fuss was about—there is no comparison between fresh and rehydrated. Teddy was disappointed to have to make the *Amatriciana* with bacon instead of pork cheek, but to Kit the food was heavenly. Eating like this every day was making her clothes start to feel a little tight, but it was worth it. She had a huge bite of pasta in her mouth when Teddy finally decided to open up.

"My parents are like your ex-girlfriend's parents," she said.

She spoke so quietly Kit had to think about her words carefully to make sense of them. She swallowed the food in her mouth a little too quickly, wanting to respond as fast as she could. Teddy was staring out the window, not making eye contact, and, instead of saying something, Kit took her hand in both of hers and squeezed. After an incredibly long pause, when Kit had convinced herself that Teddy had said all she was going to, Teddy finally met her eyes. Hers were red and brimming with tears, and Kit felt her own tear up in response.

"It happened when I was in high school," Teddy said, her voice still quiet and subdued. "It started before that, though. I knew when I was a very little girl that I wasn't like other girls. I didn't have a word for it, but I knew. I mean, even beyond being a tomboy or whatever, I was never like other kids, especially other girls. I got in trouble a couple of times when I was little, stealing jewelry and stuff from my mom for one of my crushes, but no one took it seriously then. Even my parents thought it was just a thing some young kids went through."

She broke eye contact again, and Kit could see the depth of her pain for a moment before her face became hard and tight again. Teddy seemed to force herself to go on, and Kit could tell that it was very difficult for her to talk about this.

"My family and I were always very close. I have one sister and one brother, and my parents never showed favoritism. We enjoyed spending time together as a family, and my parents were very supportive. In fact, my dad encouraged my early love of sports, even though it was kind of weird for girls to be into them at the time. We're Creole, Spanish mostly, and our family and neighbors were always pretty traditional and religious, especially back then."

She paused, and once again, Kit could tell she was willing herself to keep talking. She seemed determined to continue, so Kit didn't try to stop her, despite how badly Kit wanted to stop her and kiss away her pain.

"Things fell apart in high school," Teddy said, looking down at their clasped hands. "My crushes were starting to make my parents a little jumpy, a little wary around me, but I didn't realize that's what it was. All I could see and all I could feel was that they started to treat me a little differently, a little coldly. My dad stopped going to practice with me at the track and stopped talking about sports with me. I started to catch my mom watching me with this disgusted look on her face, but when I asked her about it, she told me I was seeing things.

"Then, on my sixteenth birthday, everything came to a head. I was seeing this girl, but we'd been pretty discreet. It was the eighties, and the whole gay thing hadn't become okay yet. No one talked about it then—at least no one I knew did. My girlfriend came over for my birthday party, and we sat apart and didn't do anything in front of my parents, but they knew anyway. When she left, they confronted me about her, and I told them the truth. I didn't know they would flip out like they did."

She was quiet again, and, unable to stop herself, Kit finally asked, "What happened?"

Teddy was crying now, but she didn't seem to be aware of the tears dripping down her face onto their clasped hands.

"My dad beat the hell out of me and my mom let him. He ended up breaking my arm. I had to take myself to the hospital, and I told the police I'd wrecked my bike. I don't think they believed me, but they couldn't do anything. The doctor wouldn't let me leave until my parents signed me out, and when they did, I just didn't go home. We didn't say anything when we all left the hospital—we just walked away from each other. I got a job in a restaurant and dropped out of school. I lived with a girlfriend and then some friends for a while until I could get a room of my own. I sued for emancipation and won. We've barely spoken to each other in the last twenty years."

Kit drew Teddy into her arms and they sat there together for a long time, clutching each other. Teddy was sobbing now, and Kit rubbed her back, speaking quiet nothings into her ear until she calmed down a little. Teddy seemed a bit shamefaced when she pulled away, and Kit felt a stab of sorrow at the bleakness in her eyes. She kissed the tears off Teddy's face and then wiped them away. Teddy looked wrung out, worn down. She'd clearly held this story inside for a long time. Kit didn't have to ask—she knew Teddy had never told anyone before. At this realization, a sharp pride pierced her sorrow. Teddy clearly trusted her.

Kit stood up and then gently pulled Teddy to her feet. She picked up the lamp and led Teddy out of the kitchen. Teddy followed her into the bedroom like someone half-alive, and Kit helped her take off her clothes and get into bed. She took her own clothes off and stood completely naked at the foot of the bed, Teddy staring at her for a long, quiet moment until some of the hopelessness drained from her eyes.

Finally, Kit climbed into the bed with her, set on comforting her any way she could. For the first time, they made love. The entire experience was different—strange, tender, and quiet. Both of them, without speaking about it, felt the shift from the way they had been to the way their lovemaking was now. They had something closer, something more intense than they'd had before. It was heavy but simultaneously lifted them up. They clasped each other for comfort and support and found it there in each other's arms and bodies.

Much later, the moonlight was so bright it could almost be daytime. Teddy had finally succumbed to fatigue, and they were spooned together, Teddy wrapped around her as she slept. Kit stared out into the dark room, tears falling from her eyes.

CHAPTER EIGHTEEN

On the Saturday after the storm, they woke up together as if by an alarm. Kit met Teddy's eyes, and they grinned at each other.

"I like waking up in your arms," Teddy said. Her voice was matter-of-fact, but her eyes were warm and tender.

Kit felt a wave of poignant joy and relief. She'd been thinking the same thing but had been afraid to say it. Suddenly scared she might cry if she responded, she kissed Teddy and they stayed in bed, not saying or doing anything for a long time. Kit had her head on Teddy's shoulder, one hand absently playing with a curl of Teddy's hair. If it were possible, she thought she would stay here in bed with her forever. This feeling, a kind of happy heartache, was crucial, vital somehow. It had been building for days, and now Kit couldn't imagine living without it. She'd never been more settled or at peace.

She heard the dogs' collars rattle and their nails click on the wood floor in the front room as all three got out of bed at the same time. This had happened before, and now she and Teddy recognized it as a signal that someone was outside. Teddy held a finger to her lips. The two of them pulled on bathrobes and went into the front room to look. Through the gap between the boards they could see two people across the street knocking on the front door of a house. They were dressed in fishing waders and hardhats, and both wore tool belts, heavy gloves, and facemasks. They shouted questions through the door, and then, after trying the door, one of them pried a board off the front window. Using flashlights, they peered into the house, again shouting questions. They were a little too far away to be heard clearly, but they were obviously searching for people. One of them went to the front door of the house, knelt down, fiddled around for a moment, and then the door was open. Kit heard Teddy gasp as they disappeared inside.

"What's happening?" Kit asked.

Teddy shook her head. "Looks like some kind of search-and-rescue operation."

A couple of minutes later, the two people reappeared and closed the door behind them. One of them took out a can of spray paint and made a large X on the wall by door, while the second one nailed the board back over the window. They painted a code in each section of the X, and, when the board on the window was back in place, they moved on to the next house and repeated the operation—knocking, peering inside, and then entering and searching.

"What should we do?" Kit asked after a while. "Should we go out and meet them?"

Teddy bit her lip, clearly conflicted. They would eventually have to meet the searchers, but Teddy didn't want anyone, particularly anyone official, to know they were here. Her fear, as she'd explained it, was that they would be forced to evacuate, and, as the two of them had been holding up fine here in the house, it didn't seem advantageous to leave yet. Nevertheless, both of them were desperate for news.

Nodding as if deciding something, Teddy said, "Yes. Once they finish that side of the street, let's go out and say hello. They don't look armed, so they shouldn't be able to force us to leave right away. It looks like no matter what we do we're going to meet them, so it would be better for us to make the first move."

Kit agreed, and they went into the bedroom to get dressed. They waited until they saw the searchers finish the last house on the other side of their block. Finally, it was time. Teddy squeezed her hand before they went outside onto the front porch. The searchers were far enough down the block that they didn't see them right away, so Teddy called out to them. Both jumped as if startled and then rushed over to Teddy and Kit.

"What in the hell are you two doing here?" the first man asked. He was older and larger than the second one. "Don't you know there's a mandatory evacuation?"

"We didn't have a way to get out of town," Teddy said, instantly defensive.

"Well, you need to leave. Immediately," the man said.

"And just how do you expect us to do that?" Teddy asked, and Kit could hear a note of anger in her voice now. "We still don't have a way to get out of town."

"They're finally starting to bring buses into downtown. Get on one of those and get the hell out of here."

"I have pets," Teddy said. "I'm not leaving them."

"Lady," the man said, his voice rising, "it's dangerous here. Your life is more important than your pets."

The younger man reached out and touched his arm. "Hey, Phil, calm down. Why don't you let me talk to them for a minute? You can get started on this side of the street. I'll join you in a minute."

Phil looked at him and then back at Kit and Teddy, his face a little calmer. "That's fine with me, Bud, but you need to get these ladies to understand that they have to leave."

"I'll do that, Phil," Bud said.

Phil turned away and stalked off down the block. A few moments later, they could hear him knocking and yelling at the house on the corner of Teddy's street.

"Sorry about that," Bud said to them. "He's kind of a hothead."

"It's fine." Teddy's voice was calmer. "I just don't understand what he expects me to do. Just leave my dogs?"

Bud shrugged. "In his mind, that's perfectly logical." He looked at Teddy and Kit for a while, obviously conflicted. "We can't do anything to make you leave, but we have to mark down that you're here. Don't you have another way out of town? Pretty soon the army will be through here—Monday or Tuesday, I think. If you're not gone when they show up, they'll force you out."

Kit and Teddy shared a look.

"We might be able to find a way," Teddy finally said. "A friend said I could use her car if I can break inside and get the keys. She has a flat tire, but there's a spare in the trunk."

Bud took off his hardhat and scratched his head. "So you didn't want to break in?"

"Basically. I'd hate to break a window. I was going to do it anyway, eventually, if I had to, but I wanted to wait until I had to."

"Well, like I said, you'll have to soon," Bud said. "The army will be here any day." He paused. "We could probably get you inside her house if it's not too far from here. We're almost done with our section for the day. We could take one of you over after we're done. You're lucky we're not one of the other search-and-rescue teams. Most of them are using crowbars to get inside, but we're unlocking the doors when we can. So where is this car?"

"Her house is about a mile away," Teddy said.

"We could do that," he said. "Phil won't be too happy about it, but he's not happy with a lot of things lately. We've both seen some fucked-up shit the last couple of days, and the bureaucrats are really screwing the pooch. He'll probably agree to it, though, if it means that you're leaving."

Teddy reluctantly agreed. "If we have the car, we'll go."

Bud nodded. "Okay. Let me go ask him. In the meantime, you two should start thinking about packing up." Bud tipped his hat to them and then walked away down the block, where he and Phil entered the house they'd just unlocked.

Teddy turned to Kit. "Okay, you heard the man. Let's get ready."

Kit's stomach dropped. All week she'd been in a kind of holding pattern. Now that it was finally time for her to take off, her earlier reluctance to go home had turned into an aching kind of dread.

"Are we leaving right away?" Kit asked.

"I don't know, but we should have the car packed up and ready. Once I get it back here, we can put a little bit of stuff in there— enough for a day or two—and then we can wait a while longer unless the army shows up before then." She paused. "Anyway—don't you want to go home?"

Kit frowned. Being back at home would mean rejoining her old life. While she had looked forward to her classes this semester, teaching was about the only thing she was interested in at home.

Everything else—her coworkers, her friends, her research, all of it—seemed unimportant now. She knew she should get back as soon as possible, but the idea made her feel lost, unmoored. Her time here with Teddy had brought her out of what now seemed like a deep sleep. Every morning that she woke up and saw Teddy, it was like her life had started again, that she had something to look forward to. If she left, what would she go home to?

Teddy was waiting for her response, her focus, as usual, searching, interested, as if Kit were the only thing that mattered in the world. If she left, Teddy would never look at her like this again. But Teddy was waiting for her to say something.

"I guess," Kit finally said.

Teddy raised an eyebrow. "You don't sound very excited about leaving. It must be pretty bad back there if sitting in a house in New Orleans in the middle of the summer without air conditioning is better."

"It's not that. It's just that…" Not knowing how to say it without revealing too much, she couldn't speak. Her life back home, while intellectually satisfying, was personally empty and barren. She hadn't felt alive, she realized, in several years. This last week was the first time she'd been genuinely interested in what was going on around her or, more specifically, who was around her, for years. Teddy made her feel this way. Teddy had brought her back to life. She didn't want to go back to her half-life and live without her again.

"I'll miss you," Kit said simply.

Teddy looked startled, and Kit blushed. It had been the wrong thing to say. While what she'd said was true, out loud it sounded more serious than she was willing to admit right now. After all, she wasn't sure if Teddy was thinking the same things about her, and she didn't want to find out yet—she wasn't ready to be disappointed.

Trying to lighten her tone, she forced a laugh. "Don't worry. I'm not asking you to marry me or anything. I like being around you. I know it would never work out…"

"No. It wouldn't," Teddy agreed, nodding firmly.

Something about her tone made Kit's stomach drop, and she turned away to hide her hurt expression. Teddy sounded so sure, and Kit's momentary sentimentality now seemed juvenile and misplaced.

"You're right," Kit said, still facing away. "I should go home."

"You should."

To Kit, it was as if she'd been punched in the stomach. They'd been so happy the last few days, especially this morning. Why was Teddy acting this way?

She needed to escape from this conversation, and, schooling herself to mimic Teddy's coolness, Kit said, "Let's get inside. We can pack a little while we wait."

They climbed up the porch and went into the living room, both of them blinking in the darkened light of the boarded-up front room. Kit didn't want to ask her next question, but she knew she had to. She swallowed a sob and forced herself to go on. "Where will we go when we leave?"

"My sister lives in Atlanta," Teddy said. "We'll have to stop somewhere before that to get a new tire—the doughnut won't make it that far. Either in Atlanta or any other city we pass, you'll have no problem getting on a plane. I don't know how much of your stuff we'll be able to fit with the dogs, but I can mail you the rest when they let me back in the city."

"Okay," Kit said, but so quietly, she wasn't sure Teddy heard her. She wanted to match Teddy's breezy attitude but failed to do so. Instead, the reality of separation, now that it was so close, put a painful knot in her throat. It wasn't, she realized, simply that she didn't want to go back home. That was only part of it. What she'd said earlier, without thinking about it, was the truth. She was going to miss Teddy. "Miss," however, wasn't quite strong enough. The thought of being separated from her made her feel ill. But what choice did she have? From the way she was acting now, Teddy didn't feel the same way as Kit, and Kit was angry for the stupidity that had allowed her to think otherwise—she'd been deluding herself all this time. Swallowing hard, Kit knew that the sooner she left, the better. Getting emotional with Teddy wouldn't help anything.

They spent the next hour planning and packing. Teddy pulled out an Atlas to look at the roads they would travel, and Kit went through her things trying to decide what was vital and what could stay behind. Having just spent several days in relative primitivism, most of her belongings now simply seemed like so much garbage. It took a great deal of concentration to decide what she would actually need immediately and what could stay behind. Her mind was a confused whirl of dread, which dampened her logic and actions. She moved slowly, as if underwater, her fingers numb and fumbling. In her first attempt to condense her belongings, she packed a single suitcase with only her underwear. Finally, after a lot of self-reproach, she made herself focus on what she was doing and managed to condense the necessities into one of her larger suitcases, repacking the others for easy shipping later.

Teddy crammed several outfits and some of her paperwork into a large, military-style duffel bag, hardly seeming to care what she was taking and what she was leaving behind. Her carelessness gave Kit a little ray of hope. Teddy looked more upset at leaving than she was letting on. She looked angry, discouraged. Almost as soon as she thought this, however, Kit decided she was projecting. If anything, Teddy was simply impatient for all of this to be over. Once Kit left, Teddy could have her bachelor pad to herself and her dogs. The needy woman who had darkened her doorway all week would be gone, and Teddy could start schmoozing lonely tourists again. That had, after all, been what she'd done with Kit. Why should Kit expect more from her now?

Bud and Phil returned to get Teddy after they'd finished checking the other houses on Teddy's block, and Teddy rode away in their truck with them. She returned about an hour later driving a small white Toyota, and Kit laughed when Teddy climbed out of it.

"How on earth are the dogs going to fit in there with us?" Kit asked.

"Very carefully." Teddy grinned and pointed at the backseat. "Jingo and Bingo will have to squish back there, and Dot will sit on the passenger's lap. Our stuff can go in the spot behind the seats."

Kit walked around to the back of the car and realized that the space behind the seats was far too small for her suitcase and Teddy's duffel bag. They were both going to have to go through their things again and whittle them down to the bare essentials.

Teddy joined her a moment later. "I can leave all my stuff here. That way, you can take more of yours."

"That's silly, Teddy. Who knows how long you'll be gone? You'll need at least some of your things. Let's go inside and sort through our bags again. I'm sure I can find some more things to leave behind."

They went back in, both of them staring at their bags for a long time.

"Maybe we should do it tomorrow," Teddy suggested.

Kit felt her heart lift and then forced the feelings back down, cursing herself. Why would I want to drag this out? she asked herself. The sooner I leave, the better. The longer I stay, the more it will hurt to say good-bye.

Steeling herself to be firm, she said, "Let's do it now. Then we can rest and get going early in the morning. With any luck, I could be on a plane tomorrow some time."

"You could. Okay. Let's get it done."

Kit wanted to hear sorrow in her voice, or, at the very least, reluctance, but instead Teddy sounded determined, clear-headed. Despite her earlier resolve to accept reality, Kit felt her spirits deflate even further. She had hoped that Teddy would say something, do something, maybe put up a fight. But Teddy wanted her to leave.

Kit went into the bathroom and cried for a long time.

CHAPTER NINETEEN

It was harder to fit the two larger dogs in the backseat than they'd anticipated. Kit knew it would be a very tight squeeze, but when Jingo climbed in, she realized it would be next to impossible—he took up almost the entire backseat on his own. Experimenting with several different scenarios, they finally managed to get Jingo, the biggest, and little Dot in the backseat, with Bingo sitting on the front passenger's lap. The situation was almost intolerably uncomfortable, but they had no other choice. As Teddy was the expert with the New Orleans area, she drove first, and Bingo's heavy, bony bottom was already painfully digging into Kit's lap after a few blocks. He was also clearly uncomfortable with the situation, as he continually yawned. She patted his side, hoping to calm him a little, but that didn't help. They were all stuck where they were for now.

Teddy made several attempts to find a way out of the city. Initially, she'd planned to head east and north toward Slidell, but the Interstate onramps near the Marigny were flooded. After attempting to reach several of them, they finally turned back toward the Quarter, hoping to find someone who knew where they could get on the highway.

"There has to be at least one entry open somewhere," Teddy said, clearly stunned by the flooding they had so far come across. It had been days since the hurricane, and nothing had changed. While they'd seen flooding and had heard on the radio that much of the city was under water, it was one thing to hear about it, and another thing entirely to see the extent of it in person.

Once through the Quarter, they saw a group of government vehicles parked along Canal, and Teddy pulled over across the street. She sat there for a moment, obviously reluctant to approach them. She glanced over, and Kit saw that she actually looked frightened.

"Do you want me to talk to them?" Kit asked.

Teddy shook her head. "You wouldn't know where to go if they told you. It would be better for me to ask."

"What's the problem?" Kit asked.

"I'm worried we'll get in trouble."

"Why?"

"Because we're not supposed to be here. There was a mandatory evacuation." Teddy shook her head. "I'm probably being irrational."

Kit squeezed Teddy's shoulder. "It'll be okay. Someone should know."

Unfortunately, as they found out, no one did—at least among the group of people Teddy talked to. Kit watched them yelling at her, Teddy clearly trying to keep her cool, and then Teddy held up her hands as if in surrender. Kit's heart dropped at the sight, as she could see that one of the officials was holding a gun across his chest. Teddy backed away slowly, hands still up, and Kit caught a fragment of what the man with the gun was shouting at her—something to do with trespassing. Eventually Teddy turned and fled, speed walking back to the car. She climbed in and slammed the door.

"Jesus," she said, her face white.

"What the hell was that?" Kit asked.

"They thought I was trying to harass them, I think. They're acting like they're in a war zone."

"So they didn't know anything?"

Teddy shook her head. "One guy managed to suggest that the police might know. So now we just need to find a policeman."

Her hands were shaking as she started the car, and they drove around the Quarter for a while looking for a cop. They were surprised to see a large number of people still around, some of them tourists, some of them locals. Most were standing around in small groups just inside the doors to bars and restaurants that were black behind them.

"Fuck this," Teddy said after they'd driven around fruitlessly for ten minutes without seeing a cop. She pulled over next to a large group of people in front of a bar.

"Hey, guys!" she called to them. They all greeted her happily. "What are you still doing here?"

Several of them shared a look, and then a large, bearded man came forward, approached Teddy's window, and leaned down.

"Shit! You guys got a whole damn zoo in there," he said, laughing. He glanced back at the crowd. "We're still here 'cause them government boys are too busy to make us leave. We got some beers, and we got some food, so we're staying 'til they force us."

"Have you heard anything about the Interstate?" Teddy asked. "I'm trying to get out of town and can't find a ramp that's not in the water."

"Where y'all headed?" he asked.

"Atlanta," Teddy said.

The man raised his eyebrows and shook his head. "You're gonna have some trouble there."

"Why's that?"

"The road to Slidell is all washed out," he said. "You can only go west from the city. The Causeway is closed, too, I think."

Teddy's face fell at the news. "Damn," she said. "That's going to put us in the wrong direction."

He nodded. "You might be able to get north on the 55. I don't know. If you can, you could get up to the 20 there, or you might need to go all the way over to Baton Rouge to pick it up. I only heard about nearby."

Teddy shook her head. "Well, thanks for the advice. Now I just have to get on the Interstate. I guess I can get on over on Canal, since that goes west."

"You can at that," he said, standing up. "Good luck, gals."

"I wish people would stop saying that," Kit said as they drove away. "All we seem to have is bad luck."

"Couldn't get much worse, could it?" Teddy asked.

Kit shrugged, sick to her stomach with sorrow and dread. The heat from the open windows and the dog on her lap weren't helping, but the main thing bringing her mood down was Teddy's urgency. She seemed to be doing everything she could to be rid of Kit as soon as she could. It bothered Kit that Teddy felt this way. As recently as yesterday morning, they'd been what anyone would call loving. Now Teddy was cold and indifferent, and had avoided contact with her all morning.

The difference, as far as Kit could tell, was simply the outside world. Together, alone, they'd become close—far closer than Kit believed was possible in such a short time. Then the world had come into their miniature sanctuary in the form of those search-and-rescue men, and everything fell apart. While it was true that reality meant that they would have to separate, Kit didn't understand why Teddy needed to act like this. Had it all been a delusion? Were Kit's feelings for Teddy one-sided? Kit didn't think so, but she couldn't be sure, either. Anyone seeing her with Teddy now would think they were basically strangers.

Teddy managed to get on the Interstate, and they headed west. The drive was one of the most surreal parts of the whole experience as, aside from a few buses and government vehicles, they had the road entirely to themselves. As the man in the Quarter had predicted, the Causeway was closed to traffic, and they were forced to continue farther west in their search for a way north. Finally, they managed to turn north on 55 and, rather than turning east right away, continued toward Jackson, Mississippi. They were occasionally waved over by police and army officials, all of whom allowed them to continue when they told them their stories. They didn't see any real traffic until they started to get close to the Jackson metropolitan area.

"Should I drop you off at the airport here?" Teddy asked as they drew near to the city.

Kit felt herself go pale. For some reason, she'd envisioned flying out of Atlanta, which would have meant another day or at least the rest of today with Teddy. There was no logic to it, however, she realized, as she could just as easily catch a flight here as anywhere.

Why should she wait until Atlanta? If she told Teddy she wanted to keep going, she would have to say why. What could she say? If she told her how horrible the idea made her feel, she would need to explain. What good could come of it? From the way Teddy had been acting, she was looking forward to getting rid of her. Kit finally forced herself to say they should check out the airport in Jackson, the words leaving a bitter tang in her mouth.

However, as they drew closer to the city, they realized the extent of the damage here. While the storm had clearly abated as it came inland, piles of branches and leaves littered the sides of the Interstate even this far north. As Kit directed Teddy toward the airport using the Atlas, they realized that it wouldn't be easy to get over there. Traffic lights were still out in parts of their path, and traffic was backed up everywhere. After an hour of fruitless attempts to reach the terminals, Teddy finally stopped trying.

"Let's just get the tire fixed and keep going. I can see planes coming and going, but you'd probably be stuck here for a while since it's so close to New Orleans. I imagine a lot of people had the same idea."

Kit relaxed with relief and nodded.

"While we get a new tire, you can call people, if you need to," Teddy said.

Kit raised her eyebrows in surprise. Not once had she thought of this. "I guess you're right," she said quietly.

Teddy was looking at her, seeming confused. "Don't you think people are missing you?"

"Y-yes," Kit said, a little reluctantly. Except for people at work, no one she cared about even knew she was here. Seeing Teddy's puzzled expression, she shook her head. "Of course they are. I'm sorry—you're right. I have calls to make."

After asking at a gas station, they were directed to a tire shop on a lonely back road. The attendant suggested that they buy two new back tires, and as Teddy haggled with him, Kit excused herself to use the pay phone.

She called work and her chair answered.

"Hey, Bill, it's me, Kit."

"Jesus Christ, Kit! Thank God. We've all been worried sick about you!" he said. "Where the hell are you? You left that mysterious message, and the news…Christ. I'm so glad you're okay."

"I'm fine. I'm a little shaken up, but I'll be okay."

"Where are you? Can I help you get back?"

The entire time they'd been on the phone, Kit had been watching Teddy outside talking to the sales attendant. It was hard not to look at her if she was nearby. Kit's eyes were drawn to her as if magnetized. Teddy looked animated and excited in the way Kit liked, and she was clearly getting her way. The attendant had his hands up, as if accepting defeat, and Kit smiled at Teddy's look of pure triumph. Realizing she'd been asked something, Kit shook her head to clear it.

"I'm sorry, Bill, what did you say?"

"I asked you if I could help you get back."

"I think I'll be okay. A…friend is driving me to Atlanta. I should be home in the next couple of days."

"So you should be able to teach next week?" Bill asked. Then, as if thinking differently, he laughed. "I'm sorry. Of course you won't be able to teach. You'll need some time to recover."

"No, it's okay, Bill," Kit said. She paused, the sinking desperation in her stomach feeling heavier for a moment, but she made herself go on. "I'm looking forward to getting back to the real world. I'll be ready by next Tuesday."

"Okay," Bill said, "but if you change your mind, don't hesitate to call. We can have Marla cover your classes for as long as you need." He paused for a long time. "Are you really okay, Kit? The stuff I've been seeing on the news…"

"I'm fine. I'm sure I'm better than most." Kit was still watching Teddy as she talked. A memory of their last time in bed together flashed through her mind, and a wave of sorrow flooded through her. She turned away from Teddy to block the memory.

Needing to end the conversation, she said, "I'll see you soon, okay, Bill?"

"Let me know when you get back into to town," he said. "And when you're ready, I'd love to hear about your experiences."

Exasperated anger flashed through Kit, and she had to fight down a snappy reply. "I'll call you soon, Bill," she managed. "Bye." She hung up.

When Kit rejoined her, Teddy still looked self-satisfied and smug.

"That cheat was trying to get me to buy four new tires," she said, grinning. "I talked him into fixing the flat one. Sonofabitch must think I just fell off the turnip truck." Seeing Kit's expression, she became serious. "Hey? You okay? You get some bad news or something?"

Kit shook her head. "No. No bad news. Just talked to my boss."

"Is he angry?"

She shook her head again. "No—it's not that. It's—it's hard to explain," she said lamely. The idea of going back, of leaving Teddy, of rejoining her empty life, left her cold inside.

Teddy pulled her into a tight hug, and Kit's heart welled up again. By the time Teddy drew back, Kit was almost crying.

"What is it? What's the matter?" Teddy asked, holding her shoulders.

Again, she couldn't say why she was so devastated about going home—at least she couldn't without telling Teddy how she felt about leaving her. She might have told her yesterday, when Teddy still seemed to like her, but not today, not after her cold indifference all morning. There was no point. She would end up feeling desperate and stupid, and Teddy would, at best, feel sorry for her and at worst be disgusted with her pathetic neediness.

Kit shook her head. "It's nothing. I'm just hormonal or something." She wiped at her eyes quickly and changed the subject. "How long until the tire's ready?"

"Half hour, maybe. I was going to take the dogs for a walk. You want to come with us?"

Smiling through her tears, Kit nodded.

"Okay. You walk Dot, and I'll take the others. That's only fair since Bingo's been on your lap the last three hours."

"Four, Teddy. Four hours," Kit said, rubbing her sore legs.

"Fair enough—the last *four* hours."

"He'll be on your lap next, so I guess I shouldn't complain too much."

They walked down the block a little, the signs of the hurricane apparent even on this side street. Tree branches and debris were piled everywhere, and they could see wind damage on some of the houses they passed.

"How long will it take to get to Atlanta?" Kit finally asked. She hadn't wanted to ask, but she needed to start facing reality—it was coming for her whether she wanted it or not.

"Barring traffic, I think it's about six hours from here."

"So close?" Kit asked. She wasn't able to keep the disappointment from her voice, and Teddy looked over at her quickly.

"Yep. You might be on a plane as early as tonight or, at the latest, tomorrow morning."

Feeling tears in her eyes again and desperate to think about something else, Kit asked, "Are you going to call your sister?"

"Yes, when we get back to the car. I'll let her know I should be there this evening."

Kit heard Teddy's "I" with a stab of pain. For the last few days, they had been a "we," and now that was ending. She'd somehow fooled herself into believing that the "we" might go on, and now, here at the end of it, she didn't feel ready to let it go. If she went back to just being herself, what did that leave her with? It seemed like nothing.

As if realizing they had nothing left to say, they turned around and walked back toward the tire shop. Soon, Kit realized, they would be on the road again. Not long after, she would be on a plane home, and they would probably never see each other again. Kit felt sick. Her entire body was suffused with dread at the idea of getting on a plane today, flying away from the only thing that seemed to matter anymore. She had never wanted to go home less than she did right now. Glancing over at Teddy, however, she could see that she was completely unfazed by their impending separation. She looked neutral, indifferent.

If she doesn't care, why should I? Kit wondered. She needed to make herself stop caring. She tried to think of something good about being home. She'd always enjoyed teaching and writing, and maybe this would be the year she would finish her new book. All of this was cold comfort, however. Her body was still heavy and sick with bleak melancholy.

As they approached the tire shop and saw that the car was waiting for them, Kit had the first flutters of angry impatience, and she grasped at it. Anger was better than sorrow any day. If she forced herself to be angry, she could put this whole experience behind her without any regrets.

CHAPTER TWENTY

The trip to Atlanta was uneventful. Kit, having lived in the Bay Area for the last few years, was used to driving fast and aggressively, and they made good time. Somewhere in Alabama they started listening to NPR, only to tune it out for music a few minutes later. Neither one of them wanted to hear about the hurricane and the destruction and death it had left behind. Kit turned to an oldies station, and the two of them sang along, Kit badly off-key. Teddy made fun of her voice a few times, but that only made Kit sing louder, a tactic she'd always used with her brother when they were little. At one point, in the middle of "American Pie," Jingo started howling along with their singing, and Kit and Teddy dissolved into near-hysterical giggles.

"He's howling for you to stop," Teddy said, gasping for breath.

This only made Kit laugh harder, and once she'd caught her breath again, she sang even louder.

They stopped on the border of Georgia in the mid-afternoon to eat and switch drivers one last time, and Kit was surprised to see how close they were to Atlanta when they saw a mile indicator a few minutes later.

"Do you want to go straight to the airport?" Teddy asked. Her voice was tight and quiet, her face impassive.

Kit felt like she'd been slapped. Despite the morning's coolness from Teddy, the last couple of hours had been jovial, and they had seemed to reclaim some of their earlier closeness. Now Teddy was back to being closed off, emotionless. What had changed? Kit continued to stare at Teddy, but Teddy was staring straight ahead, her eyes glued to the road. At this, an idea occurred to Kit for the first time. Maybe she's acting this way to make it easier for me to leave, Kit thought. She might simply be covering her feelings with her haste and coolness. There was, however, no proof of this idea, and Kit decided to dismiss it once and for all. If Teddy couldn't be honest with her, she had no reason to be honest herself.

"If we could go right to the airport, that would be great," Kit said. "I don't know if I'll be able to get a flight tonight, but maybe I can book something for tomorrow more easily if we're there in person."

Teddy nodded, her face still impassive, eyes rooted to the road. "Okay. I can call my sister again while you do that and let her know I'll be there a little later."

Once at the airport, she, Teddy, and the dogs made a spectacle of themselves as they walked into the terminal. Both she and Teddy were wrinkled and filthy, and, as always, the dogs caused a scene. People looked at them strangely, children pointed, and, as they approached the line for a ticketing agent, a security guard approached them. While Teddy was talking to him, explaining their situation, Kit excused herself and joined the line, her small backpack of belongings digging into her shoulders.

The ticketing agent was aghast when he heard her story, and he worked quickly on his computer to get her a seat.

"The airline would like to extend its sympathy to you, Miss Kelly, for your hardships and for your experience in New Orleans, by offering you a free first-class ticket home."

Kit was stunned. She'd had many, many flights cancelled in the past and had missed several planes, and had never had anything like this happened to her before.

"Thank you," she said quietly.

"Unfortunately," he said, "the earliest flight I can get you on will be tomorrow morning."

"There isn't anything sooner? I don't mind flying economy or business or whatever," Kit said. "Or paying. I just want to get home,"

Kit said. Now that she was close to leaving, she simply wanted it over with. If she had to be around Teddy for much longer, she was pretty sure she would make a fool of herself and say something she'd regret.

The ticketing agent tsked. "Unfortunately, no, Miss Kelly, as that's the only available seat for the next twenty-four hours. There was a storm system in the Midwest this morning that cancelled several flights into Atlanta, which in turn has backed us up and cancelled flights here as well." He shook his head with seeming frustration. "This has been one of the worst weeks for flight cancelations in recent history."

"That's fine. Tomorrow is fine," Kit said, her hopes sinking.

The agent continued to work on his computer for a while before printing her ticket and handing it to her.

"The flight leaves at eleven tomorrow morning, Gate A-22."

"Thank you so much," Kit said, surprised to feel tears in her eyes. The man seemed genuinely sympathetic.

"Let us know if there is anything we can do for you," he said. "I might be able to arrange to comp you a room in a hotel for the night. It's not usual, but given the circumstances…"

Kit shook her head. "It's not necessary, thank you. I have…a friend to stay with," she finished lamely.

Taking the ticket, she turned to see Teddy talking to a group of security guards. The sight initially scared her, but she realized as she drew closer that they were all simply listening to her story. Some of the men were shaking their heads as if in disbelief. All of them looked interested and sympathetic.

"Anyway," Teddy was saying as she finished, "that's why we're here, and I didn't want to leave the dogs in the car."

"It's fine, ma'am," an older guard said, patting Teddy's arm. "We can make an exception this time. Right, boys?"

The other men agreed, and several of them shook Teddy's hand before walking away.

Teddy's face lit up when she saw Kit and walked over to meet her.

"Story time?" Kit asked, smiling.

Teddy laughed. "Exactly. At first they were going to force me to leave—I guess the dogs aren't allowed in here. Then I mentioned New Orleans, and they were all ears. Some of the others came and joined us like I was the damned Pied Piper."

They shared a fond look at the menagerie, all of whom seemed terribly excited to be here.

"So," Teddy said, indicating the ticketing area, "how'd it go?"

"First class, direct flight, tomorrow morning at eleven," Kit said, holding up the ticket triumphantly.

"That's great," Teddy said, but Kit thought she sounded somewhat pained.

"Did you call your sister again?" Kit asked.

Teddy shook her head and then looked away, her face clouded with emotion. She was quiet for a long time. "Listen," she finally said, glancing at Kit and then looking away again. "When I called her earlier today, I didn't tell her you would be with me."

Kit remembered the "I" from earlier, but she was still hurt. "Why not?"

Teddy shook her head, her face still dark. "It's complicated." Seeing Kit's expression, Teddy sighed. "My whole family is there right now. They evacuated there from New Orleans. My parents, my brother…anyway, it would be one thing if it was just me, and it would also be another thing if it was just my sister and her family— they're the only sane ones in the whole lot. But with my parents and my brother there…it'll be really awkward for you."

"Awkward for me or awkward for you?" Kit asked, her temper rising.

Teddy sighed again, still not making eye contact. "Both of us," she finally said. She looked up, meeting Kit's eyes, and her expression softened. "I know this sounds terrible, especially after all we've been through together, but do you think you could get a hotel? Things could get really ugly if we show up together."

Kit saw that Teddy's eyes were slightly wet with tears. The recognition, however, didn't help temper her anger. Instead, a welling rage was beginning to build up in the pit of her stomach.

"Fine," Kit said, turning away. "It's fine. Go ahead and go." She started walking away, back toward the ticket counter.

"Wait a minute!" Teddy called after her.

Kit ignored her and kept walking.

"Jesus Christ, Kit, that's not what I meant!" Teddy called after her. "Just stop and hear me out for a second!"

Kit whirled on her so quickly Teddy almost bumped into her.

"Just who the hell do you think you are?" Kit shouted. Several people were looking at them now, but Kit ignored them.

Teddy was genuinely surprised. "What do you mean?"

"Gee, let me think," Kit said. "We just spent one of the most significant weeks in history together. We've been lovers, we've been housemates. I saved your life. You saved mine. We enjoyed each other's company. We told each other a lot about ourselves." Kit was ticking things off on her fingers as she said all of this. "Doesn't any of that mean anything to you?"

"Wait a minute," Teddy said holding up her hands, "you're confusing the issue here."

"Fuck you and your 'wait a minute,' Teddy. I was actually starting to have feelings for you," she spat. "I managed to convince myself you had feelings for me, too. I was starting to entertain the idea of leaving my job—of moving. To be with you."

Teddy was clearly stunned.

"But you've obviously just been stringing me along," Kit said, her anger evaporating as quickly as it'd come. She had to pause a moment to blink away her tears. After swallowing hard, she said, "All along, you've been looking forward to the day you could get rid of me. And now it's here, and you can't wait any longer."

"Goddamn it, Kit, it's not like that at all," Teddy said soothingly. "Just listen to me for a minute, would you?"

"No," Kit said, holding up a hand and closing her eyes. "I'm done. I'm done with this, Teddy."

Kit took a long, deep breath and opened her eyes again, her tears now falling freely. She held out her hand. "It's been wonderful to meet you, Miss Rose. I can't imagine we'll meet again, but it was a pleasure while it lasted. Good night and good luck. I hope your business revives quickly."

Teddy was clearly aghast, but, as Kit continued to hold out her hand, Teddy's expression was replaced first with anger and then with cool indifference. Teddy switched the leashes into her left hand and took Kit's, shaking it firmly and quickly.

"Good luck to you, too," Teddy said coolly. "You need it more than I do, apparently."

"I don't know what you mean," Kit said, mimicking her coolness.

"I think you do," Teddy said.

They stood staring at each other a moment longer, and then Teddy finally nodded. "Well, good-bye."

"Good-bye."

Kit stood there, rooted to the spot, watching Teddy and the dogs walk away. If Teddy turned back to look at her, she would go to her, but Teddy didn't. She did pause at the doors to wait for them to open, and only Jingo looked back, once. Long after Teddy and the dogs disappeared, Kit continued to stand in the same spot, hoping that Teddy would come back. Now that her anger had disappeared, she was left only with a deep feeling of despair.

It couldn't have just been me, could it? she wondered. Didn't she feel anything for me? Now, Kit realized, she would never find out. Perhaps, however, it was for the best. Over the last week, while she'd certainly imagined giving up her job and moving down to New Orleans—perhaps teaching in the community college or learning to work in a kitchen, like Teddy—she knew herself better than that. She was too pragmatic to make such a rash decision.

The idea was, she realized, the kind of impulsive silliness she would expect from her brother—the kind of thing she was constantly chiding him for. Why would she leave her tenured position—one she had worked hard to get—for something so ridiculous? No, it had all been a pipe dream brought on by long exposure to a hot body. In a few weeks, she told herself, she would remember the sex with fondness and perhaps even long for the experience of being cut off from the rest of the world, the only day's responsibility to warm up some water for tea or coffee. Tomorrow this would all be over, and soon, she hoped, the whole experience would simply be a series of strange memories.

It's better this way, she told herself, and, as if to make herself believe it, she turned around, away from the door where Teddy had disappeared. She squared her shoulders and got back in line at the ticketing desk, hoping to get a hotel room.

Chapter Twenty-one

K it looked out the tiny window of her office down onto the grassy quad. One of the benefits she'd received immediately upon returning was this office, one of the only ones in the English department with a view. In fact, hers was actually slightly larger than her chair's. She hadn't asked to move, hadn't even hinted that she would like a bigger office. Instead, when she'd reported for work the Monday after she returned, her boss had simply told her about it. People around here waited their whole careers for nicer offices, usually without hope, and she'd simply been given one. She'd expected bitterness and anger from her colleagues, but she had received nothing but congratulations from everyone she talked to.

And this was only one benefit of having survived Katrina. Her chair, for example, had taken her off all committee work for the academic year—something entirely unheard for an associate professor. She'd also been assigned an extra TA—again, something that never happened. Like the office, this would normally have stirred up the bitter gossip mill in her department, but no one said anything. Yes, she caught people looking at her somewhat more often than usual as she walked around campus or attended meetings, but they seemed sympathetic, or sometimes frightened, as if they imagined themselves going through the same thing. In her mailbox, colleagues from her department and across campus had also dropped off gift certificates to various restaurants, spas, and hotels. Today, she'd received an e-mail from the dean of the college asking her to speak about her experiences next week at a special campus talk series about natural disasters and climate change.

Outside of work, things were also different. Her friends were treating her in a similar manner as her colleagues. Her landlady had found out about her experience somehow and continued to bring over food and home goods. Kit was pretty sure that, should she ask, she would be allowed to skip her rent for a month or two. She was like a minor celebrity. No one seemed to understand that she simply didn't want to think or talk about Katrina anymore.

She sighed. She understood, to a certain extent, why everyone was acting this way. She'd been there—she was part of history. Not knowing how to help the people of New Orleans, but wanting to help, everyone turned their attention to her, an easy target for their charity. Soon, she hoped, the next major event would catch their attention and they would forget.

She envied the students she saw out on the quad, lounging in the autumn sun, flirting and laughing. They looked young, carefree. Remembering her own problems at that age, she smiled. All of the things that had seemed important—vital even—had faded with time. Girlfriends, exams, fights with her roommates—all of that had gone away. However, everything was relative. The feelings were the same, no matter what the problem was, no matter how old you were. This was an idea she liked to keep in mind when students told her about their lives. What they understood to be important was not, in fact, trivial, no matter what it looked like from the late side of her thirties. She liked to feel that they could tell her anything: she liked being approachable that way.

She sighed again and turned away, sitting down at her desk. She'd been back at work for over a month now, and she still hadn't gotten herself organized. Her desk contained a mountain of ungraded essays and exams. Though she was being given extra leeway and extra perks because of her "ordeal," as her chair called it, she would have to get back into the swing of things soon or risk having her students complain. Already, her lectures had been lackluster, her attitude distant and distracted. She'd be lucky if her student evaluations didn't suffer.

Picking up a nearby pile of exams, she had just grabbed her pen when someone knocked at her door. The interruption startled her badly. Her office hours didn't start for hours yet, and she and her colleagues had an unspoken rule that they weren't to disturb her while she was working.

"Yes?" she called.

Becky opened the door and stood there in the doorway. Her expression, normally open and friendly, was crestfallen, her face pale. She was clutching something knitted—a hat—twisting it in her hands, and, after one quick look into Kit's face, she couldn't meet her eyes. Her tall frame filled the doorway for a long while, as if she wasn't sure whether to come in or leave again. After an awkward pause, she finally stepped into Kit's office. Kit could hardly believe it. The sight of Becky, her supposed friend, the supposed human being who had abandoned her in the face of the hurricane, made her sick. For a moment she could vividly remember the desperate fear and horror back in the crowded hotel lobby, staring in disbelief as Becky told her there was no room in Mia's car.

"What are you doing here?" Kit asked, her voice flat with anger.

"Listen, I imagine you don't want to see me or talk to me yet, but I had to come," Becky said. "I've been trying to make myself call you for weeks now, but I couldn't. Last night I finally just booked a flight out here so I could see you in person."

"You're right," Kit said, looking down at her exams. "I don't want to see you. Please leave."

"Just give me a minute, Kit. Please."

Something in Becky's voice made Kit look up, and she was stunned to see tears in the other woman's eyes. Sighing, Kit nodded, indicating the chair across from her desk. Becky's face flushed, some of her strain apparently easing, and she sat down, putting a small bag and her hat on the floor under her chair.

"I want to apologize. What I did was inexcusable. At first, I let the blame rest solely on Mia, probably to make myself feel better, but even when we were caught in that god-awful traffic, I knew I was lying to myself. I should have insisted. I should have made her take you along."

Kit said nothing, keeping her face blank.

Becky swallowed visibly. Her face was greenish, her eyes wide and liquid. "The feeling grew worse the farther we drove away from town. When we were in Baton Rouge watching the hurricane blow in, and then all the chaos after…I felt sick. I couldn't believe we left you there. I saw pictures of my hotel, with all the windows blown out, and all the chaos at the Superdome and the Convention Center, all those bodies floating in the water…I couldn't stand thinking of you there. I couldn't believe that we'd done that to you. That *I* had done that to you just to save my own skin."

Kit continued to stay quiet, her anger now a burning pit in her stomach. She was afraid that if she said anything, she would be shouting it.

"The feeling never went away, Kit. I've been sick with disgust for weeks now. I can't sleep, I can barely eat." She shook her head and wiped at her eyes. "When I found out, through a colleague of yours, that you made it back, I felt better for a day or two, but the disgust came back. I knew I needed to see you—to tell you how sorry I am." Becky was quiet for a moment. "I think we all like to think of ourselves as heroes, Kit. We like to believe we would stand up for someone being bullied or risk our lives for others. But most of us are horrible people. This has taught me that I'm just like everyone else—a coward, a phony." Again, she was quiet for a long time. She finally cleared her throat. "Anyway, I'm sorry. I hope you'll find it in your heart to forgive me someday."

Kit, still silent, stared at Becky, who was clearly waiting for Kit to say something. After several long moments of nothing, Becky finally sighed and stood up. "I didn't expect anything else from you, Kit. Thank you for hearing me out."

As Becky turned toward the door, Kit's anger evaporated. While she'd been harboring a deep resentment for weeks now, she suddenly realized that, as no harm had come to her, she had nothing to be angry about. After all, Becky hadn't barred her from the car— Mia had.

Also, had she left then, she wouldn't have had that incredible week with Teddy.

She turned her mind away from that memory, chiding herself. She'd schooled herself not to think about Teddy anymore, though it seldom worked.

"Becky, wait."

Becky turned, her eyes hopeful.

"Come back here and sit down. Please."

Becky sat back down, crossing her hands primly on her lap.

"Listen. I don't blame you, okay? You didn't make the decision to leave me behind. If you had, I might not be able to forgive you."

"But I didn't—"

"Let me finish." Kit made a cutting gesture with her hand. "No—you didn't stand up for me. It was a dick move, no question about it. But I get it, Becky. When we were there, in the hotel before you left, you asked me if I would stay behind if our roles were reversed. Remember?"

Becky nodded.

"I've thought long and hard about that, and I would have left you there. I know it. I'm just as much a coward as you are. Everyone is an asshole, Becky. Even me." She grinned. "Although Mia is a bigger asshole than either of us."

Becky laughed. "No shit. Did you know she failed her three-year review? She finishes at Columbia at the end of the semester."

"Serves her right," Kit said, trying not to smile.

Becky beamed and then got to her feet, coming around the edge of the desk. Kit stood up and they hugged, long and hard, Becky smashing Kit's face into her breasts.

Kit finally pulled away, fighting back tears. "You did that on purpose, you perv."

"Of course I did."

They smiled at each other warmly, remembering a similar moment in the lobby of Kit's hotel in New Orleans.

"Thanks, Kit. You're a better person than I am."

Kit made a dismissive gesture. "It's nothing. Forget it and stop feeling guilty about it. It doesn't matter anymore."

"Can I at least take you to an apology lunch? I'm flying back tonight, but I have a couple of hours before I need to get to the airport."

Kit looked down at the pile of exams waiting for her and sighed. She should decline and get to work, but her heart wasn't in it.

"Just let me get my keys."

The air outside was chilly, and Kit immediately regretted leaving her jacket in the office. Reaching into her bag, she found a scarf and wrapped it around her shoulders.

"It's so much colder here than back home," Becky said. "I always forget how chilly this city is."

"'The coldest winter I ever spent was a summer in San Francisco,'" Kit said, quoting the old adage.

"Is that true?"

Kit shrugged. "It can be. Usually autumn is a little warmer, but this one is shaping up to be awful. Pretty, but awful. I hate being cold."

"Meanwhile the South is roasting. I can barely go outside, it's been so hot. Can't imagine what it's like for all those poor people back in New Orleans. Most of the city is still having problems with electricity. Imagine living there without it."

"They had that one-two punch with Katrina and Rita, and the water in the Gulf is still so warm it's possible there will be hurricanes into November." Kit shook her head.

"Meanwhile, the damn Republicans still don't believe in climate change."

"Idiots," they said together and then laughed.

They had walked off campus, and Kit led them toward a little café a couple of blocks away. It was fairly late for lunch, so when they arrived, they had the place almost entirely to themselves. After they ordered, they took their sandwiches and coffee to a small nook at the back, effectively shielding them from the rest of the room.

"We seem to always eat together in date spots," Becky said, moving her eyebrows up and down. "If I didn't know better, I would think you were trying to get me alone so you could have your way with me."

Kit turned to her food, remembering the last time she and Becky had eaten alone together. The memory caused a sharp pain. That was the beginning, she thought, remembering how Teddy had suddenly appeared at her elbow, looking at her with those dark eyes. Kit shook her head, trying to push the memory down. When she looked up again, Becky was staring at her, her expression puzzled.

"What?" Kit asked.

"You looked strange there for a moment, like you were in pain."

"It's nothing. Just a headache." Desperate to turn the conversation away, she stammered, "So how have you been? How's Duke?"

Becky launched into a long tirade about campus politics, privileged students, and dumb colleagues. Kit managed to nod along with her story, laughing at appropriate places, but her mind was elsewhere. Despite all of her efforts, she was, throughout, thinking about Teddy again. Some days, she would catch herself thinking about her for long minutes, remembering the sight of her strong, beautiful body, the sound of her low voice, the smell of her skin, the feel of her fingers clasped in hers, the taste of her lips. It seemed, no matter what she did, Kit couldn't forget her. Seeing Becky was bringing it all back, and Kit's mind was a whirl of images and sensations she'd fought desperately to suppress.

Becky had fallen silent, and Kit shook herself into the present. "I'm sorry," she said. "Spaced out there for a minute. You were telling me something about your dog?"

"That was ten minutes ago," Becky said, obviously amused. "Where did you go?"

"I'm sorry," Kit said again. She suddenly had a strong urge to cry and made herself get up quickly. "I have to pee," she explained, feeling suddenly desperate.

Becky, however, was too fast for her, and she stood up quickly, grabbing Kit's hand. "My God, Kit, what's the matter? Why does it look like you're about to burst into tears?"

In response, Kit did exactly that. Becky pulled her into an embrace, and Kit cried for a long time, sobbing into Becky's chest. Becky was rubbing her back and soothing her, all of which made Kit cry harder. It was a long time before she had calmed down enough to move away, her embarrassment finally getting the best of her.

"I'm sorry," she said again. "You must think I'm crazy."

"No, not crazy." Becky looked worried. "But you're obviously upset about something."

They sat back down, and Kit grabbed her napkin and dabbed at her eyes.

"Do you want to talk about it?" Becky asked.

Kit shook her head, voice caught in her throat.

"Does it have something to do with New Orleans?"

Kit hesitated and then nodded.

Becky's concerned-looking face cleared a moment later, understanding dawning in her eyes. "Ah," she finally said. "More like some*one* in New Orleans."

Kit didn't respond. If she said anything, she would start to cry again, and she didn't want to. She'd been crying too often as it was, and the last thing she needed was more tears.

"I'm going to take it from your silence that I'm right." Becky sighed when Kit didn't respond. "I don't know what this is about, Kit, even if I do know who it's about. What I do know, however, is that love isn't something you can forget. If it's been this long, and you still feel this way, it's love."

Kit closed her eyes. "I miss her so much, Becky. Sometimes I think my heart is going to stop beating."

"Have you talked to her since you left?"

"No. We didn't part on good terms. Anyway, she doesn't feel that way about me."

"How do you know?"

Kit shook her head. She was drained, weary. She wanted, very much, to lie down and sleep, right here in the café.

Becky leaned forward and grabbed her hands. "I don't know what went on between you two, but I do know that love very rarely exists in a vacuum. When we're young, and we fall in love, or think we fall in love, with someone that doesn't love us, we think that's love. But true love feeds on returned love. Unrequited love is something weaker, something pallid in comparison."

Kit didn't respond, and she couldn't meet Becky's eyes.

"If you love her, she loves you back. I promise you that, Kit."

Kit finally looked up, a feeling of hope surging in her stomach. "Do you think so?"

"I know it," Becky said, her face serious and stern.

Tears began leaking out of her eyes again, but she was only distantly aware that she was crying. Becky's words had struck a chord. It was as if she'd known it all along.

Hope, however, died almost as soon as it came. For weeks now, she had been waiting, hoping for a phone call. When she'd gotten back to San Francisco, she'd called the number Teddy had given her and reached her sister, but not Teddy. She'd left her home number with the woman and had been waiting ever since. She had heard nothing—no sign from Teddy at all. At first, she'd told herself it was understandable. In the chaos post-storm, Teddy would be busy. Weeks had passed, however, and Teddy hadn't even bothered to call and tell her she was okay.

It seemed Teddy didn't care for her—never had.

"I love you for trying to make me feel better, Becky." Kit wiped away the last of her tears. "I wish what you were saying were true, but I know better. I can tell when someone loves me, and this isn't that. I wish it were—I wish it more than anything in the world. But it just isn't true. She would have called—she would have done *something* to let me know by now." Kit sighed. "I just have to learn to let her go."

"But Kit—"

"It's okay, Becky. I actually feel a little better now. I just needed to tell someone about it. There hasn't been anyone who would understand." Her mind sank into memories again for a moment. She shook her head, hard, as if to clear it. "Anyway, thanks for coming. I actually feel a little better now. Maybe I can start putting it behind me now." She didn't believe a word of what she'd just said, but she also didn't want Becky's pity. It was bad enough to feel the way she did, but Becky made it clear to her just how terribly Teddy had betrayed her. Most of the time Kit felt both depressed and disgusted with herself. She should never have let her feelings get the best of her like this.

Kit stood up. "Anyway, I need to get back to my office, and you need to catch a plane."

Becky looked up at her, her face uncertain. "Are you sure? I can always get a later flight."

"I'm sure. She doesn't love me, and she never did. I need to move on."

Becky, still looking unconvinced, sighed and stood up. "Well, if what you say is true, she doesn't deserve you anyway."

Kit shook her head. "No, I guess not."

Twenty minutes later, they stood outside of Kit's building, looking at the students lying on the grassy quad for a moment.

"Can you remember what it was like to be that young?" Becky asked.

Kit shook her head. "Not really—I mean, sort of. I know it involved a lot of drama, a lot of anxiety, all the time."

"Yeah," Becky said. "I wouldn't want to go back to that."

"The dignity of middle age is so much better," Kit said, rolling her eyes.

Becky laughed, then gave her a quick hug. "Don't feel embarrassed, Kit, please. It sounds like it's her drama, not yours. I'm just sorry she did that to you. And I'm still sorry about Mia and the car, too."

"Don't be. It's fine. I'll be fine."

Becky looked at her, long and hard, then gave her one more bone-crunching hug. "I know you will be, Kit. You're stronger than anyone I know." She paused. "And you deserve to be loved. There's someone out there for you—I promise."

"Okay," Kit said, rolling her eyes. "Stop being such a sap and get out of here."

"Will I see you at MLA this Christmas?"

"Maybe. I was thinking of going home, for once, to see my dad."

"Well, hope I see you there anyway. You take care, Kit Kelly, and call me if you need someone to talk to."

"I will." Kit almost choked up. Seeing her tears, Becky gave her one last hug.

Kit watched her walk away, Becky's large figure and severe clothing catching the eye of nearly every person she passed. Kit smiled, a feeling of incredible warmth for the woman welling up inside her. She was relieved, actually. On top of everything, she'd been carrying her anger toward Becky for weeks now. She was glad to let that go, at least. It gave her hope that, with time, these other unwanted feelings would pass. As of now, her feelings for Teddy were like a sore tooth in her mind—something she couldn't forget yet something she kept touching throughout the day. Maybe Becky's visit would start to heal that pain.

Remembering her stack of papers to grade, she sighed and turned back toward the door to her building. Work would also help her forget. If she could just get her mind back into her work and research, everything else would gradually lose significance. She'd been doing that for years, after all, and it had worked marvels.

She opened the door and went upstairs.

CHAPTER TWENTY-TWO

It was definitely cold out now. When Kit had first stepped off the plane in Colorado yesterday, she'd been surprised to find it warmer than in San Francisco. But things had changed overnight, as they often did here on the Front Range. Autumn in Colorado, like the spring, was schizophrenic—warm one day, freezing and snowing the next. The sky that morning suggested snow showers might come, and Kit experienced a little thrill of excitement. It hadn't snowed in San Francisco the entire time she'd lived there, and it had been many years since she'd seen snow up close. This realization made her flush with shame—something she'd been doing a lot of since she reached her dad's place.

As she'd feared, his house needed a great deal of work. Over the last few weeks, she'd been trying to track down her brother, hoping she could get him to check in on their dad, but he'd taken the last payment she'd sent him and disappeared again. She wasn't, however, worried about him. He'd done this so many times that his disappearing acts had long worn worry thin. He fancied himself a poet and a photographer. He'd return next month, just in time for Christmas, broke and stoned and carrying a sheaf of bad poetry and several rolls of film. No, she wasn't worried about him. She was worried about her dad.

Things were worse at his place than she'd feared. Not only was her dad's house covered in a thick layer of dust and grime, from floor to ceiling, the plumbing, the roof, and the yard had problems. While trying not to show her worry when she'd first gotten in last night, she'd been taking a mental inventory of everything she would need to have done. Already, against her dad's protests, she'd arranged to have cleaners come the following day and do a top-down, and she would continue to have them come every other week after this. The rest of the house's problems would have to wait until she had some estimates and local recommendations.

When she went downstairs to the living room, her father was sitting in his armchair—his apparent permanent residence. She was fairly certain that after he got up most mornings, he simply installed himself in his chair for the day. He worried her more than the house did. Unshaven and unkempt, he had a distinct body odor that was unpleasantly sour. As she looked at him here from the stairs, he couldn't see her, and her heart sank with shame again. He was falling apart. She was going to have to hire someone to come in and take care of him. She moved and he finally looked up, his face breaking into a wide smile.

"There's my sleepyhead," he said. "You always were a deep sleeper."

"How long have you been up?" Kit pulled her robe closer, shivering a little. Either the heat was set too low or it, like the rest of the house, was malfunctioning.

He shrugged. "Long enough to watch that god-awful parade again. Everyone on that show is an idiot and talks to us like we're idiots, too. The only thing worth watching is the Rockettes."

Kit laughed. "Then why do you watch the rest of it?"

"Tradition," he said without hesitating. He tore his eyes away from the screen and rubbed his hands together. "So what are you cooking for us today?" They'd gone to the grocery store last night to pick up the ingredients for dinner as well as some general edibles— his kitchen was completely empty except for some ketchup and bad domestic beer.

"I thought I'd make some fresh bread and some pies. That's about all I have in my personal cookbook."

"Pies? Bread? What about turkey? What about cranberry sauce? Those are Thanksgiving foods. You sound positively un-American."

She could tell he was joking and rolled her eyes. "I'll make a savory turkey pie and a sweet pie with cranberries and cherries. Will that suit Your Majesty?"

He cackled and got to his feet, coming close for a hug. Again, she caught a strong whiff of his body odor and wondered how she could encourage him to bathe today. He was very frail in her arms. He'd lost a lot of weight since she'd visited last May. A wave of anger at her brother flashed through her, but she tried to dismiss it, knowing that most of her anger should be self-directed. She should never have trusted her brother to help.

As if reading her mind, her dad suddenly pulled a long face. "Jeez. I can smell myself! I'm sorry, honey. I'll go take a shower. It's been a couple of days."

Knowing it had likely been far longer than that, she said, "Sounds good."

"Do you want to go first?" he asked, indicating the bathroom.

"No, go ahead," she said. "I want to put some stuff in the oven."

Her father hugged her again and went into the bathroom, closing the door.

In the kitchen, she surveyed her ingredients, making a few notes to herself on a scrap of paper. She'd been experimenting more and more with breads and pies since her experience in Teddy's kitchen. While she no longer consciously allowed herself to think about New Orleans, or anything or anyone in it, she had continued to refine her baking skills. She liked doing it now that she wasn't scared of it. She'd been taking so many pies and loaves of bread to work, everyone had started complaining that she was fattening them up. They ate them, though, with obvious pleasure. She was surprised by how much she liked making things for people. She also found, when she was baking, that her mind cleared. Worries drifted away and everything became about what she was making—nothing else. She'd never understood why Sylvia Plath baked pies to combat writer's block, but she did now. The act of baking was soothing, meditative, mindless.

Today she was making a modified shepherd's pie, with roasted turkey instead of beef, a stuffing crust, and sour-cream potatoes for the top. Dessert would be a cranberry and cherry tart with a pecan crust. Buttery French rolls, her newest recipe, would accompany dinner. Now she just had to decide what to make first.

As she puttered around the kitchen, cleaning a little as she cooked, she smiled hearing her father singing in the shower. His singing was one of her earliest memories. Off-key with a poor sense of rhythm, he nevertheless sang his heart out both in and out of the shower. He favored show tunes, usually mixing up the words or creating his own. She frowned suddenly. She hadn't been here in half a year. She'd dropped by for a long weekend in May, and that had been the last time. No wonder he seemed so lonely, so isolated.

She'd put the turkey breast in the oven and the potatoes were boiling by the time he came out of his bedroom. The shower and shave had improved his appearance considerably. He had also chosen one of his cleaner button-up shirts, but Kit made a mental note to do his laundry for him before she left.

"Better?" he said, holding out his arms.

"Better. I'm going to take a shower now. Could you keep an eye on the potatoes for me?"

"Sure, honey. What do you need me to do?"

"Just make sure they don't boil over. If they do, turn the heat down a little bit, but not all the way."

"I can do that," he said.

"I'll be quick." She took off her apron.

The bathroom was dirty enough that she feared she'd come out just as filthy as she went in. The bathtub was covered in hair and grime, and she stood in it, gingerly, trying not to touch anything as she washed herself. The cleaners, she realized, couldn't get here fast enough. Even before her brother had taken off, just what the hell had he been doing to earn the money she was sending him? Apparently nothing. The house was a complete wreck.

When she came out of the bathroom, she sighed, seeing her father in front of the TV again. She shook her head and went back into the kitchen, not surprised to see the water on the potatoes overflowing.

After she started the next stage of cooking and baking, she had some time to relax so she decided to join her dad in the living room.

She opened the door, and the light from the kitchen penetrated the deep gloom of the living room for a moment. The light struck the side of her dad's face, casting long shadows underneath his hollowed cheekbones. She was going to have to get someone over here to feed him and soon. He looked ghoulishly thin.

"What are you watching?" Kit walked into the dark, sitting in what had been her mother's armchair.

"Some damn cooking show," he said, shaking his head in disgust. "The judges give everyone on the show something stupid to cook with, and they only have an hour to do it. It's about the most ridiculous thing you ever saw."

She laughed. "So why are you watching it?"

He sighed. "It's either this or football, and I hate both the teams playing right now."

They watched the commercials together for a while, waiting for the show to come back on. Kit let her mind drift, thinking about all the grading she should be doing right now. She'd brought a stack of papers with her, and now, this close to the end of the semester, she needed to get them back to her students to give them time for revisions. After Becky's visit, she'd managed to get her head back in her work a little more, but she was still struggling. The idea of winter break, now only two weeks away, made her lazy again. She was just about to stand up and get her workbag when the show came back on.

"Welcome back!" the host said. "The contestants have just been given their new basket of ingredients." The camera changed and panned across the four contestants, each of whom was opening a large picnic basket full of strange things. When it hit the fourth contestant in the kitchen, Kit's heart stopped.

It was Teddy.

The room, already dim, was suddenly a lot darker, and Kit's ears started ringing, loudly. Stars dancing in her vision, she felt a sickening lurch in her stomach and knew that any second she would faint. She must have made some kind of sound, as suddenly her dad was kneeling in front of her. She could see his mouth moving but couldn't hear what he was saying over the ringing in her ears. He put his hand on the back of her neck, and then he was pushing her head down and between her legs. He continued to hold it there until she could hear him again.

"Take some deep breaths, honey. In and out, nice and slow."

She obeyed, and the breathing, coupled with the position of her head, helped her mind clear again. Her dad removed his hand from the back of her neck and rubbed her back a couple of times.

"I think you can sit up now, Kit, but be careful. If you feel dizzy again, just put your head back down."

Kit sat up slowly, the room swinging for a moment before settling again. Her vision blurred with tears and she closed her eyes.

"That's good, sweetie," he said, his face grave. "Keep breathing in and out, nice and easy."

Again, she obeyed, and the breathing helped her calm her racing heart. She kept her eyes closed.

"Jesus Christ," her dad said, sitting down in his chair again. "I heard something, and when I looked over at you, you went as white as a ghost. I called out, and you didn't respond. What the hell happened? Do you faint a lot?"

"No," she said. "I don't think I've ever fainted before."

"What's the matter?"

She opened her eyes just as Teddy came back on the TV screen. Her stomach dropped again, and something in her face must have given her away. Her dad look over at the screen.

"Is it something on the TV?"

"Someone," she said quietly.

"That woman? There? On the TV?"

"Do you think you could turn it off, Dad?" she asked, her voice harsh and choked.

He clicked the television off, casting them both into near-total darkness. They sat there for a long time in silence.

Finally, feeling steadier, Kit got to her feet. "I'm sorry. I didn't mean to worry you."

"Who the hell is she, Kit?"

She shook her head wearily. "It doesn't matter anymore, Dad. Just someone I used to know."

Her father stood up and hugged her, hard. She caught a whiff of his aftershave, and a wave of sentiment washed through her. Struggling now, she blinked her tears away, desperately trying not to cry in front of him. He moved back, but seeing her face, he hugged her again. It was too much. Kit started crying, sobs wracking her body. Her dad held her throughout, rubbing her back and soothing her.

She finally managed to control herself and pulled away, wiping at her eyes with her sleeve.

"I'm sorry. I didn't mean to cause a scene. Thanks."

He raised his eyebrows. "It's fine, honey. Jeez! If I can't make my little girl feel better anymore, I wouldn't be good for anything."

He was looking at her strangely, as if waiting for her to say something. Knowing what he wanted, and half-tempted to tell him, she finally shook her head. "I don't want to talk about it," she finally said. "I wish I could, but I can't yet—maybe when I'm back at Christmas."

His face crinkled in concern, his heavy brows sinking. "Tell me one thing, at least." He indicated the TV with his chin. "That woman there. She broke your heart?"

Kit sighed, unable to say anything. Finally, she nodded.

"She ain't worth being upset about then, Kitten. Anyone who would break your heart isn't worth a damn."

Kit tried to agree and then felt tears coming again. She shook her head, clearing it. "I need to get back to dinner." Her dad looked uncertain, and Kit, realizing that he needed reassurance almost as much as she had, swallowed down her pain again. "I'm okay, really. I was just surprised."

He still looked uncertain, so Kit gave him a quick hug. "Why don't you watch something while I finish up in there? Dinner should be ready at one."

He seemed to hesitate but finally agreed. "Okay. Just let me know if you need anything."

Emotion welling up in her again, Kit turned to the kitchen to hide her anguish. She fled into it as if running for her life.

Chapter Twenty-three

K it felt significantly better about her dad by the time she walked off the plane back in San Francisco. Before she left, she'd seen the inside of the house cleaned from top to bottom by a great team of professionals, and she was certain they would continue to keep it clean and tidy during their biweekly visits. She'd talked to some of his neighbors and gotten recommendations for the plumber, roofer, and yard work, and made appointments for this week. Her dad, throughout, had been reluctant to let her arrange any of this, but when she finally explained that it would make *her* feel better to know he and the house were taken care of, he'd finally given in. Kit could tell he was, like her, relieved.

He could no longer take care of the house or himself very well, so having some helpers would be a great weight off both their minds. Kit had scheduled a couple of phone interviews later this week with some home-health-care workers, recommended by an old family friend, and the woman Kit hired would be taking care of groceries, making sure that her father had pre-prepared meals in the house, and checking that he bathed at least a couple of times a week. He didn't need more help than that yet. Kit had also sworn to herself to visit more often, and she'd managed to get the same family friend to promise to check in with him once a month. Overall, Kit knew she'd done her best and that she could stop worrying, for now. The trick would be to make sure her brother didn't mess things up again.

She'd flown out of Denver in a snowstorm, and as she stepped outside in San Francisco she realized that the weather here wasn't much better. The dark, dull sky above her was leaking sleet down on the line of taxis as she waited for hers. A stiff wind blew the sleet and dampness through her. Though it had been snowing back in Colorado, it felt much colder here because of the humidity. She pulled her wool coat closer, shuddering. Every spring in San Francisco, she forgot how cold the winter before it had been, and every winter she was surprised once again by how bitter it was here. Winter was technically three weeks away, yet she was colder than she'd been in a long time.

She climbed into the warm taxi with relief. The airport was far from her apartment, and with the weather the way it was right now, she'd be sitting in traffic for a long time. The driver, luckily, wasn't chatty, and she closed her eyes, worn out from her busy weekend. She smiled at the memory of the last time she'd slept in a taxi, and then her stomach dropped with the now-familiar dread of the memories that came after that ride. She'd made herself believe she was beginning to get over Teddy, but most of that was wishful thinking. After the dramatic fainting spell at her dad's place a few days ago, she'd wanted to believe that she'd simply been surprised to see Teddy, shocked, even. The dread was still there, as were the memories, but she hoped they had lost some of their power. All it took was a ride in a taxi to snap her back into reality. She was falling apart.

Some weeks after she'd returned to San Francisco from New Orleans, when she was floundering for purchase in her old life, she'd contemplated giving up. She'd never been suicidal, precisely, but she'd wanted to run away and give up trying, join a commune or something. All of that seemed silly now, but she still wasn't back to normal. Her job was beginning to interest her again, and she was contemplating a move to an apartment closer to the university. Everything would be fine, she told herself, if she could just keep going, making little plans and improving small things in her life. She had a new hobby she was good at, baking, and her research was finally starting to seem worthwhile again. Eventually, she would start dating again, and things would be back to normal—maybe even better than they had been before. She had, after all, survived a natural disaster. If nothing else, she was lucky to be alive.

She sat there, eyes closed, meditating on Teddy's face, trying to picture her clearly. She hadn't done this before, and it seemed very strange to allow herself to think about her. A therapist friend of hers had told her a couple of weeks ago that it would be better for her to think about Teddy than to try not to. She explained that if you actively tried to forget something, it often made it worse for a while and was not likely to help you forget anyway. Instead, she suggested that Kit think about the thing she wanted to forget for a couple of minutes a day. She also suggested visualizing Teddy walking away, waving good-bye, to help her forget. Kit tried this but was reminded of the moment in the airport when Teddy walked away, not turning around. She'd left Kit there—abandoned her, really. Kit felt a flare of anger and opened her eyes again. Maybe if she focused on her anger instead of the pain of her loss, she could start to get over her.

The cab finally stopped in front of her building, and Kit was astonished at the fare. Glancing at her watch, however, she realized she'd been in the cab for almost an hour. She paid the driver, reluctantly, and climbed out into the weather, which had switched from sleet to heavy rain. She hauled her backpack onto her shoulders and ran for the door, and, after spending several minutes in the rain looking for her keys, she was drenched. She finally stepped inside, dripping on the carpet for a moment or two, wiping her face. Her students' papers had likely been soaked as well, and she cursed under her breath. She situated the backpack more firmly on her shoulders and started climbing the stairs up to her apartment on the third floor.

As she passed the second-floor landing, a door opened, and Mrs. McKinley, her downstairs neighbor, opened the door.

"Oh, good, I thought that was you," she said, smiling. She and Kit had been in the two apartments on top of each other for years now. Mrs. McKinley kept Kit's spare key and took in her mail when she was gone.

"My goodness!" the older woman said, seeing her. "You're wet to the skin!"

"It's raining cats and dogs out there," Kit said, sighing. "I guess winter is finally here for real."

"I won't keep you, then. I'm sure you want to get out of those wet clothes. Did you have a nice trip? How's your father?"

Kit gave a quick summary of her trip, her impatience mounting. Mrs. McKinley was not someone you could have a quick chat with in the best of circumstances, and this was not the best of circumstances by a long shot. She had to suppress shudders of cold as she waited to be done.

"Say, listen—before I forget," the old woman said. She turned into her apartment and pulled something off a shelf by the door. "A friend of yours was just here, knocking for what seemed like hours. I finally opened my door and told her you were on vacation, so she left me this note for you." The woman held out a small, folded piece of paper.

Kit knew who it was from before she even took it. Holding out her own unsteady hand, she reached for the note and took it.

"Are you okay?" Mrs. McKinley came out into the hall and patted Kit's back. "You look like you've seen a ghost!"

"I'm fine," Kit said, stuttering. She still hadn't opened the note. She clutched it in her fist, and it was cutting into her palm.

"Mrs. McKinley?" Kit finally managed to ask.

"Yes?"

"How long ago did my friend drop this off?"

"Oh, let me think," she said, tapping a finger on her chin. "Maybe twenty minutes? It could have been longer. I was watching my stories, and I always lose track of time when something juicy happens."

Kit slipped her backpack off her shoulders and handed the dripping thing to her neighbor. "Could you keep this for me for a minute? I'll be right back."

Before Mrs. McKinley could say anything, Kit was racing down the stairs and out into the rain. She looked up and down her street for a moment, desperately trying to decide which way to go. To the left, she would have to climb up a very steep set of stairs set in the sidewalk. To the right, she would be heading down the hill.

Hoping that Teddy took the easy way, she ran down, reaching the corner as fast as she could. From there, however, her choices were more difficult. If she turned right, she would be heading toward a group of bars and restaurants. To the left was a large GLBTQ-centric bookstore, a soggy rainbow flag marking its entrance. Kit dashed over to the bookstore, tore through the aisles quickly, and then dashed back out into the pouring rain. She checked all of the bars, restaurants, and coffee shops on the block, then rushed down the hill and did the same on the next street. Growing increasingly desperate, Kit knew she was causing a scene every time she went inside a business to look, but she didn't care. She couldn't believe Teddy would just leave a note and disappear. She had to be somewhere nearby.

An hour later, however, tired and worn from sagging hopes and pouring rain, Kit was back at her apartment building again, her shoulders drooping with fatigue and disappointment. She opened the door slowly, the rain dripping off her, but the damp no longer registered on her radar. She walked slowly up the stairs, sloshing as she went, and decided to skip Mrs. McKinley's for now. She could get her backpack later.

Up on the third floor, she turned toward her apartment, eyes on her keys, searching for the one to her front door. When she finally looked up, she stared right into Teddy's eyes. She stopped, completely still.

"Hey there," Teddy said, her face grim.

Kit was struck dumb.

Teddy took a step closer and then stopped, her face uncertain. "I left you a note, but I thought I would come back and wait. Your neighbor—the lady downstairs?—she told me you were back from your trip, so I knew you'd be home soon."

Kit still couldn't say anything.

"Did you read my note?"

Kit managed to shake her head no. She looked down at her hands and realized that she was still clutching it in her left hand. She opened it, fingers numb.

I miss you. I love you. I'm sorry.

A local phone number and a room number were underneath this—apparently Teddy's hotel. Kit, hands shaking, read the note over and over, hardly believing what she was seeing. Finally, she managed to look up.

"I mean it," Teddy said, taking another step closer. Her face was still uncertain, confused. "I was a complete asshole to you and a complete coward. I fell in love with you the second I saw you. All you had to do was yell at me that morning in the hotel, and I was yours. I didn't want to admit it to myself, and I didn't want to say anything. I didn't think there was any point. I knew you would leave—come back here—and I would never see you again."

Kit still couldn't say anything, and her eyes were filling with tears.

Teddy took another step closer. "Then we had that week together. That awful, wonderful week together, and despite everything, I loved it. Despite the hurricane, despite the floods—none of it mattered, because you were with me." She shook her head as if disgusted with herself. "That day? When you were trying to leave the city? Before the hurricane? I went into my office at the restaurant and cried and cried. When you showed up again, and I realized you were going to be staying with me, I almost cried again. With relief. Can you believe that? How crazy that is?"

Kit managed to nod, tears now falling freely down her face.

Teddy was right in front of her now. Kit could feel her warmth, even separated from her by a few inches.

"Then, in the airport, when you told me how you felt about me, I choked. I panicked. Even before that, I was trying to push you away. I was trying not to get hurt." She laughed again, but bitterly. "Of course it didn't work. All I did was manage to ruin our last couple of days together."

She was quiet for a long time, looking into Kit's eyes. Kit's voice was still trapped in her throat. "I haven't been able to forget you, Kit," Teddy said. "I think about you every minute of every day. And now I know I don't want to forget you. I gave up hope. I decided I needed to move on. I thought I was doing it. I was busy— the restaurant needed a lot of work before it could open again. The city is in ruins. I've been helping friends with their homes and businesses all over town, working twenty-hour days. Eventually, I knew I was fooling myself. Nothing helped. Every minute of every day is haunted by you."

Kit sobbed and launched herself into Teddy's arms. They stood there, clenched together, and Kit's heart rose on a wave of triumph and relief. She was crying, Teddy was trying not to cry, and both of them were unwilling to let go. They stood, wrapped together, for several minutes.

Finally, her arms actually getting tired, Kit pulled back a little. "I suppose I should invite you inside, or something."

"I was hoping you would." Teddy moved her eyebrows up and down.

Kit shoved Teddy's shoulder, then wiped the tears off her face. "Is that all you can think about?"

Teddy pretended to ponder this question for a moment and then beamed. "When you're around, yes."

Kit grinned back at her and searched through her keys, her tears blurring her eyes too much to find the right one. Her hands were shaking badly now, and Teddy had to steady them long enough for her to locate her key and get it in the door.

Kit looked up at her, knowing that once she invited her in, things were going to change. Her life—the life she wanted—would, like the door, open in front of her.

"What are you waiting for?" Teddy asked, sounding puzzled.

Kit smiled back and unlocked the door.

EPILOGUE

On a corner along Frenchmen Street in New Orleans, you will often see a line of hungry people waiting with mounting impatience for an open table at one of New Orleans's most popular new restaurants. Since the hurricane, the reputation of this charming spot has only grown. One of the first businesses in the area to reopen after Katrina, it draws crowds made up not only of tourists and locals, but also of the great many construction workers now living and working in the area. The chef has made it a policy to give discounts and preferred seating to anyone working on the recovery of the city, which has helped make her restaurant a favorite with locals and visitors alike.

The menu has also expanded since before the storm. Customers have several new pies to choose from, including slices of a very popular savory Thanksgiving pie that's served year-round. A new baker has joined the restaurant, and her pies and bread are in incredible demand, enough so that the restaurant may expand into a neighboring building to accommodate more ovens for a new bakery.

If you wait long enough at night, after the crowds have finally stopped jostling at the door, and after the lights have finally dimmed in the dining room, you can catch the head chef and the baker leaving together, heading home together after a long day. Long-time customers say they can taste the difference in the food since the chef and baker started living together. The food, already good, is now some of the best in the city.

Whatever makes their food so incredible, you'll want to call well in advance if you want to get one of the limited reservations. They're booked up for weeks.

About the Author

Charlotte Greene grew up in the American West in a loving family that supported her earliest creative endeavors. She began writing as a teenager and has never stopped. She now holds a doctorate in English, and she teaches a wide variety of courses in literature and women's studies at a regional university in the South. When she's not teaching or writing her next novel, she enjoys playing video games, traveling, and brewing hard cider. Charlotte is a longtime lover and one-time resident of the City of New Orleans. While she no longer lives in NOLA, she visits as often as possible.

Books Available from Bold Strokes Books

Divided Nation, United Hearts by Yolanda Wallace. In a nation torn in two by a most uncivil war, can love conquer the divide? (978-1-62639-847-4)

Fury's Bridge by Brey Willows. What if your life depended on someone who didn't believe in your existence? (978-1-62639-841-2)

Lightning Strikes by Cass Sellars. When Parker Duncan and Sydney Hyatt's one-night stand turns to more, both women must fight demons past and present to cling to the relationship neither of them thought she wanted. (978-1-62639-956-3)

Love in Disaster by Charlotte Greene. A professor and a celebrity chef are drawn together by chance, but can their attraction survive a natural disaster? (978-1-62639-885-6)

Secret Hearts by Radclyffe. Can two women from different worlds find common ground while fighting their secret desires? (978-1-62639-932-7)

Sins of Our Fathers by A. Rose Mathieu. Solving gruesome murder cases is only one of Elizabeth Campbell's challenges; another is her growing attraction to the female detective who is hell-bent on keeping her client in prison. (978-1-62639-873-3)

The Sniper's Kiss by Justine Saracen. The power of a kiss: it can swell your heart with splendor, declare abject submission, and sometimes blow your brains out. (978-1-62639-839-9)

Troop 18 by Jessica L. Webb. Charged with uncovering the destructive secret that a troop of RCMP cadets has been hiding, Andy must put aside her worries about Kate and uncover the conspiracy before it's too late. (978-1-62639-934-1)

Worthy of Trust and Confidence by Kara A. McLeod. FBI Special Agent Ryan O'Connor is about to discover the hard way that when you can only handle one type of answer to a question, it really is better not to ask. (978-1-62639-889-4)

Amounting to Nothing by Karis Walsh. When mounted police officer Billie Mitchell steps in to save beautiful murder witness Merissa Karr, worlds collide on the rough city streets of Tacoma, Washington. (978-1-62639-728-6)

Becoming You by Michelle Grubb. Airlie Porter has a secret. A deep, dark, destructive secret that threatens to engulf her if she can't find the courage to face who she really is and who she really wants to be with. (978-1-62639-811-5)

Birthright by Missouri Vaun. When spies bring news that a swordswoman imprisoned in a neighboring kingdom bears the Royal mark, Princess Kathryn sets out to rescue Aiden, true heir to the Belstaff throne. (978-1-62639-485-8)

Crescent City Confidential by Aurora Rey. When romance and danger are in the air, writer Sam Torres learns the Big Easy is anything but. (978-1-62639-764-4)

Love Down Under by MJ Williamz. Wylie loves Amarina, but if Amarina isn't out, can their relationship last? (978-1-62639-726-2)

Privacy Glass by Missouri Vaun. Things heat up when Nash Wiley commandeers a limo and her best friend for a late drive out to the beach: Champagne on ice, seat belts optional, and privacy glass a must. (978-1-62639-705-7)

The Impasse by Franci McMahon. A horse packing excursion into the Montana Wilderness becomes an adventure of terrifying proportions for Miles and ten women on an outfitter led trip. (978-1-62639-781-1)

The Right Kind of Wrong by PJ Trebelhorn. Bartender Quinn Burke is happy with her life as a playgirl until she realizes she can't fight her feelings any longer for her best friend, bookstore owner Grace Everett. (978-1-62639-771-2)

Wishing on a Dream by Julie Cannon. Can two women change everything for the chance at love? (978-1-62639-762-0)

A Quiet Death by Cari Hunter. When the body of a young Pakistani girl is found out on the moors, the investigation leaves Detective Sanne Jensen facing an ordeal she may not survive. (978-1-62639-815-3)

Buried Heart by Laydin Michaels. When Drew Chambliss meets Cicely Jones, her buried past finds its way to the surface—will they survive its discovery or will their chance at love turn to dust? (978-1-62639-801-6)

Escape: Exodus Book Three by Gun Brooke. Aboard the Exodus ship *Pathfinder*, President Thea Tylio still holds Caya Lindemay, a clairvoyant changer, in protective custody, which has devastating consequences endangering their relationship and the entire Exodus mission. (978-1-62639-635-7)

Genuine Gold by Ann Aptaker. New York, 1952. Outlaw Cantor Gold is thrown back into her honky-tonk Coney Island past, where crime and passion simmer in a neon glare. (978-1-62639-730-9)

Into Thin Air by Jeannie Levig. When her girlfriend disappears, Hannah Lewis discovers her world isn't as orderly as she thought it was. (978-1-62639-722-4)

Night Voice by CF Frizzell. When talk show host Sable finally acknowledges her risqué radio relationship with a mysterious caller, she welcomes a *real* relationship with local tradeswoman Riley Burke. (978-1-62639-813-9)

Raging at the Stars by Lesley Davis. When the unbelievable theories start revealing themselves as truths, can you trust in the ones who have conspired against you from the start? (978-1-62639-720-0)

She Wolf by Sheri Lewis Wohl. When the hunter becomes the hunted, more than love might be lost. (978-1-62639-741-5)

Smothered and Covered by Missouri Vaun. The last person Nash Wiley expects to bump into over a two a.m. breakfast at Waffle House is her college crush, decked out in a curve-hugging law enforcement uniform. (978-1-62639-704-0)

The Butterfly Whisperer by Lisa Moreau. Reunited after ten years, can Jordan and Sophie heal the past and rediscover love or will differing desires keep them apart? (978-1-62639-791-0)

The Devil's Due by Ali Vali. Cain and Emma Casey are awaiting the birth of their third child, but as always in Cain's world, there are new and old enemies to face in post Katrina-ravaged New Orleans. (978-1-62639-591-6)

Widows of the Sun-Moon by Barbara Ann Wright. With immortality now out of their grasp, the gods of Calamity fight amongst themselves, egged on by the mad goddess they thought they'd left behind. (978-1-62639-777-4)

18 Months by Samantha Boyette. Alissa Reeves has only had two girlfriends and they've both gone missing. Now it's up to her to find out why. (978-1-62639-804-7)

Arrested Hearts by Holly Stratimore. A reckless cop with a secret death wish and a health nut who is afraid to die might be a perfect combination for love. (978-1-62639-809-2)

Capturing Jessica by Jane Hardee. Hyperrealist sculptor Michael tries desperately to conceal the love she holds for best friend, Jess, unaware Jess's feelings for her are changing. (978-1-62639-836-8)

Counting to Zero by AJ Quinn. NSA agent Emma Thorpe and computer hacker Paxton James must learn to trust each other as they work to stop a threat clock that's rapidly counting down to zero. (978-1-62639-783-5)

Courageous Love by KC Richardson. Two women fight a devastating disease, and their own demons, while trying to fall in love. (978-1-62639-797-2)

Pathogen by Jessica L. Webb. Can Dr. Kate Morrison navigate a deadly virus and the threat of bioterrorism, as well as her new relationship with Sergeant Andy Wyles and her own troubled past? (978-1-62639-833-7)

Rainbow Gap by Lee Lynch. Jaudon Vickers and Berry Garland, polar opposites, dream and love in this tale of lesbian lives set in Central Florida against the tapestry of societal change and the Vietnam War. (978-1-62639-799-6)

Steel and Promise by Alexa Black. Lady Nivrai's cruel desires and modified body make most of the galaxy fear her, but courtesan Cailyn Derys soon discovers the real monsters are the ones without the claws. (978-1-62639-805-4)

Swelter by D. Jackson Leigh. Teal Giovanni's mistake shines an unwanted spotlight on a small Texas ranch where August Reese is secluded until she can testify against a powerful drug kingpin. (978-1-62639-795-8)

Without Justice by Carsen Taite. Cade Kelly and Emily Sinclair must battle each other in the pursuit of justice, but can they fight their undeniable attraction outside the walls of the courtroom? (978-1-62639-560-2)